I0700031

This book is dedicated to
HT, JW, ZMG, KJP, DB, CJB, AM ,AM, KG, MB, AP,
CR, LI, JS, KH, MS, MP, ON, and many many more.
The world belongs to you, my Dear Ones.
I can't wait to see what you do with it.

And to my friend Jessica-
Thank you for being the first to experience Coranta.
This book would not be what it is without
you and your encouragement.
I square you.

DIRE MISTAKES

SUE JAMES

CHAPTER ONE

SIANA

My feet pounded on the uneven concrete of the city sidewalk as I took the turn at full speed. The sound of crying and shouting had pulled me in from a block away. The burning in my lungs was quickly overshadowed by the fire coating my heart as I approached the source of the commotion. The sight of a mother and her child being pulled from each other's arms sparked something in me that had me sprinting toward the flashing lights. Their layered clothes hung torn and tattered off of their thin frames and the sound of cloth ripping left a lump in my throat as I rounded the first police cruiser.

"Stop it! You're scaring them," I yelled. The two men

in front of me met my protest with hollow silence.

The little boy held on to his mother's shirt. A tear showed where his small hands had ripped the dark purple material. The dirt on their faces coupled with the state of their clothes were a dead giveaway that they weren't dires like most of the people surrounding them. They could feel every moment of fear and heartache running through their veins.

"Did you hear me?" I asked, speaking much slower this time. "You are scaring them."

"Please continue to your borough, Siana. The detainment of citizens who don't contribute is the law."

"Will this delay me from closing up today?" A towering man with a thin frame pointed to the shop door behind him, the words Coranta Bakery painted in large brown letters.

"Just another question and you're done." The officer took the notepad from his pocket before turning back to him. "Do you know how long they've lived in the alley next to your business?"

My eyes darted around to the others shuffling along the usually quiet street. It wasn't difficult to tell the dires from the rest. They kept walking, eyes forward and not sparing a glance at what was happening right in front of them. Everyone with an ounce of emotion, the ones who didn't have chemicals running through their veins, stared at the pair, but no sign of sympathy met their eyes. Anger bubbled up in my stomach as I gripped the sides of my jeans and tried to contain the shaking, making my body sway. My lip tasted like copper. The two men continued their conversation as if they were speaking about the weather, meanwhile the mother and child were pulled apart and placed in separate rehabilitation vans. The woman's blue eyes locked onto the van that held her son while an officer slid calmly into the driver's seat and drove away. Sounds of screaming and flesh hitting glass faded into silence as both vehicles disappeared in the distance.

As the owner of the bakery entered his shop, the smell of the freshly baked goods and cinnamon wafted through the streets and made my stomach turn. Such a pleasant and nostalgic scent had no right mingling with the heartbreak I was witnessing. My thumbs popped as I clenched my fists and glared at the police cruiser still parked on the broken gray asphalt, the writing plastered on the side a reminder of everyone's place in Coranta. A shuddering breath traveled from my head to my toes, and a tingling sensation rushed to my fingertips as I tried to let the rage drain from me. Another emotion that the human husks in front of me only learned about but would never feel. The slow breath I pulled into my lungs did little to calm me as I seethed over yet another human life destroyed by the dires. This was the second time in a week I had witnessed someone being taken away by them. Yelling would do me no good. It never did. Not in Coranta.

"Siana, proceed to your borough or I'll call for Eklund to come escort you back to E." The Dire officer took a step toward me. There wasn't a harshness to his voice, no thinly veiled threats — just hollow truth. In Coranta, the law was as unfeeling as so many of its citizens. As much as I wanted to yell and scream, I also didn't want to risk what would happen if I didn't follow an order from the officer. Slowly passing by the cruiser, I took in the words written on the doors. The same words clearly etched on the stunning marble arches of the RightCorp buildings:

Everyone Works. Everyone Strives. Everyone Gives—So the Many Survive.

The law and its reasoning were clear to everyone in Coranta. Working wasn't an option, and neither was giving. It's been that way since the Rightleys saved the continent almost a century ago. It was decided not long after, that the dires were best suited to positions where emotions could impede a defect-less outcome. Jobs of authority all went to the dires. Those void of emotion were the guardians of lives.

I didn't wait to see if the officer would be true to his word. Of course he would, and the last thing I wanted was a run in with my least favorite dire. Heart still pounding in my chest, I pointed my feet toward home, thoughts of the boy and his mother running through my mind.

As I walked down another of the city's clean but aging streets, posters of the Rightleys smiled down from their hold on the brick buildings. Each poster, more withered than the last, traced the decades of caretakers that had given everything to protect Coranta. The structures, though sturdy, echoed the posters. Each wall sported patches of mismatched bricks plastered in to cover up what time had worn down.

Somewhere deep under the slowly fading images of Ethan and Melissa Rightley sat the very first saviors of Coranta. The ones who had stood up for the people. If you peeled enough layers, you could probably find propaganda from the old government boasting the miracle drug that led us here. Dirations- a lab created cure for the famine; a replication of the most nutrient-dense foods, combined with chemical additives that would keep bodies ticking when the food source they had could no longer sustain everyone. But when the citizens who took them eventually started dying off, rumors cropped out all over Coranta, claiming that the government had purposely poisoned the population to reserve its remaining food sources for the rich and the families in power. With that, riots broke out all over the continent.

After the chaos rose RightCorp, owned by the Rightley family. A genetics and tech corporation who used their billions to correct the wrongs of a foolish and greedy government.

They built rehab facilities to house the surviving dires along with the children born to them. The damage done to the people passed on to their children. More pills were created to keep them alive, but a side effect was a loss of emotion. The dires survived as the muted versions of humanity that we have the pleasure of living with now.

As I started back toward home, I stared at the faces of the newest Rightleys as they looked out on passers-by. Both human and dires alike who probably never gave a second thought to the painful history that sat just under the surface of each smile.

"Damn it!"

Tears clouded my vision as my foot collided with the remains of a street lamp and a string of curses flowed. The metal bases were the only reminder of what had been removed and re-purposed for something else. Electricity was reserved for the areas that needed it most. RightCorp Labs, the Med Borough, the Courthouse—the places that kept the city and its people safe and thriving. Even if most of its people were heartless robots. My eyes panned over the patchwork city full of buildings long since abandoned and used for scrap to keep others from falling. The Rightley Estate, perched high on its hilly pedestal at the center of it all, looked over each borough that fanned out around it to the North.

I puffed out a breath when I finally made it to Echo Street. Lanterns hadn't been lit yet, but the people of E Borough were home for the night. The homes of dires were easy to spot—void of any character, no warmth came from them. Most of the porches already had gifts placed on them, ready to be picked up and delivered to the courthouse. Just another part of everyone gives.

The feel of the decaying metal on the old gate clung to my wet hand. Trying to compose myself, I took a moment to let my eyes wander over the aging craftsman style house. It would have been amazing to see it when it was first built. I'm sure it was beautiful. A home that had seen its fair share of birthdays, anniversaries and so many other celebrations of life, now rotting. The front door, with its blue paint covering the wooden entryway, was now chipped and faded, the frame crumbling around the edges worn by weather and time. RightCorp had encouraged their people to reuse what they could for as long as possible. There was a focus on helping each other — giving what you could to save what we still had and repair what the Coranta of the past had abused. This resulted in homes and businesses creating a patchwork of Frankenstein-like buildings across the city. We reused what we could but on the inside, the old house's bones were as brittle as the families that had once crossed its threshold and were long since dead.

"What in the name of the Rightleys are you doing coming home so late?"

My heel slammed into the frame as I took a startled step backward. The door creaked from my sudden weight on it. The already throbbing toe now pulsed in time with the rest of my aching foot.

"Gah! Aunt Jerry, what the heck?" I moaned as I slid to the floor.

Aunt Jerry's chestnut hair held streaks of flour that dusted the air with a light fog as she made her way from the kitchen toward me. She reminded me of a disheveled housewife from a book I had once read. My bag dropped with a thud. I had long since learned not to hang it up on the coat hooks. The strips of paper plastered on the wall and the now missing hook were a reminder of how heavy books can be. Working at the Library meant I could take as many as I liked for as long as I liked. Not like anyone else was going to read them, anyway.

The throbbing made its way to my head. My worn green shoes peeled away from my foot slowly as I tried to avoid touching my hurt toe, breathing in with a hiss when it came a bit too close.

"What happened to you?" She reached for my foot and squinted at me with phony rage in her eyes.

"Nothing. I stubbed my toe on the walk home and it took me a little longer to waddle my way back. That's all."

"Wow, twenty-four years old and still learning how

to use your feet." She stood and pulled my hands up with her. "Let's get you on the couch before you do anymore damage to yourself or my house."

"Ha. Ha. Ha." I gave my best impression of a dire as she made her way to the kitchen. "You scared me half to death, so if the door is broken again, that's on you."

The thick layer of blankets that Aunt Jerry used to make the old house more homey almost hid the sting of the metal spring poking me in the thigh. I shifted and slowly inhaled the fresh scent of the newly laundered blankets that now enveloped me.

"That makes absolutely no sense, Siana," she said, amidst the sound of clanking glass.

"What doesn't make sense? That you verbally assaulted me when I came in the door? I agree. Zero sense made." The smile I was trying to hide pulled at the edge of my mouth.

"So, are you going to tell me about it or not?" Aunt Jerry had always been great at reading me and calling out my bullshit. A trait that I loved and hated about her.

"I saw them haul away more people today. This time it was a mom and her little boy."

Aunt Jerry gave me a sad smile. "Siana, it's not like they are being punished. If they aren't contributing, it's because something is wrong with them or worse, they are rebels from the Sector. If they aren't helping others to thrive, then they must be removed from society until they can be rehabilitated and returned."

"It's cruel."

"It's the law. The law is above emotions. It just is. You may not like dires, but they are part of what holds our world together."

I puffed out a breath. "They're just puppets who walk around and pretend to be people."

"They're still people, Siana. They belong in this world just as much as we do." She gazed at me over the kitchen island, waiting for a response that both of us knew wouldn't be what she was looking for. I held my head high as I watched her place a pot of hot water down in front of me.

"You know, I read a book at work today. It was about the connection between emotions and the health of the physical body. It said that positive emotions are vital for remaining healthy. The same thing goes for social interaction and physical touch."

The smell of honey and cinnamon curled up from the steam. I grimaced at the once comforting aroma. The image of the mother screaming for her child sprung to my eyes. Another scene that would take up residence in my head forever. I sank my hurt foot slowly into the hot water, recoiling at the thought of the smell clinging to my skin but grateful for a slight reprieve from the throbbing pain.

I glared down at the water. "That means that the dires are just a few steps away from being the undead. They're literally dying inside."

Aunt Jerry pulled me into a hug. Her scent of lemon and flour tugged at my heart and reminded me of warm nights staying up and talking about the future with her and Nira. She squeezed tighter before pulling back to look into my brown eyes.

"You're right."

Dire Mistakes

My eyebrow just about smacked my hairline, my head tipped to the side in an open mouth stare, but my feigned surprise didn't faze her.

"They are dying inside, a little more every day, from something that was beyond their control. Something that was done to them long before they were even thought of."

And there it was. Remorse and shame washed over me like the tide from a winter sea. I thought of what the world must have been like at the start of the Crisis. No, it wasn't their fault that the dirations permanently altered them. The rehabilitation facilities had once been full of humans just learning to survive what their government had done. Medical labs working day and night to heal the hurt. A memory triggered in my mind. A harsh rim of light ringed my vision and I gagged as the sterile smell of the Med Borough stung my nose. And just like with the tide, the feelings of remorse were pulled away just as quick as they came.

The palms of my hands were warm and clammy as I pressed them to my eyes. Stars popped in the darkness behind my lids as I focused on breathing in and out, tendrils of the nauseating smell slowly unwrapping themselves from my memory.

"Are you getting another one of those migraines? Maybe we should go get you checked out."

"I'm fine." I lied.

My body tensed as the hinges on the door to the backyard squealed. A small stream of water splashed over the side of the bowl.

"How long do we have until Henry gets here, Aunt Jerry?" My sister's gentle voice floated across the space, delicate as the flowers that she tended. Nira held out a basket full of fresh flowers and placed them on the kitchen island. The fragrance of delphiniums, tea roses and freesia calmed my souring mood and brought me back from the memory.

Aunt Jerry hurried from her spot on the old sofa. A lemon scented puff of white followed her to the kitchen as she rubbed her hands on her apron.

"Siana, waddle yourself over here and help us get the Gifts ready." The tub was full of food, dried flowers, and books. Part of our contribution. Our Gift. Everyone Works, Everyone Gives.

The books Aunt Jerry suggested I collect for the Gift delivery this month were all about psychology or self-help. Although some of it was fascinating, I would be happy to start on a new genre. I got enough therapy from my best friend Josie, who worked with the police force as a reader. She worked to train the dires there to understand and maneuver through the emotions of the people they regulated. Unfortunately, she was the partner to my least favorite dire in all of Coranta.

"So, Nira, what's the news at the Rightley's? Got any scandalous gossip for us today?" Her eyes met mine from across the room, and I caught the faintest smile on her lips. Nira worked at the Rightleys' mansion, tending one of the many gardens that surrounded the palatial estate. I had been lucky enough to be placed at the Library, sorting through books, and avoiding everyone when possible. Both were jobs ordered by the Rightleys. The work our father did had been important and the Rightleys always take care of their own.

Although quiet, Nira was far from being a wallflower. She regularly came home with amazing stories of things she saw at the mansion and tales of the unbelievable work being done with the plants that grew around the estate.

"I talked to Ethan Rightley again today." She fiddled with the flowers as she spoke. "He told me that my garden was his favorite to visit. That it was one of the few places in the city where he could sit and relax without being bothered."

She continued, accompanied by a slight shake in her voice. "He said that if I wasn't careful, the other gardeners might get jealous."

I was on the edge of my seat, my mouth agape at the possibility of Ethan Rightley flirting with my sister. And why not? She was beautiful–her tall, slim frame mirrored that of the flowers which she so expertly tended. She was soft-spoken but full of life. She was the type of girl that could have songs written for her. I turned to Aunt Jerry with an excited squeal and noticed a flicker of worry accompanied by something else. Her expression shifted before I could be sure I had even seen it. We both closed in on Nira before she shrank away.

"How often does he stop by?" Aunt Jerry toyed with one of the tea roses.

"Well, it used to be his sister Melissa would come every few days to check on the blooms for collection." She stared at her hands. "But for the past month or so, he's stopped by most days instead."

"Maybe it would be best if you avoided him for a while. I don't think it's a good idea to get your hopes up or—OUCH!" Drops of red peppered the island. The rose she had been squeezing now sported a bloody thorn.

"Oh, Aunt Jerry!" Nira wrapped the hurt finger in a dishrag to stop the bleeding while I busied myself wrapping up the rest of the thorns. Aunt Jerry stared at Nira for a beat too long before looking back at the roses.

"I'm fine. Dizzy is all. I, um—I'm gonna go lay down before I destroy the entire kitchen." She laughed and hugged us both.

As soon as she was out of sight, I rose from my stool with every intention of grabbing a book and a bath. Before I could sink my hands into my bag to grab the pirate adventure, Aunt Jerry's voice shot down from the stairway.

"Deliveries are all yours tonight, Siana. Henry will be here soon, so get ready."

Nira bit her lip to keep from laughing.

"It's not funny."

"It's a little funny," she said. "Henry's not that bad."

"He is too. It's enough that I've got other cops threatening to have him cart me around. The last thing I need is for it to come from my family."

My book slid across the coffee table as I tossed it down. Deliveries to the Courthouse would take the rest of the night, which meant reading would have to wait until tomorrow. Great.

"Sorry Captain, it's looks like I'm spending my evening with a robot named Eklund." A wry smile curled my lips before turning to a pout. "Unless, of course my dear sweet older sister wants to help me out."

Nira rolled her eyes, already expecting what came next.

CHAPTER TWO

HENRY

The clock counted down. Each second gone pulled me that much closer to Echo Street.

Rain tapping on the precinct roof mimicked the steady click of officers typing up reports and gray walls matched the sky outside. Small windows let in the last bit of daylight that had squeezed its way through the clouds. My mind was fixed on Echo Street.

Echo Street. There was something about that part of my borough. Something that pulled me in. I found myself driving up and down that way more than any other. As if I was set to repeat.

"Hey, Henry." Josie's curly hair bounced as she crossed the room to our shared desk and tossed a stack of stiff brown folders on it. The papers slid out, showing a lineup of faces covered in dirt at various levels of unkempt.

"What are you working on now?" I said. She wrinkled her nose and pinched her bottom lip. An expression that meant she was conflicted. That something was bothering her. "What about these files is making you… worry?"

Her expression smoothed as she looked up from her newest assignment with a smile.

"Nice read, buddy."

"Thanks. So what's going on? The last thing I need is a Reader who can't focus on her job because she's too focused on her own emotions."

"You were so close." Her expression changed again. Eyebrows drawn together and corners of mouth pulled down—sadness, maybe?

She shuffled through the files. The tiny keepsakes she kept on her side of the desk rattled with each stack of papers she taped on the metal to align.

"The number of rehabilitations in Coranta are on the rise," She took a breath and bit her lip, "Sheridan and the RightCorp both think that it may be connected to the Sector. That they might be planning something big and planting their group throughout the city for it. I'm just going through the files of everyone who we've picked up. Take a look at the two that just came in." I grabbed the few papers she had shuffled through and slid my way. There were two photos in the pile.

"Female; mid-30's, 5'2", blond hair, blue eyes, purple

shirt. The second a juvenile male; blond hair, brown eyes, 3'7", large dark brown jacket. Notes say female was taken to RightCorp Labs for conditioning and the juvenile was taken to a rehab facility outside of Coranta." I looked at her. "I don't understand the reason for your emotions. It looks like a by the book detainment."

"If these two are from the Sector, it means that they're using children." The soft quiet tone of her voice meant something, but the pile of work in my intake bin meant I wasn't about to make her expand on it. Deliveries for E borough were tonight and getting the work done before heading out was top priority. The Gifts had to be delivered.

"Eklund," Sheridan had stepped just outside of her office to address me over the clatter and click of the bullpen, "We just got a message over from Jerry. She's feeling unwell, so you'll be making the deliveries with her niece tonight. You'd better get over there if you don't want your borough docked." Without another word, Sheridan went back into her office. I didn't need any other clarification to know which niece she meant. If she felt she needed to warn me, it could only mean Siana would be joining me.

"Thanks for the update, Chief." My fingers curled around the full bottle of Soterapine in my pocket.

"I wish I didn't have so much work or I would come." Josie gave me a full smile and laughed. "Tell Sia that I will see her later for the play-by-play. I'm sure I'm gonna to enjoy this one."

The empty porch was a clear sign that tonight wouldn't go as smoothly as usual. Jerry usually had the gifts on the porch when I arrived. Schedules for Gift delivery were preset based on the borough and Siana's absence now was further sign that, to her, protocol did not matter. I was in for a long night.

An uneven but steady thumping sound was coming from the house. I moved closer to the window to find the source. The same window Siana had thrown my badge through just a few weeks prior. She was enraged when I said that family was not a necessity for a person's survival. Just moments before, she had said that I was the product of unmarried parents. This was true of most dires, so I assumed we were trading pertinent information about the topic. I pointed out that she was too, since her parents were dead. This was when she took my badge and launched it at my head, missing me altogether and sending it crashing through the window instead. I spent a week after that taking extra emotion classes with Josie.

A loud thud came from the house.

"You owe me for the storm incident!" Siana's voice snapped through the boarded window.

Nira's soft voice was barely audible compared to her sisters. "You have used that same excuse for the last three times I've bailed you out of something. I definitely do not owe you anymore."

"Aunt Jerry made me clean the kitchen for three hours because of that mess! I am owed a few extra get out of jail free cards for that alone."

I had never taken Siana to jail before. Was she planning on doing something illegal tonight? I needed to stop her before she made a mistake that she couldn't take back. A steady sound of thumping from inside the house, coupled with loud outbursts from both sisters, carried my feet to the door that much faster. I turned the handle without knocking and was hit in the face. The pillow that had just assaulted me lay on the ground at my feet and the culprit stared at me with a wide grin. The smile was short-lived.

"I know it must be difficult to understand basic human courtesy, but I thought you would at least follow your own laws. Knocking is required before entering."

"Usually you would be right, Ms. Turpin. However, when an officer has probable cause, they may enter without being permitted. Your admission of wanting to commit a crime, along with the sound of what I could interpret as a struggle, were all I needed to investigate."

Assured that she and her sister would see my reasoning and continue on with our scheduled duty, I walked toward the kitchen island which held this month's deliveries. The second pillow hit me in the back of the head.

"Siana, behaving this way toward me is a mild offense."

"Be glad I wasn't holding a book, jackass."

"If you are trying out incarceration to get out of your responsibility to assist me tonight, I can tell you–you will not be getting a 'get out of jail free card'. By the way, there is no such thing."

"You're an idiot. I didn't realize those pills messed with your IQ as well." She shouldered past me and made her way to the items meant for the courthouse. "Let's get this over with. Oh, and just so you know, eavesdropping is rude."

Dire Mistakes

We made our way back out the door and into the truck without another word spoken. A buzzing sound in my ears was my only company for the long task. Stopping by the other pickups in the neighborhood was slow going. Siana took the time to talk to every person along our route. That, coupled with an unscheduled stop to drop off soup for Josie, meant we were now over an hour behind schedule.

CHAPTER THREE

SIANA

The docking bays behind the courthouse were already being cleared of each borough's gifts when Henry pulled the truck in. Dragging my feet, though satisfying, may have been counterproductive. The sky was getting dark and several official looking people were leaving the monstrous structure now.

"You better get inside and file your paperwork, Eklund. Your boroughs gonna end up being docked if you don't."

The coverall clad man opened the sliding door to the truck and began unloading our gifts. Pulling out a stained rag from his pocket, he wiped off the sweat that was rolling down his brow.

"It's protocol to help you unload the truck." Henry lifted himself up on the concrete platform and began grabbing boxes.

"But the Gifts are here. Why would we be punished just because some papers don't get signed?" I asked.

"Because the Rightleys don't have time to come down and check everything themselves. They rely on this to make sure everyone thrives. There are people out there who need these things. Depend on them." He took the box from Henry, gesturing with his head toward the Courthouse.

The courthouse loomed up ahead. Another white marble building like the RightCorp factories, but somehow, where the factories seemed to give off hope and light, the courthouse drained it. We traveled up the abundance of steps with paperwork in hand.

"So if we didn't file our paperwork and inventory for the neighborhood's gifts, it would be as if we never dropped them off?" A gnawing settled in the pit of my stomach. My shoes were a green blur as we ascended toward the entrance.

"Yes. The entire neighborhood would be reprimanded for it." Henry spoke just over my shoulder. I hadn't even noticed he had moved in so close.

The massive arches that hunched over the entryway seemed to judge all who passed beneath them.

"Are you feeling unwell?"

"Nope. I'm fine. Why wouldn't I be?" The chills that ran down my spine would have given me away to anyone else but a dire.

Rarely did I have to make this trip. Anytime that I

had before, there seemed to be whole boroughs dropping off at once. It was silent. The usual crowds were long gone, leaving the already cold building feeling void of life. The harsh sound of our feet slapping against the cold hard floor echoed uncomfortably off of the tomb like walls. For a place used for charity and justice, it inspired little hope.

"Signing off for E Borough." Henry's deep voice reverberated through the cavernous room. My body gave an involuntary shudder as another set of chills, like skeletal fingers, ran up my spine. The shrill woman behind the counter stared at Henry as if he were a rat. It made me wonder if they had met before. If so, the look was most likely warranted.

"You missed your check in time. I can't help you. You're going to have to go upstairs and talk to the Rightley's bookkeeper, if he's still here." By the time her voice faded from the room, it was as if she had forgotten we were there.

"I can take care of this if you would like to go wait in the truck." Henry mimicked concern pretty believably. The feigned emotion on his face was nothing more than a product of empathy classes Josie had made him go to. And they were paying off. It almost seemed genuine. A puff of air came out instead of the laugh I had intended to give him.

"No, Officer Eklund. I made us late so I will go upstairs and take care of the paperwork. Why don't you go and wait in the truck?" The hands on my hips were for show, but my stubbornness came naturally. I was nothing if not fully aware of my faults. The twisting in my gut continued as an itch trailed its way across my collarbone and up my neck. It would be my fault if the borough was punished.

"Alright." Henry gave a slight shrug before handing me a brown folder and slowly but steadily heading back under the arches and down the steps. Soon, he was out of sight. My lips sputtered as I let out an exasperated breath. Damn it.

"Great job, Siana. Now you get to go upstairs in the creepy, lifeless building all by yourself. And after this maybe you will want to go jogging in a haunted forest at night, or maybe buy a possessed doll, oh or maybe a Ouija board. I hear those are lots of fun. Idiot. Idiot. Idiot."

The clerk cleared her throat. "Third-floor, fourth hallway, second door on the left. You'd better hurry before he leaves for the night. Oh, and the elevators are out of order."

I gave her a nod of thanks and made my way to the left side of the staircase that flanked her desk.

"Thanks. I'll be right back." My head hung down over my chest as I exhaled, "I seriously just said that I will be right back? Great, I'm definitely getting ax murdered today."

Visions of every murder and monster I had ever read about bounced around my head as I hurried to escape the frigid glare of the clerk.

The shadows along the third floor landing were suffocating. The growing pounding in my chest echoed through my ears. My feet, woefully unaware of the beat the rest of my body was pulsing to, planted themselves in the dark space. The urge to turn around and clod back downstairs was strong.

How many horrible souls have waited for sentencing in the courtroom just below my feet? I remembered a story that had taken over every conversation for months when I was younger. A man from V Borough had gone on a killing spree, taking out dires left and right. He poisoned their Soterapine, causing them to suffer a slow, painful death over the course of a week. He was arrested quickly, but the damage was already done and an entire borough of dires was wiped out. Anyone not working had showed up to watch the trial. Those that were there said that he showed zero remorse for what he had done–until they handed the sentence down, that is. When the guilty verdict was read, rage consumed him and he attacked his attorney. That was perhaps one of the good things about the dires–they didn't murder. It was the rest of mankind that you had to worry about.

A soft thud funneled down the closest hallway, and I took a slow step back toward the stairs. No. My borough wouldn't be punished because of me. With a new steel in my step, I marched forward toward the only light source coming from any of the many connecting hallways.

Did the clerk say fourth door? Was I even in the right hall? The click of a door closing behind me made my ears prick up and sent my feet turning to run. Before I could make a full turn to book it out of there, I slammed into something solid, warm and unmoving. I knew when I lifted my head that I would be face to face with another human and for a moment, I hoped that face would belong to Eklund, coming back to help me.

"Henry?" I said shakily as I looked up at the looming figure. The shadows that encased him left his sharp features in outline, and despite the darkness, I could tell that this was not my officer.

"Not Henry." The deep timbre of the voice reverberated through my hands, which were still planted on the unmoving chest in front of me. The realization of how inappropriate this was hit me and shocked me out of my frozen stupor.

"Are you lost?"

"Nope. Nope. I'm playing hide and seek with the clerk downstairs and if you don't scram, you're going to lose the game for me." My attempt at humor may have gone over well if my eyes hadn't been searching for the nearest escape route. The man in front of me didn't make any effort to move and instead leaned against the door frame to his right. The light coming from behind him left his face in shadow while illuminating the nameplate on his door. *Rhett Willulf- Attorney at Law*.

"Mr. Willulf is it? That's a cool last name. I wouldn't mind having that as a last name." I took a sharp intake of breath as I realized what I just said. "My last name is just fine for me, though. It's Turpin by the way–I'm Siana Turpin."

Feeling like a complete jackass, I extended my hand to him. He looked at it and tilted his head, taking me in.

"Rhett. Is your friend Henry also playing?"

The already chilly hallway took a sharp dip. Rhett closed the minuscule distance between us and my breath hitched in my throat. The hairs on the back of my neck stood on end as he stared me down, the shadows seeming to freeze me in place. My internal alarm went off as a slow smile spread across his face. I fucking called it. He may not have had an ax, but who knows what kind of horrible things he might be hiding in that briefcase.

"As a matter of fact, yes, he is. He's a cop, so, you know, he's great at finding things that go missing. Like people who disappear–in a creepy building, when they should be at home, binge reading and eating a whole loaf of Aunt Jerry's rye bread while lounging on the couch." If the word vomit didn't give me away, the tremble in my voice sure as hell would. A glint in his eye left me thinking that he knew.

"Well, I know of a few places in the building that are great for not being found–Conference rooms, parking garage, the records room in the basement."

The gravel in his tone was making my insides war against each other. A strange mixture of excitement and fear enveloped me as I continued to stare at the man in front of me. One of three things was happening. Either he was;

1. Flirting with me. (Which was kinda scary and made me want to run and hide)

2. An ax murderer detailing the places he will hide my body after hacking me to bits (Which was really scary and made me want to run and hide) or

3. Genuinely giving me hide and seek tips (which was sad and made me want to run and hide under a rock.)

"Let me guess what's happening here. You were late with your delivery and you went down the wrong hall-way trying to find the bookkeeper who has already left for the night. Leaving you unable to make your drop off. Is that about right?" He spoke as if he didn't know that every syllable he let escape his lips was making me want to freeze and run at the same time. The ugly gray carpet made a dull scratching sound as my feet shifted back and forth.

"I think you have grossly underestimated my commitment to this game that--" My heart plunged and sent a wave of nausea rushing up my throat. "The bookkeeper has already left for the night?" Despite the frigid hallway, a dampness veiled my palms and forehead.

"He has to drop off the reports to Mr. Rightley. He's the first one out the door." The hand not gripping his briefcase slid into his tailored suit pocket.

A gnawing sawed at my insides as the floor seemed to drop out from under me. Whatever happened to my borough would be my fault. Would they dock everyone's pay? Would they send me and Henry to a rehab center? I couldn't remember a time when a borough hadn't delivered. "If you would please excuse me, I'm going to show myself out." I sidestepped his massive frame, only to have his looming presence follow me down the hall.

"I'll walk you out. I'm heading that way myself." I nodded without taking another glance behind me. From the shift in the air, I could tell he was following. As we started down the stairs, which there now seemed to be infinitely more of, I took the chance and looked back at the stranger that was now haunting my descent. Dark eyes stared right back at me. A momentary jolt had my feet forgetting they weren't on level ground and I stumbled forward, missing my next step. Rhett moved fast–arms around my waist, holding me up from a fall that would rival any of my past oafish moments, but not before I let out a very unladylike scream. No. Scream wouldn't be the right word for the sound that was now playing on repeat as it echoed through the monstrous chamber below us. It was more of a cross between a squeal and a honk. A smile broke out across my savior's face as he straightened and placed me on the step beside him.

"I'm curious as to how you made it up the stairs in the first place?" He asked–a haughty expression plastered on his face. "You may have fared better taking the elevator."

"Trust me, if I could have avoided all the climbing, I would have. The clerk downstairs said that the elevators are broken." I couldn't help but steal glances at him now that we were in the light. He really was the poster child for tall, dark, and handsome. It seemed as if the shadows that had surrounded us upstairs had clung to him, resulting in his long, dark hair. His tailored suit hugged his frame just enough to tell that, unlike me, he probably enjoyed taking the stairs every day. Why do you have to be so cliche, Mr. Willulf?

My stomach coiled again. "What's going to happen now that our deliveries weren't reported?"

"Well, what's going to happen is that you're going to meet me at the Rightley's estate tomorrow morning. The courthouse is closed tomorrow, but I do business there on Saturdays. I can get your inventory on the books before Ethan does his final check. You'll just need to meet me there to sign everything." He had stopped walking and was staring down at me.

"That would be amazing. But I couldn't ask you to do that for me. I don't even know you." If the flush of heat that I could feel shooting up my ears wasn't enough to give me away, the thudding in my chest had to be. He smiled as if he knew what I was thinking.

"It's my job. I help the Rightleys with anything they may need. That includes helping their people, which includes Nira's little sister."

A trickle of cold rushed down my spine as my feet hit the entry hall floor. He must have known that my sister worked at the estate. It's not like Turpin is a super common name.

His gaze shifted behind me. "It looks like you lost this time, Siana." My breath hitched as he leaned down, hand still in his pocket to whisper in my ear. "You've been found."

The sound of footsteps brought me out of my stupor.

"Is there a problem in here? I could have sworn I heard an animal dying somewhere in the building." Henry approached from the archways.

"That dying animal you heard was me almost eating the lobby floor and this kind gentleman stopping that from happening." A ping sounded behind me. I turned to find Rhett already inside the elevator.

"I seemed to have forgotten something very important in my office. Come see me tomorrow and we will get you all situated. Have a good night, Miss Turpin."

Before I could respond, the elevator doors closed, and he was gone. So many questions were bombarding my thoughts that they left me with only one clear certainty. That clerk was ass for making me take the stairs.

CHAPTER FOUR

SIANA

Josie had been questioning me about the entire courthouse debacle since I had Henry drop me off at her house.

"Hold on just a minute! You told Rhett Willulf, the Rightley's personal attorney, that you were playing hide and seek in one of the most important buildings in the city?"

Josie's place gave a feeling of warmth, just like her. When I first started getting a clear read on Josie, her house made me realize I could trust her, since working side by side with one of the soulless humans wasn't one of her redeeming qualities.

The outside was just like any other in our borough. A quilt work structure that was pieced together to hold the important things housed within it. At first glance, when you stepped inside, everything was colorful and chaotic—but when you took the time to take it all in, it was easy to see that everything was done with purpose–meticulously well thought out. It was a perfect reflection of Josie. Usually.

The strain of whatever she had been working on was clear. Her curly hair was starting to frizz around her face from where she had massaged her scalp too many times. The red marks at her temples were a clear sign of a headache that had already taken root.

"He looked like he could use a laugh." I said. Josie smiled at me despite obviously feeling sick. "Do you want me to brush your hair? That always helps when I get a headache."

"I already feel like hot garbage. You want me to look like it too?" She scrunched her face at me when I let out a small chuckle. The memory of what her curls looked like the one time I had ever seen them brushed out danced in my head.

"I know why you're laughing, jerk." She let out a breathy laugh as well before getting back to Rhett and the Courthouse. "I still can't believe you did that. You like to put your foot in your mouth, don't you?"

"Well, can you blame me? Look at how cute my toes are!" I inched my feet towards her, knowing full well what her reaction would be.

"Uh! No! Do not touch me with those things. I'll throw my soup at you. Aren't you supposed to be nice to me when I'm sick?"

I put on my serious face for her. "You're right. How could I be so careless with my best friend? Do you need your pillows fluffed? Want me to read you a bedtime story? Do you need a lullaby to fall gently into dreamland?"

"The only thing that I need is for you to tell me you stayed out of trouble for the rest of the night before you got here." Now it was her turn to give me the serious face.

"Yes, Mom. I was a good girl." Even though I knew she was worried, I couldn't help but poke at her a little.

"What was Henry doing during all of this?"

"My shadow wasn't being very helpful, so I told him to go wait in the car." As soon as I said it, I knew I was in for a lecture.

"Henry just wants to help you. Why are you always so mean to him? He's a great guy once you get to know him. Whether you want to believe that the dires have feelings or not is your prerogative, but they aren't as heartless as you would like to think. They still have some emotions. They just run too far below the surface for us to see. And I think Henry cares for your family, even if neither you nor him actually understands what that means. And I'm just going to say it again. I think you could stand to go talk to someone about these feelings that you have. You don't need to keep living with this hatred."

I stared at the wall behind Josie—not wanting to look her in the eye. All the playful banter had left me. My head fell back as the start of a yawn built in my chest. The chaos of the day was catching up.

"I just want to understand. It doesn't seem right that

someone as caring as you could hold on to so much malice. And for people who have done nothing to earn it."

An uncomfortable itch branched out under my scalp and an electric buzz hummed as white light and the sterile smell of bleach brought water to my eyes. Not again.

"Could we just change the subject, please? You're giving me your headache."

Josie took a deep gulp of her soup and coughed. Large brown spots blotted her white button-up shirt.

"First day with your new mouth?" The lighthearted response not giving off the air I had intended.

"Either Aunt Jerry lost her knack for cooking, or I forgot to rinse off these bowls. It tastes like I just swallowed a bottle of soap." She rose to return the offending meal to the kitchen.

"I'm gonna grab some tea to wash this taste out of my mouth. You want some?"

The sound of dishes rattling in the kitchen set my already frayed nerves on edge. The white light ringing my vision pulsed and my tongue felt too large in my mouth. Struggling to swallow the lump stuck in my throat, I squeezed my eyes shut as hard as I could and focused on filling my lungs with air. My chest rose as I pulled in each breath— in through the nose and out through the mouth. The tingling sensation in my head eased as I opened my eyes, the bright light dissipating.

"Did you know Nira broke her arm when she was eleven?"

"And I suppose a dire was responsible for that somehow." Although she was trying to sound annoyed, I could hear the concern in her voice.

"No." I smiled. "The arm was my fault. Aunt Jerry had just brought us a bike and Nira was being a jerk and hogging it. She rode up and down the street so many times and each time she passed the house, I begged to have a turn. She ignored me over and over again until I picked up a stick and threw it at her. It missed her, but ended up getting caught in the spokes. The wheels locked up, and threw her over the handlebars and she slammed into the pavement."

"We rushed to the med borough, and a doctor saw us almost immediately. The fall had broken her arm. He said it was going to be painful to reset and heal, but that she would have full use of it again. He was straightforward, no nonsense. She was going to be okay. We would just have to wait while a nurse took her for the procedure."

"While we waited for her to come back, they brought in a man. He was covered in blood—frantically crying. A doctor came, a dire of course, and told him to be silent so that he could help him, but he kept begging to know about his wife and child. Without missing a beat, the doctor told him they didn't make it to the hospital."

"The sound of the man's crying scared me. I waited for a long time, thinking about whether I should go over to him. I worked up enough courage to hold his hand. Just as I reached out to grab it, the machine beside his bed cried out, mocking me—telling me I took too long. I was too scared to even move. Aunt Jerry found me later, huddled up in a ball, crying beside the lifeless body of a man that I didn't know."

I found my eyes searching for Josie. My vision clouded by the tears that I hadn't yet let fall and her face slick with the tears she had already shed.

"I always wondered after that. Is that what happened when my parents died? Was their last moment with a heartless dire, too busy to show them that, in their last breath, they weren't alone?"

Josie spoke so softly. "Whatever happened to your parents, they weren't alone. Your aunt said that they were together. So no matter what, they had each other."

That thought broke the dam. Before I could release my first guttural sob, Josie had her arms around me, hugging me. I breathed in her jasmine soap mixing with the smell of vegetable soup she had spilled on herself. I took a deep breath and felt the world around me shift. Everything became brighter with Josie.

"You've held on to this for sixteen years. I think it's time to let someone else carry it." Josie had always given expert advice right when I needed it.

"And maybe, with some help, you will see the dires as friends. Like I do with Henry."

Almost always.

I stayed at Josie's, not wanting to face Aunt Jerry to tell her I hadn't signed off our borough's gifts. Avoiding the lecture that she was bound to give me was my top priority. Besides, it would all get fixed when I saw Rhett. Do I call him Rhett or Mr. Willulf? Both seemed weird. I was pretty sure that he asked me to call him Rhett. Or did my mind add that in one of the many times that I replayed our meeting in my head?

Work was going to drag today. There was too much clutter in my head to really appreciate my surroundings.

Working in the Coranta Library was a dream job. I was required to read through the many books that came through and catalog them for the RightCorp. Most of my day were spent on the second floor taking in as much literature as I could. Tucked away in an older section that was usually covered in dust and cobwebs. It was technically also my job to clean and keep the library in pristine order, but the smell of the old books combined with the feel of a dust covered jacket were my idea of serenity. It meant that I was the first person to delve into this particular world in ages and there was something sad but hopeful about that. I pulled another book down from the stacks and began my newest journey. Losing myself in this new world of dragons and magic was my goal, and I was very good at getting lost. So much so that I didn't notice when three o'clock passed and I still hadn't left yet to go meet up with Rhett at the Rightley's place.

At first, I didn't even notice when an older man wearing tattered clothes entered the library. Even the group of officers that followed a few minutes later went unnoticed by yours truly. In fact, it wasn't until a stack of books across the room fell that I was pulled from the fantasy kingdom that I had been trekking through. I looked up to find the older gentleman picking up the stack of books and unceremoniously throwing them back on the shelf in front of him.

"Oh sir, don't worry about that." The look of horror on his face was strangely out of place.

"It's really alright–I don't mind. Cleaning this up is my job." He grabbed my forearms and pulled me in close before I could process what was happening.

"You work here? Please, please tell me where I can find a place to hide. They can't find me. I know what they do to people who don't work–don't contribute and make gifts. It's not what everyone thinks. The dires aren't what everyone thinks, and neither are the Rightleys. Please, they can't find me again." The look in the old man's eyes spoke of pain and fear. Whatever information he was holding on to–whatever he was running from—I wanted to know all about it. It wasn't even a choice to hide him. It was a necessity.

"Hurry sir, follow me." My heart raced as we rounded the end of the bookcase. The sound of a police radio and footsteps pounded up the stairs and in our direction. I knew this library better than anyone else, which meant I also knew that there wasn't a place to hide that these officers would not find if they looked hard enough.

"Go to the end of the mystery section and wait for my signal. Once they're distracted, head back downstairs. There is a door behind the stairs that leads to a storeroom with a window that leads to the alley behind the building. If you're careful and quiet, you should be able to get pretty far before they realize you're gone."

Making my way back to my original spot just as an officer made it to the top of the stairs, I settled on the first plan that came to mind. If only I had time for another plan to come to mind, but I had to make sure that I had his complete attention. I turned my back to the stairs and waited for him to approach me. I could only hope that he would focus on me first instead of searching for the old man. The second the officer's hand connected with my shoulder, I screamed. And if only my brain had stopped formulating a plan there, but no. The books that I began chucking toward the unsuspecting dire made a sad thud as they bounced off of his chest and hit the floor.

Throughout the chaos, I didn't notice the old man slip away and as the officer escorted me downstairs, I couldn't help but grin at our little victory over the dires that pursued him.

"So tell me again why you were throwing books at Officer Kindolf's head?" Neither Henry nor Josie were amused when I was brought in for questioning. Henry was his same level of vanilla as he paced around the desk, accompanied by the familiar rattle of pills in his pocket, while Josie sat on the opposite side of me, arms crossed and seething.

"He scared me. Who just walks up behind someone like that? I can't control when I get scared. You know, if dires like you would spend a bit more time trying to understand the rest of us instead of just regulating and rehabilitating, you might get that."

Henry stared. "Our job is to regulate and rehabilitate. I don't understand your argument."

"Just because you don't understand something, doesn't mean you can't respect it."

Before he had a chance to say something stupid, Chief Sheridan called him to her office. Her dark brown eyes met mine, and I sat up a little straighter in Henry's chair. Although she was a dire, she usually still felt warm. None of that warmth showed now, as she closed the door behind her.

Josie's silent rage had apparently hit its limit. "You

know that if anyone finds out that you helped him, that you could be sent to a detainment facility as well."

"For the last time, I didn't see anyone except for the jerk that scared the shit out of me and ruined my book. It's not my fault he decided to barge into the room and make a scene." I stared at the floor, knowing Josie saw right through it.

"You attacked an officer, Siana! What aren't you getting?"

The air in my lungs punched out of me. Would they send me away too? Would Josie let them? Would she even have a choice? Nausea radiated through me while the questions I wanted to ask caught in my throat. The reality of the situation was settling in heavy as the feeling in my stomach.

She lowered her voice after realizing her outburst had gained the attention of the rest of the room. "The old man that they caught doesn't just live without contributing– they also caught him stealing gifts."

They had caught him, after all. Disappointment wound through my chest, along with anger. Why would someone steal gifts? It made little sense. Not contributing was one thing, but then stealing what others had given was unthinkable. I needed to talk to this man because if I just traded my freedom to help him; I needed to know why.

CHAPTER FIVE

HENRY

My feet shuffled under me as I moved around in the warm gray office chair. I respected the law, and the law had been broken. How hard was that for her to understand? She had sent my head spinning yet again. What was it about this woman? I woke up in the morning and the first thought of my day was usually; I wonder what Siana will do today? What paperwork will I need to fill out because of Siana? A dull ache in my chest usually accompanied the thought that would take all morning to subside. Until I saw her and it happened all over again. I needed to ask my doctor if you caould be allergic to a person. Maybe it was something that she wore.

She's had to come down to the precinct before, but

it's never been this serious—only minor offenses that most of the time didn't even warrant a report. This was different. I was certain that she helped that criminal, but figuring out the reason for it was absolutely escaping me. None of it made sense. She knew it was the law for everyone to contribute to the good of the people. Everyone works. Everyone Strives, Everyone Gives, So the Many Survive. It was our most sacred law and teaching. There was no reason for her to help this man, which means she either didn't or she didn't know what he had done.

Sheridan's voice cut through my thoughts. "The Rightleys aren't happy. Keep your borough in line or they will find a new use for you. The people of Coranta rely on us to keep them safe. So keep them safe, Henry."

"Will she be rehabilitated?" The urge to get up and leave before Sheridan gave me an answer was overwhelming.

"My recommendation was to send her to a detainment facility along with the old man. They, however, would prefer she stay here with close supervision, while Mr. Finley will be taken back to RightCorp. Apparently, he escaped during one of the Rightleys' visits and they would like him returned for his own safety."

My body relaxed and stilled again until her focus turned back to me. She didn't say a word, but just stared at me with furrowed brows.

"Chief?"

"Take her home, Officer Eklund." She started on the report in front of her as I got up to leave the room.

"Yes, Chief."

A pulsing in my throat distracted me as I left Sheridan's office and glanced over to Siana, sitting at my desk, drinking my coffee. Siana looked up at me as I crossed the room back to where she sat. What I knew to be anger rested on her face. It didn't sit well with me to see her like this for some reason. I made a mental note to ask Josie about that later.

"Siana, I don't understand why you are so upset about this. He stole Gifts in transit from the courthouse. He deserves to be in a detainment facility." Siana's eyes held fire in them when she looked back up at me. And for a split second, I swore I could smell smoke.

"Of course you don't understand. You would need to know compassion and for that, you are missing one vital thing." Siana downed the rest of my coffee and slammed the mug back down on my desk before standing. I'm sure that the gesture had some significance to what she was saying, but it was lost on me. I'd ask Josie about that too.

My hand slipped into my pocket, a subconscious gesture now, to check my pills. They had been rattling in my pocket when I walked lately. A sign that it was time to refill. A commotion behind me pulled me from my conversation.

"Please! I can't go back there! You don't know! None of you know!" They were transporting the old man with some difficulty. Despite his age, he was putting up a good fight. They were about to pass my desk, and I could see the look in Siana's eyes. She would not stand there silently as they hauled him away.

"Stop being so rough with him! He's not going to hurt anyone! He's just scared." Siana's voice carried a desperate tone that I had never heard before. Rushing over, she put her hands on his shoulders and whispered something to him. The old man's body and expression softened again. A strange smell filled the air. Everyone in the room was focused on the old man and Siana, but as soon as he relaxed, half the room went back to work as if nothing had happened. It must have been some kind of emotional cue that I hadn't learned. Siana had let the man go to be led away.

"Let me drive you home." I expected for her to turn down the offer. With a simple nod, she accepted and with that, we got in my cruiser and drove back to Echo Street with a familiar ache in my chest.

CHAPTER SIX

SIANA

I couldn't make my mind leave the station. My hands tingled from rubbing them on the rough fabric of my faded jeans and the taste of copper settled in my mouth thanks to the broken skin on my lip. The half hour drive home had done nothing to calm my nerves and the words of the old man were consuming my every thought. He had been near breaking down. I had seen it, recognized it immediately. Wherever they were taking him, he had been there before and the thought of going back had him in a panic. But that wasn't what I was caught up on. When I went to him, something happened. I wanted to help ease his worry. My whole body ached to hug him and assure him that everything would be alright. Like Aunt Jerry used to do for me when I was younger and would get frightened.

An overpowering smell of tea and lemon came over me and I felt him relax under my hands. I couldn't figure out how he had done it. The entire room went quiet for those few moments. And before they took him away, he leaned in to whisper so that only I could hear. Not that it mattered, if I didn't even understand what he said.

"Tell the wolf it's with Doyle in Baskerville."

It made zero freaking sense.

"Why is Willulf on your front porch?" Henry's question broke me free of my current puzzlement and threw me headfirst into another one. Without answering him, I opened the door and went straight for the porch. To my dismay, Henry followed.

"Mr. Willulf, what are you doing at my house? How do you know where I live?" Even as the words left my head, I only partially cared about the answer. Night had fallen while we were at the precinct, and an unseasonable chill hung in the air. My arms wrapped around themselves. My eyes darted to the boarded-up window, the thought of the couch and blankets on the other side so tempting, and I wanted nothing more than to go inside and cuddle up.

"Please, call me Rhett. I was under the impression that I would be seeing you at the Rightley's estate today." He leaned against the post and it let out an uncomfortable creak under his weight.

"Oh, shit! I'm so sorry. Please come in." Shame

washed over me as I realized the reason for his visit. "I can't believe you wasted your time to come here to help me." The rambling didn't stop as I ushered him inside the house, Officer shadow right on his heels.

"Sure, Henry, come in too." Rhett sat his briefcase on the coffee table in front of the couch. He came all this way just to help me. Maybe he was flirting with me back in the courthouse. A girl could dream, right? As I made my way to sit beside him, Henry launched himself into my chosen spot. Robot asshole. Yanking the soft crochet blanket from behind him, I tossed him a glare and crossed to the other side of the table from Rhett. The lumpy armchair was rarely used. Despite the occasional spring popping out, the couch felt like sitting on a cloud of marshmallows compared to this old thing. My tongue traced the backs of my teeth while I inhaled a slow breath through my nose. The familiar smell of fresh bread made my jaw go slack.

Rhett pulled several papers from his briefcase and laid them out on the table.

"It's not a waste of my time. The Rightleys are adamant about the records being straight before they transport gifts. The trucks move out to the rehab facilities on Sunday evenings. Ethan won't ask for the reports until tomorrow afternoon, so as long as we take care of everything now, I can get them in tonight." He looked up from his briefcase, his eyebrows arched. "I rarely make house calls, but seeing as how I've never been stood up before, I thought I'd make an exception." Rhett didn't take his eyes off of me the entire time he spoke.

"Aren't you their lawyer?" Henry was quick to jump in and ruin the moment. Why wouldn't he when he had little to no understanding of social cues and even less of flirting? Was Rhett flirting? My nerves were still shot over what had happened earlier.

I sat up straight as a spark ignited itself inside my brain.

"Wait. Did you say the trucks don't leave until Sunday?"

"Always. To make sure everything is as efficient as possible, we keep a very rigid schedule."

He didn't realize it, but Rhett had just added gasoline to the spark, and a blazing fire was raging through my veins. I turned to Henry this time.

"How could that old man have stolen gifts in transit if there were no gifts in transit today?" I stared at Henry, a look of confusion coating his face.

"That's not right. Mr. Wilullf must be mistaken. There would be no reason for anyone in the precinct to lie about it. The old man was already going to be arrested for not contributing. There's no need to add a false charge." Although he said the words with conviction, his expression never strayed from confusion. Rhett's face, however, was unreadable as he listened to our exchange.

"What old man?" He asked.

"There was this man who came into the library today. He was scared and begged me to help him." I wriggled my legs beneath me as my body sank further into the uncomfortable chair.

"I knew you helped him." Henry dead panned out.

"You're very smart. Now shut up." I felt a twinge of guilt for being mean to him. Despite that, I kept explaining.

"They claimed he had stolen gifts from one transport, but he couldn't have. Not if they don't go out until tomorrow. When I spoke to him, before they took him away, he was scared–which is probably why I can't make any sense of what he said to me." Word vomit again.

"What did he say to you before they took him?" Rhett spoke with an even tone, but something seemed off. Before I could explore any further, Henry chimed in.

"What did he tell you, Siana?" Both men were staring at me. My skin began to itch from all the attention and made me want to sink back into the cushions and throw a blanket over my face.

"Tell the wolf it's with Doyle in Baskerville."

A soft rattle grabbed my attention as Rhett pulled a stack of papers from his briefcase. An all too familiar pill bottle had fallen with them. The little orange pills tumbled around as the bottle rolled across the coffee table. Rhett was a dire? How did I not see that one coming? As if on cue, Henry checked his own pocket. Another wave of panic consumed me. Had I just told the Rightleys' enforcer I had helped the old man? It was one thing to tell someone who I thought could at least sympathize, but if he was a dire—before I even had time to process what that meant, Aunt Jerry and Nira came home and provided a welcome distraction from the confusion running through my brain.

"What's going on here?" Aunt Jerry didn't hide the suspicion in her tone.

"Mr. Wilullf, were you looking for me?" Nira's expression dropped as she took in Rhett. I could tell from the way she kept her eyes locked on him that something was off. It was almost as if she was frightened of him.

"No, Miss Turpin. I came here to see your sister." He looked at me as if expecting me to finish his sentence. The whole situation weirded me out too much to respond, so he continued.

"We met at the courthouse last night. Since we weren't able to conclude our business there, she was supposed to have met me at the Rightley's; however, when she didn't show, I thought it would be best to make a house call."

Nira came to stand behind me as Aunt Jerry made her way to the kitchen. Probably to fetch some kind of snack for our guests.

"Well, it's a little late for business, so maybe it would be best if you left now. I'll be sure to let Ethan know you stopped by tonight." Nira's soft voice came out with a bite. Rhett stood.

"You are absolutely right, Nira. It is late and I should get back. I would keep this visit between us, though. I would hate for Mr. Rightley to bother himself with something so trivial, don't you think?" The steel in his voice wasn't for show.

"Officer Eklund, would you please follow me out? I have something to discuss with you before I leave." Having sat there for the last 5 minutes without muttering a single word, Henry stood as well. After they had both left, Nira came to sit beside me.

"You need to stay away from him, Sia." There was a snap to her words I had never heard from her before tonight.

"He came here to help us. I was late to the courthouse last night . He brought the paperwork for me to sign so that the neighborhood wouldn't get into trouble for it." My head still spun, trying to find the reason he had to help if he didn't feel sorry for me.

"He may seem all nice and friendly at first, but there is a reason that the Rightley's use him as their personal attorney. Not everyone is a fan of them, and he is great at making problems disappear." Nira brought her eyes level with mine.

"How do you know so much about him?"

"Ethan. He tells me a lot–when it's just me and him." Nira's face flushed. Her body shifted into the nearest seat.

"What do you mean, when it's just you and him? Nira, are you seeing Ethan Rightley?" A confusing mix of pride and fear surged through me. If I could have so thoroughly misread Rhett, could she be misreading Ethan as well? Ignoring my question, Nira continued.

"Listen to me. Rhett is a wolf in very expensive sheep's clothing. Ethan and Melissa use him because they are too kindhearted. He can be ruthless so that they don't have to be. And believe me, from what I've seen and been told, he is ruthless." Nira kept her eyes trained on me and her voice low, as if he would rush back inside at any minute and drag me away from her.

"He's a dire. I'm not interested." I was still living in the disappointment of that fact.

"You realize that I can read you better than any other person on this continent, right? I was only in the room with the both of you for five minutes and I could see how you looked at him. Sia, you don't want to get caught up in his drama." I wanted nothing more than to shift the subject away from me and my poor taste in men.

"Speaking of drama, tell me more about Ethan. How long have you been seeing him and why am I just now finding out?" The sound of Rhett's and Henry's muffled voices outside filtered through the windows as we spoke.

"Well, I told you he likes to visit my garden. That's how it started, I would be working and Ethan would come to sit and read. He started off telling me about the types of plants that they had assigned me and how impressed he was with how well I kept them alive when the other gardeners couldn't." Nira was blushing, and I had to admit that the look suited her well.

"Before I knew it, we were talking about everything. We talked about my job, my family, how I enjoy living in E Borough, how we came to live in Coranta, we even talked about you and your work."

My nose pinched with uncertainty. She was on a cloud and I really hated to bring her back down.

"What did he tell you about himself and his family? It kinda sounds like the only other person you talked about from you was Rhett. I'm not a relationship guru or anything, but that seems a bit off, don't you think?"

I took a quick breath when she didn't immediately look hurt, but there was a distant look in her eyes. Like she had thought of this before and had never said it out loud.

"I think he wanted to get a break from all of that. Last time he came to see me, Rhett showed up, and he got so angry. Ethan stormed out of the garden with him, and I could hear them yelling. When he came back without Rhett, Ethan warned me to stay away from him."

"Nira, I don't know if you should keep seeing–"

"He told me he loves me. Yesterday before I left to come home. He kissed me and told me he loves me." There it was again, a look that didn't belong on the face of someone who had just learned that the man she loves feels the same way.

"Oh. Is that not a good thing?" Heat was building in my chest.

"It's nothing, just. He almost seemed disappointed after he told me. I said it back, and I really meant it, Sia. I love him–but he stood there staring at me, almost like he was waiting for something else to happen. He was called away right after. I haven't seen or heard from him since."

I hated hearing the joy drain from her voice. Something about the entire situation seemed wrong.

"It's only been a day, and he's a Rightley. He's probably been super busy." Even as I spoke the words, I felt my blood boil. The air in the room thickened and Nira moved uncomfortably in her chair across from me.

"Do you smell that?"

I didn't. "What?"

She brushed her hand through her hair. "There must be a storm about to pass through. It smells like rain." Nira rose from her chair looking confused, like the conversation we just had didn't happen. "That's so weird. Maybe Aunt Jerry is cooking something?" She started her way to the kitchen, only making it a few steps before she began to sway.

"Nira?"

She fell to the ground, unconscious. Throwing myself out of my chair and on to the ground next to her, I shoved my hands under her head.

"Nira!" I yelled, louder this time, hoping it would rouse her. It didn't.

"Aunt Jerry!" I could hear her making her way downstairs. The front door burst open and in stormed Henry and Rhett.

"What's wrong with her?" Henry was at my side in an instant.

"I don't know. We were just talking, and she started acting weird and passed out." I couldn't take my eyes off of my sister with so much worry coursing through me.

"What do you mean? Be more specific." I didn't have to look up to know that Rhett was standing over us.

"She was talking about feeling or smelling something. Do you think she might be having a stroke? Henry, should you radio for an ambulance?" Without a word, Henry made for the door.

"No, Henry!" Aunt Jerry chimed in, finally, but it wasn't what I expected to hear. "I think she just needs some rest. She's been stressed lately and I don't think a trip to the med borough is what any of us need right now."

I could feel my anger welling up again, but the panic I felt for my sister overtook the feeling. Rhett made a sound above me, the confusion and rage I momentarily felt for my Aunt now focused on him.

"Before she went down, did she say she smelled a storm?"

"Were you creeping at the door?" I looked up at him and for a dire, he had the look of concern down pat.

A strange look passed between him and Aunt Jerry as the temperature in the room dropped.

"Please let me know when Nira wakes. I'm sure she will be just fine." He turned quickly and slammed into Henry on the way out, making the pill bottle Henry had in his hand fall to the floor. A weight lifted from my hands and I looked down to find Nira, lifting herself up with one hand and rubbing her temple with the other.

"Are you alright? You just scared the shit out of me. Do you need to go see a doctor?"

"What are you talking about?" Nira stared out of the door that Rhett had left wide open in his hurry to leave.

CHAPTER SEVEN

HENRY

"I could have sworn I needed a refill."

Driving home after the flurry of events at the Turpin house had me exhausted. Most nights I would be fast asleep well before now. Instead, I stared at the bedside table that housed my badge, gun, and pills. I slid the drawer open for the third time and examined the bottle there, studying the prescription details.

A product of RightCorp. Soterapine- take one pill daily

So many of us take them they don't even bother with names on the bottles anymore. There aren't any side effects, besides avoiding death for dires, that there hasn't been a need to regulate them. I used to go to the court-house once a month along with every dire in my borough. They would check where we were on our medication and either top off the bottle or give us a new one. Now, I just get them from the precinct. I'm sure there is a system to it. They run a very tidy operation. RightCorp is methodical in all of its dealings.

My dose for the night already taken, I sat staring at the sealed bottle.

My stomach turned. The food Jerry sent me home with was waiting for me in the kitchen. That was it–I hadn't had dinner tonight. The lights in the wood paneled kitchen were just about non-existent but I had more than enough to see by. Jerry Turpin had insisted that I take the leftover stew and bread that she had made for dinner as a thank you for bringing Siana home. I never understood her need to thank me when something like this happened. It was part of my job. Sometimes she would even leave it in my car if I refused it, like she had done tonight.

My knee jumped up and down, making the metal stool I sat on rattle while I finished the last of the food. The conversation with Rhett before Nira had her episode wasn't a new one. Both he and Captain Sheridan instructed me to keep close tabs on the Turpin's long before Siana had had run-ins with the Coranta police. They had always been in-sistent that I keep it between the three of us and now Rhett had not only made contact with her at the courthouse but showed up at the Turpin house. He had mentioned that I should be very careful around both Siana and Nira, more so than usual and to report everything to him. It made sense. Siana was constantly getting into trouble wherever she went and Nira worked closely enough to the Rightleys, the association could affect them. It made the most sense to agree. My stomach twisted and raged at me. I glared down at what was left of the stew and bread. They must have gone bad in the car.

CHAPTER EIGHT

RHETT

"I have it all handled, sir. I understand that the time line is closing in, but if we rush this before we are sure…" the line went dead.

I drove home with the familiar smell of leather coming off of my seats. As I sped around the last corner leading to the house next to the Rightley's, I couldn't help but wonder if Nira really would be alright. The smell that had permeated the Turpin house was a memory that clung to my senses.

The library would have to wait until tomorrow. The sisters location had been confirmed and so much closer than we had ever expected. Hopefully, Officer Eklund would listen to my warning and keep them close.

Lucky for us, I had already taken extra steps to ensure he wouldn't have a choice.

CHAPTER NINE

SIANA

I stayed with Nira most of the day. As long as I still got a few hours of work in, I wouldn't be in any trouble. Aunt Jerry had already called the Rightley estate to tell them that Nira wouldn't be in today. It took some arguing, but she finally gave in. Both she and Aunt Jerry insisted that going on like it never happened was the best course of action. I know Nira was just saying that because she hated to break the rules, but Aunt Jerry's reasoning sounded a bit off for her, if I'm being honest. Usually she would be all about feeding her until she was about to pop and then sending her to bed with an out of tune song stuck in her head. Not today- not that it mattered, because this was one fight I decided to win.

After Aunt Jerry left for work, Nira and I hunkered down in the living room. We spent a good bit of the morning pigging out on whatever we found in the pantry and I read one of my books that I borrowed from the library while she brushed my long hair. The feeling had always been so comforting. A memory that I couldn't quite make surface stalled in my head. Something from when we were both little. Letting it fade again, I acted out the story I was reading to Nira. Jumping on and off the couch with an imaginary sword in my hand, I fought off pirates, saved the damsel in distress and returned a chest full of gold back to the king, all in the span of morning.

"What a compelling tale! And what a daring hero you make!" Nira was struggling to get her words out through the laughter. My sweet sister loved seeing me make an idiot of myself, and I had no problem with it if it made her laugh.

"And it doesn't hurt that I am also quite dashing." She got the most devious look I could muster. "I may make a great hero, but the villains always have the best back stories." I launched a pillow at her face before she had time to roll away. Fighting in the small living room was a dangerous game, and I had already hit my leg on the coffee table more than once. Nira took my distraction as an opening and pounced.

"You can't tickle! That's cheating!" Despite her sweet and cuddly exterior, Nira was a fighter who always went for the cheap shots. Tickling was as cheap as you could get.

"I was enjoying a nice epic pirate saga before you

attacked me unprovoked! You are a no good scalawag who deserves whatever she gets!" Laughter still laced her voice when I finally got loose and wrapped my arms around her, keeping those diabolical hands from any more assaults.

"Say that you give and that I'm the superior sister! Say it or I won't let you–OUCH!" A sharp pain went through my arm and a split second later Nira was checking every inch of it. "I'm pretty sure this table hates me."

"You'll live." she smacked the angry red spot. "And what I think what you meant to say is that I am, in fact, the superior sister." Despite what she was saying, she spoke the words with all the love she had and I thought about last night and how grateful I was that she was alright. Nevertheless, she wouldn't steal my title.

"Never! And if you don't stop tickling me, I'm going to pee and neither of us wants to have to explain to Aunt Jerry why her living room rug has a new stain." I was half sure that I was bluffing.

"Truce?" She didn't demand her victory, although I'm pretty sure we both knew she had already won.

"Truce." It wasn't hard to see why everyone who could fell in love with Nira so fast. She was amazing, and I was so grateful that I got to call her my sister. She reached out and pulled me in for a hug. A warm sense of calm fell over me as we sat there in amiable silence, neither one making the slightest attempt to move for a long time.

"I hope you realize that's gonna bruise, jerk."

"That sounds a lot like admitting defeat. I must be the superior sister, after all." A chuckle escaped both of us and I'm not sure who squeezed in closer first.

I begrudgingly left my sister and made my way to work just after noon. My morning with Nira had been just what I had needed and, honestly, long overdue. And after seeing how well she seemed after the episode last night and all this morning, I stopped picking at my nails at the thought of leaving her.

The warm sunlight soaked into the beautiful aged stone of the library building as I made my way into work. The book Nira and I had finished rested in my hands, it's faded green cover worn at the edges. The thought of Henry playing the part of the evil pirate from my story, big feather and all had a chuckle clawing at my throat. A yellow haze floated on the edge of my vision broken by sudden laughter in front of me. A couple, obviously not dires, sat on one of the many stone benches outside of the Library. Their laughter left just as suddenly as it came replaced by looks of confusion that shadowed both of their youthful faces. A strange feeling washed over me as I ascended the stone steps.

Like usual, the old space was void of life except for Manny, the librarian, who was working hard sorting through the boxes of donations; a task that I was desperately trying to avoid today. Since the Crisis, with much of humanity wasted away, only the jobs that served the preservation of the many stuck around. Unfortunately, writing and printing of books didn't make the list. Obviously, the best people of society had not been consulted on this change. The only new printed material now focused on our history and the family that saved us all. The library relied on the donation of relics found in attics, garages and forgotten boxes to stock our shelves.

Usually, the thought of slowly making my way through each stack made my heart flutter. The thought of finding some forgotten tome equal to that of a pirate queen finding a glistening treasure. Not today. Today I wanted nothing more than to retreat to my usual corner and cuddle up with a familiar book. The upstairs area was still disheveled from the happenings of yesterday. Was it really just yesterday? It felt like an eternity since the strange scene between myself and the old man played out.

"Where do you think you're going, young lady?" Manny caught me right before my foot hit the first step. The old librarian's voice, though friendly enough, still belonged to a dire. I often wondered if his almost human like banter was owed to his job. If anything could make the unfeeling more human, it would be books.

My body itched to run upstairs. "I thought I would let you have the fun today."

"You're so kind. Don't worry, I've already gone through all the good stuff. But I saved this beautiful box of deliveries for you." Manny patted the top of the old cardboard box. Its darkened corners were a sure sign that their previous owner had stored them somewhere dark, damp, and musty. Removing the top flap made both my stomach and lips pinch in. My heart sank. It would take hours to properly clean and air out these poor things.

By the time I emerged from the back, my skin crawled with the layers of filth that clung to me. The moldy grime mixed with the smell of warm vinegar coated the inside of my nostrils, and I longed for a scalding hot bath. Boiling off the top layer of skin was just the only way to get this stench off of me. But before I could take a step toward cleaning myself, I needed to clean my sanctuary upstairs.

After whispering a heartfelt apology to each of the books that I had launched at Officer Kindolf's head, I made my way around the room, placing each one back in its home. Making my way down the mystery section, I could almost smell the rose and mint soap that was waiting for me at home. I rushed through the rest of my task in a hurry to grab my book from yesterday. As the last few tomes slid into place, my gaze snagged on the last one, jutting out on the shelf. Unlike the rest of my friends scattered about the aisle, someone had already tried to put this one back. My body froze. The unease that was working its way through my veins had nothing to do with the grime that covered me.

"This is not where you go, Mr. Holmes." The copy of Sherlock Holmes and the Case of the Hound of Baskerville had somehow made it to the opposite side of the section. My mind raced as the puzzle pieces shoved themselves into place. Doyle and Baskerville! The old man had said to tell the wolf it's with Doyle in Baskerville. My hands shaking, I flipped through the book. My heart gave a jolt as several pages fell from it, and although many of the books here lost pages from years of neglect, these didn't belong. Adrenaline pulsed through my veins as I reached down to collect my treasure. My heart was beating so loudly that I would have felt the need to shush myself if it weren't for the fact that there was no one else up here for me to disturb. I fidgeted with the papers in my hand before quickly shoving the book back into place. My eyes darted around the room. The old man left these pages here for someone named the Wolf to find.

I unfolded the tanned, wrinkled pages with shaking hands. This was what the old man was trying desperately to keep hidden, and now I would know what was so important that he risked so much for.

75 and 76 didn't thrive. Subjects terminated by Hartlem. 77 and 78 already in Coranta. Ready for activation. Be advised to detain upon transition. Terminate if not active.

The pages that followed were filled with numbers and letters, some with a long strike through them. Maybe I was reading into it too much, or maybe it was my overactive imagination combined with the mafia mystery novels that had come in last week's donation haul, but this letter read a lot like a hit list. The thought crossed my mind that maybe I should have left this for Wolf to find. No. Whoever this Wolf person was, the people on this list needed me to keep them safe and away from him.

If my feet hadn't already been itching to make the long trek home, they would have been now. All I wanted was to get back to Aunt Jerry and Nira. Josie would be my first stop after that, though. She was undoubtedly still pissed at me for yesterday, but there was no way she would turn down a chance to help. As much as she was a stickler for the rules, if someone was really in trouble, she would do anything to save them. She would know exactly what to do.

The walk home was faster than usual. The orange sunset was casting a hauntingly beautiful background to juxtapose the all night rave, hopping around through my brain and chest. My thoughts bumbled around between mafia to rebels to an undead legion about to take over all of Coranta. With my thoughts planted firmly on the tantalizing, if not foreboding, and cryptic letter, I didn't smell the smoke until I was turning down my street. I didn't see the smoke and flames for a few minutes more. That wasn't my house–it couldn't be.

It wasn't possible that the place that held every part of my heart was going up in flames. I opened my mouth and let out a silent scream, my brain unable to process moving and making a sound at the same time. Feet firmly frozen in place, I scanned the ever-growing crowd around me. Hands were on my shoulders, and someone was turning me to face them. A worried voice was trying to break through the fog that I had found myself in.

"Where's Nira and your aunt?"

Everything snapped back as the tunnel I had been falling through shattered. Nira never went to work today. I made her stay at home. Looking up at the owner of the concern, I found Henry.

"Siana, are they still in the house?" His voice was steady, but the fear was clear in his eyes.

"I don't know. I was at work and I just got here and I don't..." My voice cracked as the panic gained momentum inside of me. Without another word, I raced toward the house. Henry got to the porch first.

"Stop!" He grabbed me around the waist before I could take another step. "Tony! Come, take her and do not let go. No matter what, do not let go of her. Do you hear me?" One of my many neighbors stepped forward before

I could move and hauled me back toward the rusty gate. Suddenly my frozen shock was gone and in its place, a caged animal clawed at my insides.

"Let me go! I have to find my sister! Please! Please! Let me go!" With the adrenaline, fear, and rage pumping through my veins, I fought.

"Henry, I will kill you if you don't make him let me go!" Kicking and screaming, I did all I could to try to fight my way back to the burning house. Even when I saw Henry, only seconds after I was hauled away, run head first into the fiery hell that was once my home. Arms grabbed me and pulled me in tight. The smell of lemon and flour was barely detectable over the oppressive smoke. She didn't say a word as we both stood there staring at the house. Waiting, hoping, wishing for a miracle.

"Siana!" It was Henry. Was he calling to me from behind the house? Bolting, I flew to where Henry's call was still coming from, with Aunt Jerry close behind. The only light here coming from the fire behind me.

"You found her!" Henry laid Nira on the ground in front of me and began giving her mouth to mouth. Soot covered her too pale face in patches. Although it didn't seem that she had been touched by any of the flames, the smell of burnt hair and char clung to her. Painfully aware of how still she was, I moved myself to the ground beside her. Henry worked at trying to resuscitate her for what felt like an eternity until finally–Aunt Jerry stopped him. She and Henry spoke, but I couldn't hear any of it. It was as if the world had been plunged underwater, leaving me to drown in the muted chaos around me, unable to pull my eyes away from the hands that I now held in my own. The bubbling murmur of the crowd out front was making its way to us again, and before I realized what was happening, Aunt Jerry was gone.

"Nira? Nira, please." Reaching for my sister, I placed my hands beneath her head, just as I had the night before. But I knew, this time, she wouldn't be getting back up. This time, there would be no junk food and pirate stories afterwards. No horse-playing or declarations of victory. Henry took Nira's hands without looking at me.

"She was still conscious. I tried, Siana. I swear I thought I could get her out." The pleading in his voice matched his expression. "She called for you."

I broke.

Sobs retched their way through my body as I rocked back and forth, holding the person I loved most in this world. She was by herself in the end and the only one to come to her side in her last breath was an unfeeling dire. The irony was not lost on me. As the still burning flames crackled and mocked me, my sorrow turned to a thick rage that rolled off of me and mimicked the smoke–encasing us. My head felt as though it might tear apart as another scream built in my chest, but this one would be far from silent. As I raged into the night sky, I could hear distant screams and hollow thuds as chaos erupted again. Henry stared at me with eyes wide before falling to the ground. My vision blackened, my body felt heavy, and I fell willingly into the void. And just before I let it fully take me under, I heard Nira calling me back.

CHAPTER TEN

HENRY

I woke with a pounding in my head that pulsed in time with the metallic beeping coming from a large silver box at my bedside. The device looked like something from the med borough and was attached to a large battery. The room spun as I pulled myself to a sitting position, the tug of tubes and wires pulling at me from the device. The harsh sound of my feet dragging against the thread bare carpet of my room scratched at my brain as I walked to the mirror. The tubes and wires I was hooked up to created a cage like suit across my torso and chest. The smoke I had breathed in had done a number on me and I felt the need to empty the contents of my stomach; although, from the angry sounds coming from it, I'm pretty sure I would have nothing to purge. What had even happened? It was my job to keep my zone safe. As an officer of E borough, it was on me to make sure that everyone thrived. It had always been a simple task. Make sure everyone works. Make sure everyone gives. Of course, bad things had happened before, but this was different. I'm not sure why, but I knew that this was different. I could feel it.

After what felt like an eternity, I emerged from my room free of the medical equipment. I'm sure Siana would have a field day if she saw me hooked up like an actual robot. Siana. A tightening in my stomach began to churn as it crept its way into my chest.

The smell of fresh coffee and something sweet curled its way through the old house and beckoned me down the lit hallway. As I passed the usually empty guest room another of the machines I had been attached to was laying in a pile just outside. I stared through the slight opening in the faded green door. A pile of clothes laid folded on the beat up wood dresser opposite the hallway where I stood dumbfounded. Siana's clothes. Knowing that the almost guaranteed probability of physical harm lay just on the other side of the door, I reached for the knob.

"What are you doing?" The strain in her voice sounded painful. The hollowness accompanying it hurt in a different way. Siana stood at the end of the hallway, mug in hand, staring—her eyes void of the usual fire and disdain that she so often saved for me. It's a strange concept that flame could extinguish flame. Mind racing, heart hammering inside my chest and stomach, on the verge of emptying itself all over my hallway rug, I open the door the rest of the way for her.

"Your hands look full. Let me get the door for you?" She slowly made her way toward me, not stopping to offer a retort or even glance in my direction. My tongue felt huge in my dry mouth. The silence in the house was suffocating, so I let myself say the thing that was lingering on the edge of mind. It was an itching inside my chest that felt as if it would shred my lungs if I didn't voice it.

"I'm so sorry, Siana." As soon as it left my lips, I could feel I had done something wrong, but she didn't throw anything, didn't berate or attack me with a barrage of insults. She slowly eased her way down on the creaking bed, looking so much older than she was.

"You don't know what it means to be sorry. Shut the door, please." She lay the still steaming mug on the side table and slowly folded in on herself. Not knowing what else to do or say, I closed the door. And as the sharp angles of darkness cut her off from the light outside the room, I felt a vice tightening around my chest. It didn't feel right to leave her alone, but I wasn't able to offer her anything that could soothe her pain, a pain that I had never and would never feel. My pill bottle rattled as I crossed the distance to the kitchen.

Dire Mistakes

CHAPTER ELEVEN

SIANA

The small room had filled with darkness while I sat staring at the floor. The bed was spinning again. I took a sip of the cold coffee after already letting most of it spill on the comforter. It didn't feel like she was gone. It did feel like winter had permeated every inch of the room I now occupied. It didn't feel like she was gone. It did feel like I was suffocating under the weight of the surrounding darkness. It didn't feel like she was gone. It did feel like the flames that had engulfed my home were now pouring down my throat. It didn't feel like she was gone. She wasn't gone. She couldn't be gone.

Dire Mistakes

Blankets and coffee went haphazardly flying around the room as I fought for air. Panicking, I plunged forward toward the light switch, tripping in the debris from the bed, and slammed my shoulder into the wall. Flicking on the switch, I rubbed my now aching shoulder. As I surveyed my hurt arm, a patch of skin caught my eye. A faint discoloration that she had given me what felt like an eternity ago. It seems to have healed much faster than it should have. She had only given it to me yesterday, and yet the colors were already fading into a pale yellow. With a sharp piercing in my chest, I slammed my fist into the bruise. Over and over again, until I was sure that the blood would come to the surface just under my skin. And with that, I could breathe again–if only for a moment.

CHAPTER TWELVE

RHETT

The phone was beginning to overheat as it rested against my cheek. This conversation had gone on long enough and with each new question my rage continued to climb. It was dangerous to continue the conversation this way.

I snapped across the line. "We can run the tests back at the facility when she is at full strength. I'm on my way now to check in on Siana and Mr. Eklund to see if there has been any change."

Slipping the phone back into my pocket, I stared at the rubble and char of what used to be a home. The clean-up crew hadn't done more than collapse the rest of the structure. So much for everyone works. Despite being free of flames, it had looked so much worse in the daylight. The mess that we had found when myself and the Rightley's clean-up crew had arrived was unfortunate. Unconscious bodies filled the street in front of the house, but most of this borough being dires meant that a tedious cover up wasn't necessary. Without emotion, the mind will believe any plausible story. Within an hour of removing Siana and Nira from the area, the rest of the onlookers woke up no worse than before. Henry, on the other hand, didn't fare as well and continued to sleep the same as Siana. If this continues for too long, Henry will be the one who suffers next.

It had taken no small amount of back and forth to have them both set up at Henry's house to heal.

With more time, the fire would have been avoidable. I could see that, but what would happen next wouldn't be. She was going to find out what happened to her sister, eventually. She would continue to be forged until someone discovered how to wield her. But by who, remained to be seen.

CHAPTER THIRTEEN

SIANA

Sleeping on the hard floor left a dull ache in my neck. I wasn't sure when I had finally nodded off, but I was grateful for the dreamless rest. My stomach growled loudly as I propped myself up on my elbows. The ache in my neck was overshadowed by the ache in my stomach. The soft glow of moonlight reflected off of the floor as I made my way down the unfamiliar hallway. It reminded me of when Nira and I had first come to live with Aunt Jerry. I don't remember our parents; I don't remember much about where we lived before, but I remember the feeling of my little feet on the cold wood floor when I woke one night soon after we arrived, confused and scared not remembering how I had gotten there. And I remember the way Aunt Jerry led me to the kitchen and warmed my soul with a bowl of hot soup, humming all the while. The thought pulled me down the hall and into what I had expected to be an empty kitchen.

I stood in the doorway silently staring at Henry, his head in hands and looking much worse for wear. My usual need to pester him lay dormant. There was something about the way he sat there. Maybe it was his posture–free of confidence- that bothered me. Something was bothering him too, although how that was possible was beyond me. Maybe dires did feel loss like the rest of us. Maybe that was something that even decades of brain altering chemicals couldn't take from them. The thought of that was utterly cruel.

The cold from the room had seeped its way into my bones. I walked straight to the kettle to fill it again. The little drops of water that splashed onto my hands sent a chill shivering its way up my spine. He didn't say a word.

"I've read so many books that talk about something called a funeral. It was a kind of sad celebration of the life of whoever died. They put them in this box and lowered them into the ground while everyone looked down at them and cried. I always thought it was kinda sick." Why was I telling him this? After the Crisis society realized the need to use every resource. The need for graveyards became a thing of the past. And when they were all cleared out to make way for fresh growth, they were a sentiment that only remained in stories.

He didn't move as I continued. "After a while, I started skipping past anything in my reading that included funerals or graveyards. It was too difficult to grasp why, but I think I get it now. They weren't some kind of beautiful tribute to the dead. They weren't about the dead at all. They were about the ones that were left behind to face each day. So that they could have a place to go to release their pain and anger instead of having to scream at an empty sky. That's why the graveyards in books are always haunted. Not because of the ghosts of the dead, but the anguish of the living."

The scraping of chair legs on wood was the only warning I got before Henry closed his arms around me. Not realizing how much I needed this before, I returned the embrace. Tears streamed down my face and soaked through his gray shirt. He didn't seem to mind, and neither did I. We stayed that way until the kettle started screaming for us to part. As we did, I looked up at Henry's face. The face that I had dreamed about punching countless times. The face that had garnered so much rage and disdain from me. The face that was now wet with tears. There was something there that I knew wasn't the result of some lesson. It was real and heartbreaking, and he was feeling it. He was feeling. Reaching my hand to him, I wiped the tears from his cheeks, and he returned the gesture.

"Why does this hurt?" He stared into my eyes, pleading for an answer that I had no way to give. Tears flowed again as I fell back into his arms. I had hated this man and when I came to my senses, I probably still would. But for now, I didn't care to think too hard about it. I had found an unexpected comfort, and I lost myself in our mutual heartache.

Dire Mistakes

The black breakfast tea that we enjoyed throughout our talk had left a delicious smell radiating through the kitchen and living room where we had moved to sometime during our talk. A comforting glow radiated through my skin as the morning sun peeked through the windows. I had spent the night telling Henry every story about Nira that I could think of, even the bad ones. We decided to go back to the house at daylight to search through the rubble and find some remaining item of my sisters to bury. It may not have been rational, but it felt right. Henry was looking at the angry bruise on my arm when a knock on the door sounded. We both jolted upright, Henry leaving his chair to get to the door. Josie didn't wait to be invited in–rushing over to smother me in her arms.

"You're both awake. I was starting to worry that you would waste a way in here. I've been going crazy waiting around to see you both." Josie never broke contact with me as she spoke. "Where is your aunt?"

"I'm not sure. She was here when I woke up the morning after the fire, but I haven't seen her since."

"What do you mean, morning after? Sia, you've both been asleep for a week. I wanted to take you to the Med Borough, but Aunt Jerry thought it would be better just to let you rest. I wasn't allowed in to see you. The only people allowed in were the doctors from RightCorp. From what your aunt told me, they said that the fumes from the fire did a number on the two of you. Your bodies were so in shock that you just slept and healed." There was no holding back tears as she spoke. "I just kept hoping that somehow, you knew we were here and ready to help. Whatever you need, I'm here for you."

"A week? I've been asleep for a week?"

"There was some kind of toxin or something that was released in the fire and knocked everyone out. The police haven't figured out exactly what yet, but they think it may be the paint used when your house was originally built. Either way, everyone else woke up within an hour of the fire except for you and Henry." Josie kept explaining, but a ringing in my ears was drowning her out. A sudden wave of nausea descended on me as the smell of burning plastic filled the space. Josie jumped up from her chair and ran to the kitchen. Grabbing my hand, Henry stood as well. The sudden contact caused the panic to drain from me and took the toxic smell with it.

"Josie, is it the kettle?" Henry's face hid none of the fear he was feeling. Josie came back to the living room, a look of worry plastered to her usually gentle features.

"Everything is fine. I don't smell it anymore." Josie and Henry both took a deep breath.

"Have you washed the clothes you were both wearing that night yet? It might be lingering on them. Henry, go collect everything that you, Siana, and Aunt Jerry were wearing and I'll do a load of laundry." Fear made Josie bossy, but Henry didn't seem to mind. He left the room and went straight to work on his task.

Josie turned to me. "What would you like for breakfast?"

"Pancakes and honey?"

"Coming right up."

Despite the shock of learning I had been asleep for almost a week, after breakfast, I went to my room to rest. Josie's pancakes sat heavy in my stomach, and the comforting feeling of being full had my eyelashes brushing against my cheeks. A gold sheen covered the room and the smell of black breakfast tea lulled me to sleep.

Later that day, we stood in front of the charred and broken bones of my home, the memories that were made there already feeling as though they belonged to someone else. I instinctively ran my hand over the bruise on my arm and squeezed. Time wouldn't take her memory from me. Henry, Josie, and I spent the next hour sifting through the wreckage. The search was difficult as the structure still standing after the blaze died was torn down for the safety of the borough. It felt surreal to be sure.

"Sia, I found something," Josie said standing at what could have been the stairway. The layout of the house seemed so much smaller now that the walls were gone. Holding a spring I found in the living room, I went to Josie, my heart racing. She held up a metal box for me that was covered in the residue of something that had melted in the flames. It was unrecognizable. The only purpose it served now was to keep the contents of the box trapped inside. Henry took it and gently shifted it back and forth.

"We can pry it open back at the house. Do you want to keep looking?" Henry gave me a look that said he saw how much this was breaking me.

Spring still in hand, I answered, "Not yet. I want to find something of hers to bury. I don't want to scream at the sky."

We kept searching until, finally; I found a pile of seashells. Aunt Jerry told us about it when we were younger. She and our mother had lived near a coast when they were young girls and our mother would collect them and place them around the house for protection. She must have given them to Nira to remind her of our mother. We buried the shells under a rosebush in the backyard. The green branches and bright pink blooms were completely untouched by the destruction that had robbed me of so much.

Back at Henry's, I clung to the rose I had snapped from what would forever be Niras' grave. I thought about how her body must have already been recycled and given back to the land to help it thrive. I squeezed the rose tightly in my hand at the thought, the sting of the thorns, just the pain I needed to help me focus as a drop rolled down and onto the brown carpet of Henry's living room. I didn't want the world to thrive without Nira in it. For all I cared, the entire thing could rot and I would sit and watch it all crumble, feeling nothing.

"Do you have anything to drink?" Josie had said nothing since we had gotten back. "My mouth tastes like pennies and dirt." She used her shirt to scrape her tongue, and the look on her face told me she immediately regretted it.

"It must have been something in the house. I can taste it too." Henry and Josie continued their conversation to the kitchen, but for me, the world fell silent. I looked down at my hands. Grave dirt lined my nails along with a trickle of blood from the rose's thorn.

The laundry Josie had finished before she left lay folded in the basket. The smell of smoke still lingered on them, so despite her best efforts, I went to the kitchen and tossed them all the trash. I'm sure Henry wouldn't miss them. A few folded papers that were at the bottom of the basket lay now on top of the trash pile. Josie must have taken them from the pocket of my pants before washing them. I had forgotten about the old man's cryptic pages and for good reason, but now I could use a distraction. I opened the garage door to the sound of heavy scraping as Henry was taking a handsaw to the plastic encasing the metal box we had found. The sound of scrapping and sawing invaded every inch of the garage as I tried to get his attention.

"Henry, I need your opinion on something." As if he was waiting for a reprieve from the task, he dropped both the saw and the box on the workbench.

"Anything for you, Siana. That's not what I meant, not how I meant for that to come out. I didn't think you, yep–what do you need?" Was that embarrassment coloring his cheeks?

"Henry, are you alright?" Taking a few cautious steps forward, I put my hand to his head to check for a fever. He leaned in to the touch before I snatched my hand back.

"I'm fine. I just haven't taken my pills in a little while. Apparently, I slept the week away with you—not with you, near you. I was also asleep when you were also asleep. What is happening?"

It was more serious than I had thought. How had I not realized what was going on before this? He had been off of his Soterapine for too long and whether it was withdrawal or the dire chemicals now taking over, Henry was showing signs of being without it.

"Oh shit, are you going to be alright?" I looked toward the pill bottle he kept in his pocket. "Do you need to take them now? I can go get you something to drink." I left the room before he answered.

Why had no one thought to give him his pills while he was out? I would have thought Josie of all people would have made it a point to keep him safe. This made the whole Henry acting like a human thing make sense, though. I was fuming by the time I came back with his tea, sitting it down on the workbench beside where he had been struggling just moments before. He had won the battle while I had been in the house, and a smile was now spreading from ear to ear. My own hands were itching to take them, but that could wait a second more.

"Take your pill first and then we'll go through it together."

His hand went to his pocket. "I left them in my room. I'll take them when we're done, promise." The smile that covered his face was a surprise. I suddenly dreaded the thought of that smile fading, knowing it was only a matter of time before his pills robbed him of that grin.

Although I was worried about Henry, my eyes wandered from his to the box sitting on the workbench. I wasn't sure if it was calling to me or mocking me. Henry slowly lifted the lid and paused.

"If you want, I can leave. If you need to do this yourself." He wasn't looking at me. Reaching for the hand that he had on the lid, we opened it together. Inside was a collection of what looked like letters, small tokens from mine and Nira's childhood, and a small journal. Henry thumbed through the letters as I picked up a hospital tag. It was from when Nira broke her arm; there were also several tubes that contained what seemed to be baby teeth and locks of hair and then, underneath it all, a picture. Staring down at the image, I felt something click inside of me. A very pregnant woman stood beside a very tiny Nira who couldn't have been over four years old. The face that had my heart racing wasn't that of my mother or my sister, but of the man beside them. Glowing with pride and happiness for the women surrounding him was my father. The look he gave was filled with so much love that my heart ached for their loss. Looking at the picture, I could almost remember the feeling of him holding my hand. Warmth spread from my fingertips, through my palm, and up my arm.

"Let's go inside while we look through this. It's getting a little stuffy in here and I don't know about you, but I could use some food." Henry didn't wait for my answer as he carried the box inside. After bringing us two bowls piled high with butter noodles, we got back to sifting through Nira's belongings.

"Henry, listen to this letter and tell me if you can make sense of it."

Be advised that all property belonging to the Rightley family, RightCorp and its stakeholders, is subject to review. The care of said property will result in compensation on a growing scale until such a time that your services are no longer required. A non-disclosure agreement is compulsory for the safety and well being of all parties involved. Any damage to the property or violation of said agreement will result in immediate and permanent action against the employee/perpetrator. The Rightley family thanks you for your continued service.

The Law Offices of RightCorp

"That's a really weird way to say, hey come plant

flowers on my land and make sure they don't die, right? Oh and also, if you see us do anything weird, keep it to yourself."

"The Rightleys laced their employment contracts with thinly veiled threats. Did your sister ever tell you about her work there?"

"Of course she did. She's my sister. She told me everything." A weird clarity settled over me. "She did just tell me about something going on between her and Ethan Rightley. Do you think the Rightleys could have done something?" Nausea and disbelief volleyed for dominance within me. Henry didn't answer as we searched through the remaining documents. Most were medical files or other strange correspondence from the Right-Corp.

"Everything else in this box seems to be directly connected to you or Nira except for this." Henry held the small journal for me to inspect. The handwriting inside was difficult to decipher but seemed to be some kind of code. It felt oddly familiar. Each code was paired with a random number, followed by an address. I pulled several papers from my pocket.   "What's that?"

"Remember that nice old man that you and your friends carted off?" The accusation in my voice was unmistakable. Despite the change of demeanor, Henry was still a part of the system that punished innocent people for no reason.

"This is the message that he left for the Wolf. I found it planted in a book when I went back to work." As I unfolded the paper, I started to see the connections. Every code on the old man's page was listed in the journal. We scanned the first line together:

BR4-6 / CH4-6 77&78 24 Shelling Lane, Ocean Borough, Port Hartlem Region 54

A sinking feeling in my gut told me that this had something to do with Nira's death. But why? Why would RightCorp want to hurt Nira. She couldn't have been a threat to them.

Another knock sounded at the door. I rummaged through the rest of the journal while Henry answered it. I was in the middle of trying to decipher what looked to be the page out of a completely different journal when he came back.

"We've been asked to come down to the station for questioning. It seems that the Rightley's want a thorough investigation into your sister's death."

"Alright. Let me find a good place for Nira's things first."

"No, Siana, they want us to bring the box as well."

I clutched the metal box to my chest. The hollow shuffle of papers and tubes inside seemed far away.

"How do they even know about it?"

"A representative for RightCorp came by earlier while you were in the shower. They asked me a few questions about what we had done since waking up, so I told them about going to Echo street, finding the box, and Nira's grave."

"Why would you tell them any of that?" A red ocean boiled behind my already watering eyes. I couldn't give them the only clue I had at making this right.

"Because they asked. This is still a possible murder investigation and I am still a police officer of Coranta."

And there he was. The jackass dire that I loved to hate.

Rhett walked into the interrogation room without an ounce of reserve. I guess that's a plus about being a dire—you don't have to care about invading other people's space if you have no concept of it. He crossed the room in only a few steps and reached out to Henry to hand him the metal box. Items were tossed onto the table as he rifled through its contents. My mouth hung open wide, unable to form the words that I was screaming inside my head. Henry didn't flush red with anger or even let out an exasperated sigh. This was the law, and he was all business again and with Josie busy, I was all on my own.

"What are you doing?" The question barreled out of me, coated in all the disgust and rage I could muster.

He didn't even look in my direction. "Everything in this box is the property of RightCorp. I will let you keep anything that may not be pertinent." After throwing out the last of what he deemed 'not pertinent' he finally turned his gaze toward me. "Where is the journal?"

No. Giving this muscle puppet anything that belonged to Nira wasn't happening. I wouldn't let them cover this up. Some part of me took great pleasure in slamming the metal box closed on his curled fingers.

"Gah! Damn it! What is wrong with you?" Rhett paced back and forth like a hurt animal nursing his hand. I had seen dires hurt before, and although they felt pain, their reaction was nothing like what I was seeing in Rhett.

"If you need to file an assault report, I can write up a

statement. Although I'm sure Ms. Turpin's actions were merely an unfortunate accident." In that moment, I came very close to assaulting two men in in one day. Henry had no idea how close his face came to the same fate as Rhett's fingers.

A shift happened in Rhett's expression. He must have aced those human emotion classes because the look he was giving me was nothing but pure human emotion. The room was getting uncomfortably hot as I stared at the man who was trying to tear my world apart. Rhett took a step forward. He placed his hands on the table in front of me and despite the sweltering heat permeating the room, I froze. Was he actually mad? Was that even possible? Could this husk of a human actually feel something or did the Rightley's just train him well in the art of intimidation? My insides turned as heat radiated from my chest and throat. A mixture of anticipation and fear consumed me as he leaned in close enough for me to feel his breath on my neck as he spoke.

"That won't be necessary, Henry. I'm sure Miss Viteri won't be trying anything like that again." He reached for my water, the sweat on the outside of the glass dripping on me as he raised it to his lips. A smirk curling around from the lip of the glass as he finished it off.

"Thank you for your time." He started to leave.

"My name is Turpin, asshole. If you're going to try to intimidate someone, you should probably know who you are dealing with."

He turned back to me, the muscle in his jaw twitched as an unspoken challenge raged in his eyes. "Trust me, I know exactly what I'm dealing with."

CHAPTER FOURTEEN

HENRY

We found ourselves in our far too familiar spot of her sitting in my seat and drinking my coffee as I stood close by. Siana refused to look at me, but I couldn't take my eyes off of her. It had been nearly impossible to not smile from ear to ear when she slammed Willulf's hand in that box. She had done what my entire body had been aching to do. Well, almost. When he leaned in close to her in the interrogation room, I had the strongest urge to slam his head into the table. She didn't need me to protect her; I knew that, but I couldn't help but think it would have made her smile. The Turpin's had been made a priority some time ago, so it wasn't new to have the Rightley's check in on them. This, however, was different. Willulf hadn't been involved until recently and none of them had ever interacted with the Turpin's directly. Nira's passing must have had a bigger impact than I had thought. Even Chief Sheridan seemed to be working more closely with Willulf.

Rhett Willulf had always just seemed like another superior to me, checking in, collecting my reports, and dropping off my Soterapine. But something about his interactions had changed. I could feel in my gut that whatever his end goal was, it wasn't good. Whether it was because I was finally able to read his emotions or because I was learning how to trust my own, I didn't know.

Viteri. He had called her Ms. Viteri. It seemed strange that he would make such an obvious mistake, especially when he had been so intent on knowing everything about the girls these past few months. It was a strange mistake to make. One that neither myself nor Siana seemed to understand.

A worried feeling had my head in fog as I stared at the desk where I had sat so many times, not worrying about anything. Paperwork had been piling up since the fire, but I had no desire to return to it anytime soon. That was new. I couldn't think of a time when I had left anything unfinished. It just made sense to get it done before, but now the only thing that made sense was helping Siana. Something coiled through my chest every time I thought about her hurting, and she was hurting now.

"Eklund, come see me before you head home." Chief Sheridan had already disappeared into her office before I could answer.

She was sitting back at her desk as I stepped into the dark gray office, her dark hair sitting in tight curls around her shoulders.

"First of all, the Rightleys would like me to thank you on their behalf for your continued service watching over the Turpin's. Against my guidance and despite your inability to protect the eldest sister, they have decided not to have you sent to a rehabilitation center at this time."

"Against your guidance? You asked them to send me to a rehabilitation center?"

"Yes. Henry, if you are unable to perform your job for the betterment of Coranta, then that's where you should want to be." She narrowed her dark green eyes at me. "It's my hope that they'll reconsider. If they do, I will let you know immediately."

A wave of nausea coursed its way up my chest. The room began to spin as I fought the urge to run and find Siana. Sheridan kept speaking, but the pressure building in my ears made it seem as though she were in another room altogether.

"Until that happens, for your lack of contribution this past week, you will be required to give your next one hundred and eighty four hours of wages to help Coranta to thrive."

The thought of being hauled off to a rehab center right when I was starting to figure out my part in all of this. I couldn't stomach it. I would do whatever it took to make sure Siana and I both got our answers.

Sheridan narrowed her eyes at me. "You don't look well. When was the last time that you took your Soterapine?"

"I have a full bottle at home."

"Here," her unwavering stare never left mine as she reached to open a drawer, hand emerging a second later with a familiar looking bottle. She reached to place it in front of me. "Just use this one instead. You can get rid of the other one once you get home."

I stared at the bottle of toxins, not wanting to touch the thing that would have me thinking exactly like her: like every other dire in Coranta. I left it on the desk knowing fully that without it, my heart would stop. I promised myself, as soon as I started to feel sick, I would take them again. For now, I needed information.

"Which rehabilitation center might I be sent to? Would it be the one in the Hartlem region? And how long would a trip like that even take?"

"To my knowledge, there aren't any centers there. It's just an old shipping town and port. How do you know about that fraction of the continent?"

A tightening in my chest made me nauseous as I thought about her question. "Siana works at the Library. She, uh, found some info about it in a book. It seemed interesting. Do you know anything about it?"

Sheridan turned in her chair to reach for the wall of cabinets behind her, each filled to the brim with cases and information about Coranta and its people. When she fixed her attention on me again, it was with a cardboard tube in hand. I leaned in forward as she pulled the large stopper from one side of the red cylinder marked with the word 'RESTRICTED'.

"Chief?" My eyes bounced from the roll of paper she

was flatting out to her as a flapping sensation tumbled about in my chest. A map of the continent was laid out before me and there, drawn out a mere six inches or so away from Coranta, sat Port Hartlem.

She cast another hollow look my way before a loud knock on the door took her attention from me. I took a long, settling breath as she rounded her desk, feet clacking on the concrete floor. Rhett opened the door and walked in before she had the chance to turn the handle.

"Officer Eklund, the Rightleys have made it clear that they want your Soterapine levels returned to normal before you have any further interaction with the remaining Turpin sister. You are to report to RightCorp tomorrow morning for testing and injections."

My heart was a lead weight in my chest as I answered him. "I don't understand why they would have any interest in either myself or Siana."

"Because the Rightley's care about all of their contributors, Henry." The smile he gave had me balling my hands into fists as I imagined what he would look like with a few missing teeth; but instead, the vision of Siana crushing his hand left me smiling right back at him. Rhett tilted his head toward me at me before glancing at the open map.

"Sheridan, a word." He left the room without another spare glance in my direction.

"Stay put." Sheridan said before exiting behind him. They hadn't gone far, but their muffled voiced were too low to make anything out.

Circling the desk, I memorized as much of the map as I possibly could, with a plan forming in my mind. Unfortunately, the door swung open again before I could make much sense of what I was looking at. I stared, dumbfounded and not sure how to cover as Sheridan, still in partial conversation with Willulf, stood in the doorway, facing away from me.

"Henry, put the map on my desk back."

The door slammed closed, leaving me scratching at the stubble that lined my open jaw. Did she know what I was doing? Before she had a chance to come back and complete the task herself, I stuffed the now folded map in my shirt and placed the empty tube back in the drawer. My palms were slick with sweat as I wiped a bead from my brow. What I had in mind was absolutely insane, but so was falling back into a fog and being carted off. No. I wouldn't let myself be wiped away until I helped. I owed her that much—for Nira.

I wasn't familiar with any of the land outside of Coranta. No one really was. There was no reason for anyone to leave the city except for the officers making the Gift deliveries or citizens being taken for either rehabilitation or recycling. From what we had been told, there wasn't much to see beyond Coranta besides dilapidated roadways and decaying buildings.

The map I had stolen from Sheridan showed one mostly straight road leading straight out of Coranta on the East side of Z Borough. There were several roads that branched off at intervals labeled with different names–Akerman, Renbrough, Fuller, Willulf and there at the very end, where the road ran into blue ink–Hartlem. Siana and

Josie sat in the back seat of my car as we drove through each borough.

Glancing in the rear-view mirror for the millionth time, I studied her; shoulder leaning against the car door, head on the glass, staring out into the dark sky that was yet to see the morning sun. Leaving Coranta wasn't something that was done except by the escorts that carry the people or Gifts to the Rehab centers. Without any official leave paperwork, I held my breath as we drove through the final borough. The disappointment that would be on Siana's face if we had to turn around was plastered in my mind, but as we approached the final road that led out of town, there was nothing stopping us. No guards, no gates, not even a single camera that I could see. The road was clear in front of us and I took it without pause.

As the car ran over pothole after pothole on the old crumbling road, a familiar shake made me reach for my pocket. I hadn't taken one since before the fire. I felt different without them. Everything seemed sharper. As the pills ran out of my system, everything tasted and smelled stronger. I could see new colors that I didn't know were possible. It had to be a side effect of the dire chemicals taking over, corrupting my brain without the Soterapine there to stop them from degrading my mind. I kept telling myself that when I started really feeling sick, I'd take them. I didn't want to die, but the thought of losing this feeling of finally being awake made me feel trapped all over again. But this time, I could feel what I wanted. And there was this overwhelming feeling that Siana needed me. Helping her was something that I was meant to do. I knew it and sickness be damned, I was going to help her.

CHAPTER FIFTEEN

SIANA

None of the papers I brought made any sense. I'd been looking at them since we left the house, or at least trying to. A feeling of triumph had overcome me and Henry when we had discovered the connection between the journal and the old man's papers, but now that we were making the trek to find out what was hiding in Hartlem, I couldn't have felt more lost. Nira was into something that I couldn't yet fathom, and Aunt Jerry may never forgive me for making her stay home the day of the fire. She must blame me for what happened; that was the only thing that explained why I hadn't heard from her since I woke up. According to Rhett, she had been reassigned to a new job that better suited her, whatever that meant.

The trip to the police station last night had frayed every last nerve I still had. So much so that when Henry had vehemently suggested that we make the trip to Hartlem, I almost turned the idea down. The look in his eyes when he begged me and Josie to take the trip was heartbreaking. Something inside me knew that he needed this too. I wondered if he felt responsible for the old man or Nira. If the new feeling of guilt was hitting him so hard that he had to do this. Both Josie and I had the sneaking suspicious that he would go by himself if we said no. And honestly, I was relieved when he fought so hard for it. He was doing exactly what I wanted to do. Fighting for Nira.

But now that we were on our way to break several Coranta laws, I felt a wave of dizziness pass over me. My gut twisted as the car dove into another pothole. What were we even going to do if we did find answers? What power did I have to make whoever did this pay? None. I shoved my thumb into the tender purple bruise on my arm and took a breath. Josie's warm hand gripped the one digging into my skin.

"I'm here and we are going to figure this out together." Josie didn't let go of my hand as we continued to drive. I didn't realize I nodded off until the sound of laughter entered my dreams. Keeping my eyes closed, I listened to Henry and Josie as her short burst of laughter continued to fill the car. I listened in awe of the joyful sound: wanting to join in, but knowing the second I opened my eyes, the concern would seep back into both of theirs and strip them of the one uncomplicated moment they have had in the past week.

"Come on, that was good. Okay, what about this one?" The laughter in Josie's voice was there, but I could taste a sour note in her tone. "What do you call a bee that can't make up its mind?... A maybe." The laugh that rolled from Henry seemed to shock even him. I would miss him when the pills started taking over again. My nose was flooded by the smell of black breakfast tea and honey, and I fought the urge to join in, not wanting to risk missing another laugh.

"I knew it! You haven't started taking your pills again, have you?" Her hushed tones were just sharp enough to read that she was pissed. The air in that car soured again and took the comforting taste I had started to revel in with it. The silence that followed was an answer in itself.

"Why, Henry? You know what will happen if you don't take those pills. And if the station finds out that you aren't taking them, you'll lose your job. They will ship you off like that crazy old man." The temperature in the car turned icy as my heavy heartbeat began to drown out the sounds of the road.

"Josie, just drop it for now, please."

"No. I will not just drop the fact that you couldn't care less about a serious problem."

"Trust me. I care and that's the problem." Henry exhaled a loud and shaky breath. "Sheridan want's me sent off for rehabilitation. The Rightley's want me to report to RightCorp."

"Turn the car around right now, Henry. You can take your pills and we can convince Sheridan that you're fine."

"We both know, the second I step into RightCorp, I won't be back. Something is going on and Siana is stuck in the middle of it. We are all she has, Josie. I can't go back.

Not yet." Henry was almost inaudible as he spoke and even with my eyes closed and resting against the frigid window, I could feel his warm eyes on me. He and Josie must have come to some kind of understanding, because neither of them said a word. If I let them know I was awake now, I would feel like I intruded on a private moment, so a quick glance over as the heater kicked on was all I was going to risk. Henry's hand covered the one that Josie had placed on his shoulder.

It had always confused me how she could see a dire as a friend but looking at them both, so content in each other's silence, I envied that friendship almost as much as I envied the comfort they had with being so close to one another. It was hard to reconcile that the cold, unfeeling, dire and the compassionate if not confused human were the same person. I couldn't stand the thought of him being back to his old robocop self, but it would be better than the alternative. He couldn't stay like this if he had any chance of staying alive. If anyone could get him to see the reasoning behind taking his pills, it would be Josie.

The thought of losing the person he was becoming was too much after I had just lost Nira. My breaths rushed out of me in short, jagged bursts as my chest fought itself. Flashbacks of the fire flooded my brain. Smoke seemed to cloud my vision and force itself down my lungs and unable to hide that I was awake any longer, I bolted up straight in my seat. As Josie grabbed at her own chest, I caught Henry's face in the rear-view mirror, gasping for only a second before smoke completely obscured my vision. The car started swerving back and forth and the panic that had already set in cranked into overdrive. I tried to scramble my way over the seat and to Henry's side as the car careened off to the side of the road. I slammed my foot on the brake, but the car kept sliding before finally coming to a jarring stop with the help of a large metal pole. Both Henry and Josie looked as sick as I was feeling. I slid across the seat and out the door, ready to empty my stomach just outside the battered car. Henry and Josie followed suit immediately after.

"I'm so sorry. The car must have started overheating and I lost control," Henry gasped out as Josie checked him and myself over. "Do you think someone could have messed with it? What are the chances that someone at the station knew we were leaving?"

"It's fine, Henry, and so are we. Cars just break sometimes. There's a reason they aren't used by the many."

Henry stared at his cruiser. "Why isn't it still smoking?"

The acrid taste of smoke in my mouth was almost as nauseating as the earth swaying around me. There was something very wrong with me but what I was thinking was insane. The car just overheated. That was all.

Josie's voice sounded muddled and far away when she spoke, "We need to start walking. According to the map we shouldn't have too much farther before we reach a town."

"As long as that part isn't wrong too." Henry voice was still shaky as he reached for my hand.

I took it to help lift myself from the hard ground. "There's only one way to find out."

It was one thing to drive down the unused road, but

walking down it was another story. Although it looked to me that the car was just a little crumblier than it started out, Henry couldn't get it to start after it made friends with the big pole.

"How far are we from the Hartlem Region?" My feet were aching from walking on the old pavement and twisting my fair share of ankles on the giant cracks that lined it. It was hard to believe that a car that could drive over all of this got taken out by an old billboard.

"I wish I could tell you we will be there soon, but I honestly have no idea. The map I got from the Chief has all the Regions outside of Coranta, but the problem is, the roads that are supposed to connect them are nowhere in sight. We passed a road for the rehabilitation facility a half hour outside of the city, but other than that, we haven't passed another one." Henry stared down at the map for the hundredth time as Josie chimed in.

"We should have passed four different turn offs before Henry lost control of the car."

"I don't know what happened. I couldn't see for a minute and my body just froze."

"Henry, you have to take-"

He didn't wait for Josie to finish.

"Look up there."

I wasn't sure if he was purposely cutting her off or if he really saw something at first, but when he picked up speed, we followed as closely as we could. The smell hit me before I saw it, and a memory tried to bob its way to the surface. Out in the distance, the ocean lay beckoning us forward and, for some unexplainable reason, a wave of calm passed over me.

CHAPTER SIXTEEN

RHETT

I struggled to cover the strain in my voice as I spoke. "If we push her too far now it could ruin everything. We already know she has the chemical present in her blood. She's a Viteri. Just be patient." I slid the phone in my pocket before continuing my walk around the lush sprawling grounds of the estate. The torrent inside my head began to calm with each step. Before long, I found myself standing in Nira's garden– a mixture of contempt and disgust rolled through me as I glared down at the once colorful blooms. My rage steadily built again as I plucked a petal off of its stem, the edges started to curl and harden with lack of care. The garden was decaying faster than it should have been. I opened the shed and wiped the oily layer of film that transferred to my hand off on the door frame. The inside, more like that of a small lab than a shed, was clear of all signs of life. The work Nira had been doing had already been processed and moved to RightCorp. The involuntary twitch in my eyebrow grew as I continued to scan the shelves for anything left behind. Ethan's workers had done their job well; nothing remained of the work that had been done here.

Siana's face held in her death sleep flooded my mind. She had been cold as ice laying there in a room at Eklund's house, unmoving. Very much unlike the woman that had been pure fire as she stared me down in the interrogation room while pretending to not have what she thought was her sister's journal hidden under her shirt.

The aunt had done her job for the Rightleys well. She had raised the girls and kept them healthy until they were old enough to access their abilities. Because of her, the Rightleys had kept the girls well enough hidden from the Sector but it was only a matter of time before they took them back.

CHAPTER SEVENTEEN

SIANA

"Do you really think the Rightleys had something to do with the fire?" Josie didn't look at me as we sat on the old bench that looked out on the town. It's what one of my books would have called a ghost town at first glance. Time had weathered the small port. Shutters covered windows; remnants of a storm that had long since passed. While Coranta covered its decay with patches and paint, this place had been swallowed by it.

"Nira told me she had been seeing Ethan Rightley." She made a gentle gasp. She was as shocked as Aunt Jerry and I had been when she told us. "But I'm not sure that it was what she thought it was—or what she wanted."

I crossed my arms over my chest and searched in the distance for Henry. No sign of him meant his mission to find a better map wasn't going as well as he had hoped.

"A few days before the fire, they had met in her garden and he told her he loved her."

"That's beautiful! I knew Ethan Rightley was handsome, but who knew he was romantic, too? He must be heartbroken."

"I don't know. Nira said he was acting really strange after. Like he didn't get the reaction he wanted. Then she didn't hear from him at all, which may or may not have something to do with Rhett Willulf coming in and acting all menacing right after."

"Wait! Maybe it was a love triangle. Is it possible that Rhett was in love with Nira, too?"

"Judging by the way they acted toward each other the night before, I would say that's a hard no. But what do I really know about any of this?" Movement to my right caught my attention. I spotted Henry leaving what used to be a hardware store and moving toward another building a few yards away. This one, shuttered like the rest, had two large wooden doors resting between ornate pillars. A chill wrapped my spine as I shifted toward Josie. It reminded me too much of the Courthouse.

"This whole thing is surreal, but I know that it's all connected. Nira must have known something, and the Rightleys did something permanent about it. I don't know if they meant to kill her, but I just can't believe that they didn't have a part in it."

Josie took my hand in hers. "It's hard to imagine the Rightleys would do something like that. They saved us,

Siana. They saved everyone."

"No, they didn't. Decades ago, their ancestors saved the continent. I'm not convinced these are the same Rightleys." Josie looked deep in thought for a moment before something behind me caught her eye. I turned to see Henry striding toward us–an unknown woman at his side.

CHAPTER EIGHTEEN

HENRY

"I'm not threatening you, ma'am. All I'm saying is that we have probable cause to search the house in question." Siana gave me an exasperated look. She had already told me more than once that I was 'using my cop voice again.' I only have one voice.

"And I'm telling you, you need to go back to wherever you came from." The woman standing a few feet away from me was around five and a half feet, average build, dark olive complexion, and had to be somewhere in her late forties or early fifties. My usual interactions were a bit more cut and dry even without Josie assisting, but I could sense something about this woman that put me on edge. Realizing that I was way out of my comfort zone with this feeling, Josie jumped in.

"We are here on business from the Rightleys. There may be proprietary information in the residence."

"Hartlem won't be happy that you are here unannounced. Like any of the other Overseers, the Rightleys have to answer them." My attention had drifted back to Siana. She looked as though she needed to rest again. Staying focused was crucial to getting what we needed. "Overseer?"

She seemed to assess me before deciding to speak again. Her eyes pinched at the corners. "What are you really doing here?" Her gaze lingered over each of us in turn.

"We just want to see the house." Siana's voice held a note of pleading in it. A faint feeling of tightness rolled over me as something, not unlike that of a fog, closed in around us. The woman's entire demeanor changed as she took a step toward her. I didn't let her take more than one.

"What's your name?" The question was only meant for one of us.

When she didn't try to move any closer, Siana replied, "Siana Turpin."

The woman paused and took a deep breath. "I'm Livia. Names are important, Siana. And it's important that you know yours. Come--I'll show you home."

CHAPTER NINETEEN

SIANA

We had walked without her saying a word to us for at least half an hour before finding this place. Josie seemed to be taking in the scenery. Henry's eyes were darting around, checking for threats behind every ditch and hill. All the while I was trying to keep my head from exploding with all the questions I had bouncing around my skull. The main one being, where are we going? Which I asked. Several times. With no response. I kept thinking that if this were a horror story, we would be headed straight to our own sacrifice. The last leg of our journey was taken in complete silence while Livia's words sat uncomfortably on the edge of my mind. I didn't understand them until now. A feeling of familiarity and dread trickled through my body like slow-moving patches of ice just spreading on a water's surface. With a snap, I froze in place. She hadn't meant her home.

The house was battered by time, but not like the houses found in Coranta. There were no patchwork windows, no scrap and saves turned into livable spaces. The blue paint was only visible in cracks along the wooden siding and signs of corrosion, either from time or termites, made it clear that the old dwelling was not livable. The smell of the ocean continued to knock on the door of a memory that was firmly locked. With no fence to halt our intrusion, we pressed forward. A walkway, which at first glance seemed to be pebbles, crunched under our feet–seashells. The entire pathway and porch had been covered with them. Something Aunt Jerry had said came to the forefront of my mind. My mother had done the same thing when they were younger. An unease settled over me as my heart began to pound. The realization that I misunderstood Livia was setting in.

"Who lived here?" The question hung in the air between us.

"I think that you should go in and have a look around. When you're ready for answers, I will be waiting on the beach for you. I won't go anywhere, so take as long as you need." And with that, Livia turned back down the pathway; the soft crunching of shells accompanied her as she headed toward the water. Josie's hand was in mine as we stepped on to the sagging porch. I said nothing as we approached the door.

"So, is anyone else gonna address the fact that we are

about to break into a house on the instruction of a complete stranger that just so happened to be in the middle of a desolate town that no one knew was there at the exact moment that we showed up? I could always just arrest her and save us the time." Despite the welcome change in his general demeanor, it seemed Henry still needed to learn the subtleties of reading the damn room.

"Henry, what the heck?" Josie and I both turned back as she began to berate him.

"Even before you stopped the pills, we talked about this. Sometimes people need space or silence to process. Give her space."

"Ok, I think I get that, but what I don't get is how the two of you are planning to get inside when the door has a lock and chain on it. Also, don't know if you've noticed, but the windows are boarded up too. So there is that."

"You're kind of smart ass when you're not on your meds." Josie stepped back off the porch, leaving me to my thoughts. "Come on, wise guy, let's go see if we can find something to pry this door open." She turned to me. "See if you can figure out that lock while we're looking, huh?"

And with that, they disappeared around the side of the house. Taking the paper and journal out of my bag, I stared at them—trying to make sense of what it all meant. Still not feeling like I could even think about the obvious connection, I moved to peek through a small opening where one of the boards sealing up the windows had split. The house was too dark to make out much of anything. The small amount of light coming from a hole in the roof offered strange silhouettes of unusable furniture. I stood there, staring into the darkness, until the sound of footsteps alerted me that Henry and Josie were coming back. As I turned away from the window, a dim glow caught my eye. It seemed to be coming from the end of the short hallway and left a soft red light, barely visible on the far wall.

"We found a metal pipe. I think I can use it to pry the boards off of one of the windows." He held the pipe in his hand proudly while crossing to the window in front of me. The next few moments were filled with the sound of screeching nails being wrenched away from their age-old task. Henry threw the old wood over the side of the porch as each piece came away, revealing more of what looked like a small kitchen and living room joined together by long shadows.

When the last of the boards and glass were cleared, Josie didn't hesitate to reach for Henry to help hoist her through the now cleared frame. Turning my back to them, I stared down at the beach where Livia had gone to wait. A dizziness clouded my head as I looked out, half tempted to follow instead of rummaging through the old beach house. Everything had already changed so rapidly and somehow, I knew what taking that first step inside meant.

I knew that it meant opening up a world that had been closed to me so long ago. A world that had my mom, dad, and most of all, Nira in it. We had nights where we would stay up trying to remember what they were like. Imagining what kind of gray hair Dad would have or what kind of concoction Mom would cook us up for dinner. For me, it was all imaginary. I couldn't remember anything but faint tastes and smells. Nira was a bit older and whether she did it for me or genuinely remembered was anyone's guess now. It felt wrong to go in without her. Henry's hand on my shoulder sent a warm wave through me.

"We can't get to the bottom of what happened to your sister if we don't first jump inside." The sound of Josie already rummaging through the rooms knocked me out of my trance.

"Alright, toss me over, robocop."

He smiled. "You know you are going to have to stop calling me that. At least until it's true again." Henry kneeled in front of the window–hand raised out to me. My chest tightened as I took his hand and used his raised knee to boost myself over the window ledge, almost tangling my feet up in a small collapsed table when I landed. Henry reached out through the open frame and caught me before I fell. After the initial drop in my stomach, a laugh escaped both of us.

"Nah, you'll always be robocop to me." I smiled back at Henry. His hands were still holding me up when Josie cleared her throat somewhere in the dark living area.

There was an unfamiliar tremor in my voice when I spoke to him. "It might not be a bad idea for you to clear the window on the other side, too. We could really use the extra light to have a good look around." And with that, Henry let me go slowly, making sure I wasn't going to trip over my own feet before releasing me completely. He smiled as he picked up his makeshift pry bar and began work on the other window. When I turned to Josie, despite the shadows cast around the room, I could see a wide grin plastered on her face.

"What?"

"It's just kind of funny, is all. Despite your disdain for all dires, I didn't think it would take this long for you and Henry to become friends. I'm pretty certain, deep down, even he realized he felt something." Josie stopped to look at me.

It was hard to reconcile the husk he was before with the person he was now. I didn't see him as the same person at all. He wasn't the same person.

"No. I have disdain for what he was. He isn't that anymore. And he couldn't have felt anything before. Dires don't feel."

"Just because you refused to see anything but the worst in anyone who isn't like you, it doesn't make what you say right. And even if they truly didn't feel anything, like you think, that's not their fault." Anger and pain seeped through her words. "You're wrong. Henry is the same person."

Shame coiled around my chest as I avoided her gaze. "I'm sorry. I just—"

"Siana, he hasn't been taking his Soterapine. I know it's because he feels for you. I could see it before he ever went off of them. He doesn't know how to hide any of his emotions yet. It's clear on his face every time he looks at you."

Just then, Henry released a large board from its hold on the window and a sharp ray of light split the space between us. We didn't speak as we continued searching and Henry continued along outside, uncovering windows and giving us more light to work by. The kitchen and living room were void of anything more than old furniture in disarray, but we turned every piece over and examined it from top to bottom before moving on to the next task. A short hallway connected two rooms to the living space. A quick search of the wall and surrounding floor yielded no source of the red light I had seen before.

Henry finally joined us as we searched the two small bedrooms. A step into the dark space to the left had my heart pounding as my foot collided with several glass bottles.

"Looks like somebody had a drinking problem." My eyes stung as I gave a low chuckle.

"The baby." Henry's humor wasn't much better than mine. In his defense, he was new to it. He crossed the room and raised the bottle I had kicked. Returning to my side, he held out a glass baby bottle nestled in his palms.

A thick layer of dust suffocated the room and even the cobwebs had fallen prey to it. Several books rested on a table in the opposite corner of the bedroom and my fingers were already itching to flip through them. The first book looked to be a children's story. Moisture had curved and hardened the edges, but the yellowing paper was still mostly legible. The story was called Little Red Riding Hood.

Of all the books that came to the library, children's books were the ones I liked the least. There was something unsettling about children going off to face evil by themselves. Children should be protected, not sent out into the world to save themselves.

"Anything good?" Josie peeked over my shoulder.

"Oh look, she gets eaten by a wolf. Wonderful." I handed the book to Josie before moving to the next. It was a scrapbook with one word embossed into the cover.

VITERI. The same name Rhett had called me by at the station. It was filled with children's drawings and an occasional picture, and there staring back at me was an image of Nira, me, and a tall man with dark hair and round framed glasses. Nira and I had to be close to the age when we moved in with Aunt Jerry. Henry sat beside me on the bed as I looked through the forgotten memories.

"Who's that?" Henry leaned over to see more closely.

"I'm pretty sure that's my dad." A numbness washed over me as I searched the images. Of the few pictures scattered throughout the album, there wasn't a single one of my mother. There weren't even any pictures of Nira before I was born.

The room opposite the hall didn't turn up much else. Another bedroom, this one the same set up, only covered in various broken clay pots and what seemed to be cookbooks. I wasn't about to start going through each of those, no matter how much I enjoyed reading. I would leave the cooking to Aunt Jerry when I got back. That is, if she wasn't still avoiding me.

We had spent most of the day going through what I knew now was once my family's home. The setting sun was giving way to the shadows that came to claim the space again. I left Josie and Henry on the porch and made my way down the shell pathway and on to the beach.

"How the hell do people walk on this stuff?" Complaining to no one but myself as I slogged through the sand.

"It helps quite a bit to take your shoes off." Livia was sitting a short distance away on a log that must have been there for years. I couldn't help but wonder if it had seen the old house when it was full. I crossed the distance, the sound of gentle waves lapping at the sand beside me. The watery seat looked far from comfortable, but I took it anyway, trying not to look straight at the woman who undoubtedly held answers about my past.

No words escaped me. Whether from her own wonder or pity, she was silent for a long time as well.

I thought I had set out to save some unknown strangers and find out why Nira had been taken from me. Now, I knew that I had been too late. I had had the warning in my hand without knowing it. Because I did nothing, Nira was gone.

"I remember Nira."

I hadn't realized I had said her name out loud.

"The two of you used to play along this beach with my son." The smile in her voice was overshadowed by the sadness peering out through her eyes.

"You were all so little then." Finding the words had never been this difficult before. There was always a joke within reach to shield off any unwanted thoughts. That was me, the girl that could take whatever was thrown and toss it right back with a witty retort. But the girl that found herself on this beach, trembling and unsure of what came next–I didn't know her.

"Are you ready?" The question was simple. Yes or no was all that was needed and yet I couldn't force either syllable out. I inhaled and nodded my head–it was the best I could do right now.

"First thing you need to know is the dires are not the monsters that you believe them to be. I can feel you rolling your eyes at me, Siana Viteri." Maybe she really did know me. "How much do you know about what happened after the Crisis?"

We all learned the history of Coranta in our first training lessons. It was almost automatic to repeat the short of it back to her.

"The world was in trouble and famine hit. The governing power almost killed the people with their Dirations. When the food that was supposed to save them started poisoning them instead, the RightCorp stepped in and saved everyone."

"It may have been the government that made and distributed the Dirations, but it was RightCorp that created the chemical that went into it."

"No. The RightCorp created the rehab centers. They created Soterapine. They helped the people in the rebellion to destroy the ones that did all of this to the people and they solved the famine."

"When the continent started to upturn, RightCorp used pull from several very powerful families to overturn the government and take control. When they started hauling people off to the rehab facilities, they already had the cure in hand, unfortunately they hadn't found a way to profit off of it yet. With the first round of dires gone, their children could be manipulated to believe anything they told them. And for a while, they did. Families were sifted through facilities and, being pumped full of Soterapine, they didn't have the heart to care. As testing groups were narrowed down, thousands were expelled back into the regions and put to work."

"Everyone Works. Everyone Thrives." The mantra

never felt right, but now the words tasted like ash on my tongue. Livia gave me a knowing look.

"We'll get to that part soon enough." I had the feeling that she wasn't talking about the mantra.

"The small groups that remained in the facilities were put through the worst of the testing."

"Testing for what? If they had already found a solution for the food shortage and a cure for the chemicals the dirations left behind, what else could they need to test for?"

"One of the side effects of taking Dirations used to be death. Taking them directly without the Soterapine was a death sentence. They altered the first round's brain chemistry in ways that took the researchers decades to understand."

"It used to be a death sentence? I'm going to need you to elaborate on that part." I let the small mound of sand I had been holding fall back to the beach as I shifted to look at her again.

"Dirations altered the brain chemicals for the children of dires as well, but in all subsequent generations, the effects were no longer fatal. In fact, in a select few, the new makeup caused certain abilities to surface, once triggered. When RightCorp found this out, they took advantage of the opportunity it provided them." Livia looked straight at me without a hint of hesitation in her voice.

"My family and yours were part of those select few."

"What opportunity?" I asked.

"Everyone has been told that the start of the Crisis was the famine, but it was actually a great war. A war that has never stopped."

"A war? Really. Why wouldn't we have seen any sign of it? If it's been going on for so long, there would be stories about it. There is no way that a war that has been happening for a hundred years wouldn't have affected Coranta."

"No one said it didn't affect Coranta. Everyone contributes to it every day. The families put in place, the Overseeing families, came up with the Gifts to support Hartlem and keep them from spilling over onto the continent. Eventually, with the discovery of these new altered abilities, they started trading their people for that protection."

"When you say abilities?" My brain was racing with the possibilities.

"Once you have trained, you should be able to have full cognitive and physical control over some of your senses." Livia peered at me with a knowing gaze. Her wise face took me in as her work-worn hands held mine. She was giving me time to adjust to the knowledge that she had just bestowed upon me.

"The fuck does that mean?"

Livia chuckled. Either from surprise or relief, I didn't know.

"You have the ability to amplify your senses and to absorb those of others around you. I've already experienced it myself. You thought about ash earlier when you said the RightCorp mantra. I tasted it too. It seems that you can amplify taste and most likely smell as well."

"That sounds a lot like something I would read at the Library in Coranta." Although I kept my tone laced with disbelief, my thoughts swirled and my chest tightened at the thought of having some kind of special powers.

A deep sadness overwhelmed Livia's face. The worry lines there made her seem much older. At least, much older that I had thought she was. "RightCorp has done many horrible things during its existence. Some of the worst has been their work with children. I truly am sorry to say that you and Nira, among others, were subjected to some of the worst of it. Your family was caught up in a great deal of it. Your family is also the reason why we made it here. We were able to build a life here in hiding because of what they did. However, what was done was done. The children that left RightCorp labs were already permanently altered. Not all with abilities and none for the better." She looked down at her hands as a bitter taste dripped down the back of my throat.

"If something like that happened to me, I would remember it. And Nira would have remembered it too."

She held my hand. "You were young, and the mind does what it can to protect it from things that it can't and shouldn't have to handle. Especially in one so young as you were."

"But Nira."

"Nira probably had a great many things that she didn't want you to be hurt by. And anything she kept from you was certainly to protect you."

The sand that was still stuck to my hand made my skin crawl as I slowly pulled mine from hers.

"What did they do to us?"

"I'm not entirely sure of every experiment. I only know the results."

A knot formed in my throat and refused to let go as

I stared at Livia.

"Have you ever been overwhelmed by a smell when you were angry? Or been around someone who was elated and suddenly you tasted something you know you have never had before?"

All the time, but more so lately. "It wasn't this strong before."

"Which means that you have been triggered."

"You make it sound like I'm some kind of weapon."

"To them, you are. You were created to fight a war for them and once they needed more power, they activated you. It's not right but it's what happened to you. And to many more before you."

The wood snagged at my pants as I turned, trying to spot Henry and Josie by the old beach house. Darkness had fallen over the coast and the glow of a lantern was all there was to reassure me that they were still there and safe. She followed my gaze back to the beam of light. "It's important that you keep this to yourself. Your friends seem lovely, but you need to be very careful in whom you trust. You don't realize it yet Siana, but great sacrifice was made by both sides to ensure that the Viteri sisters came to be."

"Sacrifices? I don't want anyone to sacrifice anything for me."

"And I'm sorry to say that what was done wasn't for you—well, not just for you. It was for the people and there will be more tears to shed before it's all over."

My shoulders curled forward as Livia placed her shawl around me. All I could think of was Nira. Closing my eyes, I could see the backyard. Smell the dirt under the rose bushes.

"It's called a sense shift. It allows you to project things you have experienced onto someone else. It will be difficult to control at first. You have to let yourself fall into it. Start with the strongest sense and take it from there. Almost as if you are turning over an hourglass. The sand on top is where you are and on the bottom is where the memory is. You have to sift out everything around you to find the memory and then push it out."

"Any memory?"

"Eventually, yes. Right now, memories that have had the greatest effect on you will be the easiest to push out to others."

"What happens?"

"Well, I should be able to smell or taste anything that you are experiencing during your sense shift. Just focus on a memory that has a strong connection to smell."

I took a deep breath as I let myself start to trickle into a memory. I tried to think of one that wasn't connected to the fire. A slight smile tugged up my face. My shoulders fell as each of the coiled nerves controlling my body began to loosen their grip. As I slowly pulled the smell of floral soap into my lungs, a shallow sigh left my throat.

The kitchen in Aunt Jerry's house was warm and inviting. The smell of dinner was still hanging in the air as a much younger Nira and I finished up the dishes. Water splashed my face as she dropped a huge pot into the sink. Bubbles floated up and along the shelves surrounding us as laughter rung out through the room. As I grabbed a handful of soap shavings to add to the already foamy basin, another splash of water cascaded into the surrounding air, soaking me and drenching the already slippery floor. Aunt Jerry was going to be so mad when she saw the mess we had made. I laughed anyway. My hands formed twisty tornadoes under the warm water, expelling giant mountains of frothy floral bubbles, which I scooped up to blow at her. My heart bubbled with laughter until the sound of glass shattering sliced through it. I looked down to find red tendrils leaching their way through the water puddling on the tile floor. A jagged shard had broken off of the dropped mug—the blood covering it, already being watered down and washed away.

Breaking free of the memory, a heaviness lay against me. Livia's body, slumped forward over on the cold wet sand, was being held up by my leg. Fumbling forward, I grabbed her shoulders and pushed her back into a sitting position.

"Livia! Are you okay? Please be okay." Tears stung my eyes as I held her at arm's length. "Livia, please—"

My stomach dropped the second a pained hiss escaped her lips. She grabbed at the inside arch of her foot. The exact same place where the broken mug had slashed skin.

"Did I hurt you?" I grabbed at her arm, my breathing ragged and spots popping around my eyes. "I didn't mean to. I don't know how…"

She placed a gentle hand on my shoulder before pointing to her unharmed skin, but the pinched look on her face told a different story.

"I'm fine, see."

"But it's hurting you."

"For all its complexities, the mind is one of the easiest things in the world to fool. It will believe whatever it's master tells it to. And when you sense shift, you—Siana— are in control."

I didn't want to master anyone. To take control of someone—to use their own body to hurt them was unimaginable. "I could have killed you."

"But you wouldn't."

The ease I had felt around Livia immediately seeped away.

"Was it natural or brought on by RightCorp?" Her voice was soft, but I found no comfort in it as I had before. She didn't need to explain what she meant—I knew exactly what she was asking.

"Nira, my older sister, I lost her. There was a fire, and I lost her." There was the smoke again.

"Great loss is a guaranteed trigger. Anything that causes a deep emotional response is. I wouldn't be surprised if the RightCorp had something to do with it. Though, it would be strange of them to risk Nira when she could easily have had shifts as well. It makes me wonder why they would only try to activate you."

The gears in my mind were turning. Maybe it wasn't the RightCorp. Although the letter of employment I found of Nira's was far from cordial. And a relationship with Ethan Rightley had to have put a target on her. But if we really were so important to some evil mastermind plan, why would he even risk being with her? And besides all that, he was in love with her.

He was in love.

He was acting strange because he was in love.

I snapped.

"He was pretending to love her to try to push her into a shift. That's why he was so cold after she said it back. He didn't love her. He used her feelings to try to break her and when that didn't work, he used her to break me."

This time, as the shift closed in around me, I didn't ignore it. Instead, I honed in on every single sense and sat in awe of it and what it meant.

My vision blurred.

Smoke filled my nostrils.

Ash coated my tongue.

The crackle of the flames hissed in my ears.

My fingertips burned like hot coals as heat scorched through my entire body.

This didn't come from the Rightley's fire. This was mine and I would use every bit of this new part of me to burn their world to the ground.

CHAPTER TWENTY

HENRY

With the night already fallen and the car miles away and out of service, we stayed with Livia. She was having a friend fix our car and bring it to town in the morning. They were very good at staying hidden. In the hours that we had been here, I hadn't seen a single person besides our trio and Livia.

Siana had been uncharacteristically quiet since she had returned from the beach. I was still trying to wrap my brain around all the information myself. It all sounded like a bit of a stretch, but what did I know, really? I had been asleep my entire life. RightCorp had been lying to us this entire time, using us to help keep their rich partners in Hartlem living in luxury. A wave of gratitude came over me as I looked at Livia. Because of her, I knew the truth. I would never take Soterapine again.

A gentle creak accompanied Josie's reemergence as she claimed the wooden stool at the counter beside me.

"How was the talk with Livia?"

"Enlightening. I believe her when she says that she wants to help, but she is definitely hiding something."

"Do you have any idea what?"

"Not yet, and she wasn't very forthcoming when I asked her about it."

"What exactly did you ask her?"

"The same things you and Siana would have asked her. How did she know so much about Siana's past? Why was she here at the same moment we arrived since it's obvious that she doesn't actually live here full time?"

"That's what I would ask. What would Siana ask?"

"Was she planning to ax murder us in our sleep?"

A familiar sense of pride surged through me as she tossed me a crooked smile. Josie and I had always been close, but it elated me to know that she was my friend. She put her hands in her lap and looked over to where Siana was sitting on the floor, her gaze fixed on something in the distance. She hadn't moved from her spot on the floor of the living room since we had gotten here. The only conversation once we arrived was her telling us she needed space to think. She had even gone as far as pulling what little furniture was in the room around closer to block off any access to her.

A knot had formed in my throat. "Do you think she will be alright?"

"She's been the strongest person I've known since the day I met her. She'll pull herself out of this. She has to."

"And RightCorp? The Rightley's? What do we do about them?" Knowing that she would have no straightforward way to answer the questions, I asked them anyway.

"We take it one day at a time. It's going to be hard to get any kind of information without getting much closer to them."

Siana's mouth had slid into a slight smile. Her eyes were closed as she had raised her hand to her mouth. She was lost in her thoughts, and I found myself hoping I was in them. I wondered where we would be. Maybe in a castle from one of those books that she reads. Or back on the beach with the breeze off of the waves rolling over us and filling our senses with the smell of salt and fresh air. I inhaled the scent, more real than if I were standing on the beach at that very moment.

"What the..." My shoes were sinking into the wet sand as Siana walked toward me, her hair a beautiful mess of dark locks whipping around in the now raging wind. A feeling of wrongness crept up my spine, but I brushed it off as quickly as it came. A tingle at the base of my skull felt like a warning. I wasn't supposed to be here. As I continued to stare in amazement at the woman in front of me, her smile contorted into one of pain. The scent in the air shifted to that of acrid smoke that filled my nostrils and made it difficult to breathe. Gasping for air like one of the many fish now flopping onto the sand from the violent waves, my head spun as my knees collided with the ground. This was fear: raw and untethered, storming through my veins with all the ferocity of the raging sea.

"Henry!" Her lips didn't move, but her voice was clear and ringing in my ears. I sank further into the sand. The cold, wet sludge compressed every inch of my body until it had swallowed all traces of light from my vision. The sound of her muffled calls barely made it to my ears as the darkness overtook my senses and the world was abruptly pulled away.

Voices softly thudded in my ears. The ground under me was soft and free of any dampness. They had moved me from the sand and into a bedroom. A drum was pulsing inside my skull with every breath.

"It's vital that you don't tell them anything until you know you can trust them. I know you feel bad about what happened to him, but once you have a bit more practice, you will wield it more effectively."

"I wasn't wielding anything. I don't even know how it happened. I was sitting there minding my business, thinking of a freaking lemon cake. I was just doing your hour glass thingy and when I looked up, there I was, standing on a beach, with Henry drowning in the sand right in front of me. "

"I know it's scary, but you have to try to focus on honing it. It's important that, for now, you only focus on sending out your own memories. Sense shifts are dangerous enough when you have a clear reference."

"What do I tell him? How do I explain why this is happening?"

"His body and mind have been through a lot in the past week."

"I was killing him and you think he is just going to be-lieve that he passed out from what–exhaustion?" Siana's quip was void of its usual snark. An air of defeat that I had never heard in her clung to each word. Footsteps and the retreating sound of her voice signaled her exit, "He may be a dire, but he's not an idiot."

There was a shuffling of feet far too heavy to be Josie or Siana. Livia's voice was barely a whisper as she spoke to whoever was still in the room. "What she described wasn't a memory."

"She shouldn't be able to push new senses on anyone yet." he said.

"I know. We need to be very careful with her. I need to go check on some things. If I'm not back before morn-ing, make sure they are safe and that they have a way home."

A door slammed in the distance, the sound echoing back and bouncing around my head. Breathing deeply un-til the thrumming faded, I put away thoughts of what hap-pened and faded with it.

CHAPTER TWENTY-ONE

RHETT

The dark gray walls of the training gym stood dull and void of any character, with no motivational posters or mirrors to encourage progress. That was fine. I had a very vivid imagination and the vision of Henry Eklund getting the shit beat out of him was all the encouragement I needed.

The benches lining the far wall would usually be covered in workout bags and bottles, but today, there was only my jacket and button up. After my morning meeting with the Rightleys had gone south, I made an unexpected trip here to try to calm down. Everyone cleared out without me having to say a word. That was one good thing about being the Rightley's beast–no one questioned me. Sliding another fifty pounds on each side of the bar, I began my reps, envisioning the look on Ethan's face when I brought the cop in myself. He had no idea how close they had come to being stopped at the gate. I wanted nothing more than to make him pay for their little trip.

The sound of the heavy weights clanked through the open room as I dropped them to the ground. I had done everything in my power to make sure they had stayed hidden and that the Sector was kept at a safe distance. Henry led me to believe that he cared more for his place in Coranta than the girl. He hadn't been off of the Soterapine long enough to lie, which means that she must have been having an effect on him sooner than expected. There would be no denying that the stimulus worked and Siana had been activated.

The towel I grabbed to dry myself off was already soaked–fuck. There would be no avoiding going back to the manor and cleaning myself up. The courthouse was a half hour drive and I would need that time to get my anger in check. The facade I held was breaking more and more these days. Being so close to the final stages had me on edge and Eklund's newfound feels were getting in the way of my planning.

The thud of the towel hitting the trash can barely registered before the bench that held my belongings collided with the wall behind it.

I had always thought the Rightleys were idiots. Their predecessors were at least vicious and brutal, but this iteration of them was nothing but a pack of smiling morons. They jumped at the chance to have a Willulf work for them. As if I could be squeezed under their thumb. When my father contacted them about me coming to guide their legal operations years ago, they had thought it was a chance to get a hold on our fraction of the continent. Without a sliver of brain cells between the lot of them, they had no idea that I was here to overthrow theirs. When you live in a fog brought on by your own drugs, it's difficult to see more than a few steps ahead of you. Only Ethan Rightley and his sister were the exception to this rule. No matter how much encouragement I had given him, he never took the bait.

A familiar ring sounded. I despised the small black box that glared at me from the floor. Ethan used them to keep track of all of his high ups. Early on, I had made an almost fatal mistake trying to make contact with my family. Not realizing yet that Ethan could zero in on any conversation, I was just able to talk my way out of a toxic situation. He kept close tabs on me since then. Plugging in the hearing piece and placing it in my ear, I answered the call, well aware of the ears that could be listening along. I put my flat-line demeanor back in place. The Soterapine haze that I had mastered fell over me and I played the part of the cold hearted beast again.

"Hello, Glinda. Has my one o'clock been confirmed?" The moment of silence on the other end left me checking to be sure my phone didn't need repair again. The courthouse clerk was eerily soft spoken when she finally answered.

"I sent a messenger to cancel your meetings today, Mr. Willulf, just like you asked."

I hadn't asked her to do that, which meant one thing.

"Thank you. I should be at the Courthouse in about half an hour so we can get started on that paperwork." A hurried sign off and one brisk walk later, I was behind the wheel of my car, speeding my way through Coranta's unkempt streets. A myriad of rusted buildings went by in flashes. For all the pomp and circumstance that the Rightley's and RightCorp put on for the other overseers, you would have thought that their city was built of gold. My father always spoke of them with a high level of abhorrence, and I could see why. Although their facilities were pristine- carved out of white marble that blazed in the daylight, the rest of this fraction of the continent lived like vultures, picking at the carcasses of their families, only to build desolate shelters for themselves. The irony of that thought was far from lost on me. Our city was sterile and clean despite housing the remains of all of Coranta's dead. The Willulf overseers had long since stopped trying to hold on to a past that no longer served their purposes.

As I slowed to pass an elderly couple in the late years of their life, I thought about the RightCorp mantra. Many here didn't thrive. Watching them picking up the trash and debris out of an alley entrance, I couldn't help but wonder if they would thank me when I burned this entire city to the ground. If time was kind, they would live long enough to see me do just that.

Glinda was waiting in the parking garage when I finally arrived at the Courthouse.

"I tried to tell her to go home, but she insisted that it was worth the risk." The sound of the city outside combined with the echo of engines did nothing to hide the worry in her voice. The cold grimy walls of the parking garage amplified her words and carried them into every dark crevasse. This was the only parking garage in the city that received regular upkeep, and yet it still felt like an ancient relic, only a matter of time before its years of use broke it down and took the people who used it down with it. We walked slowly through the ever present puddles that seemed to materialize from nowhere. Glinda forced her steps to match mine, and I could sense the racing of her pulse. The smell of stringent cleaner filled the small space as we entered the white marble elevator.

"You have to calm down." The glow from the buttons matched the red that had bloomed on Glinda's chest and ears.

"That's easy for you to say. You're not the one that had to come up with a convincing lie and four different messengers at the drop of a hat just because she couldn't follow protocol."

I had to admit, this was more than a little inconvenient. As the elevator slowed to a stop, I turned to the clerk and placed a hand on her shoulder. She didn't pull away from me but instead took a step closer despite her foul mood. A warmth covered my hand, and she relaxed just a bit.

"I will admit that it isn't the best timing. However, if she is here, it's because something has happened–and whatever it is, we'll probably need to move quickly." A hint of determination stirred in her eyes as we walked down the dark carpeted halls. The pattern had always reminded me of a snake, winding around itself over and over until it was lost in its own twists and turns–unable to strike at its prey. Fitting that it should rest in the Rightly's so called place of justice. The place where another one of their supposed sheep, stalked their every turn, waiting for the chance to lunge at their throats. The visual had put a smile on my lips as I parted ways with Glinda.

I pushed open the heavy wooded door to my private offices. The dark sitting area that greeted me was barely touched by the hallway's light. Instead, the only source of illumination was cast by a single green stained glass lamp that sat on one of the ebony side tables. The woman sitting in one of the leather-back chairs seemed frozen in its iridescent glow as it colored the gray strands that ran through her hair a sickly green. She looked up from the book she had been reading to stare me straight in the eye. A gesture that she accomplished without an ounce of fear or reservation. A feat that most here in Coranta would not think of chancing even in their wildest dreams. I took a step into the sitting area, but not before making sure no one else was in the hall, closing the door and locking it behind me.

"I believe I've found something you've been looking for." She smiled, the warmth of it lost in the darkness of the room.

"I can't imagine anything that would warrant you risking everything to come here." The anger that I had tamped back down since my outburst at the gym bubbled to the surface again.

"Keep it up and I won't tell you a damn thing. You may lead this charge, but don't forget who put you there. Now, if you're done being an alpha male, you can come sit over here and I can fill you in on our progress."

"I'm not being unreasonable in asking that you stick

to protocol. You should have at least waited until a Gift shipment went out so the East gate would have been cleared." The frustration coming off of me in tendrils was palpable and filled the room with an icy chill.

"We don't have enough time to be waiting on empty gates." She stood and walked to the high counter that housed a pneumatic tube system, jotted something on a piece of paper, and sent it down the tube. I rubbed my hands on my temples, my irritation steadily rising while the temperature of the room continued to drop.

"We need to make a decision."

"Where is she now?"

She smiled as she nodded toward me. "I'd venture a guess that she is still currently sleeping in your old bed. She definitely has the potential to help us take it all back. I think she has all five senses. She almost killed her cop friend with only a few weeks' worth of being activated and with only one guided shift." Serves him right for being an unpredictable ass.

She crossed the room and placed her hand on my shoulder.

"We stand to gain the most advantage with her."

"Well, what kind of son would I be if I ignored the advice of my elders? I need her back in the city, though. I'm not done here yet." A key turned in the lock to the office door and Glinda entered with a steaming cup of dark liquid.

"Sorry Livia, we have nothing to add to it right now."

"That's alright, it's not for me. It's for Rhett—to warm

himself up before heading back to the viper's den. Besides, my Little Wolf has always preferred his coffee black."

CHAPTER TWENTY-TWO

SIANA

Nothing felt right. I kicked my way out of the slippery soft sheets lining the bed and rolled to my side, taking in the dark space. Looking around the room, I could tell whoever had lived here before hadn't used it in a very long time. It was slightly larger than the house my family had claimed, and with more rooms. Even so, Josie insisted she room with me after everything that had happened with Henry. I didn't disagree.

A worn set of wooden balls was lined up on a shelf closest to the door. They were arranged from smallest to largest and several other wooden shapes were spread out among them, including several animals and what looked to be some trees as well. If you really think about it, it's kind of morbid that someone would carve a tree out of a tree. To each their own, I guess. This space had obviously once belonged to a child. Everything that they would have played with, including the wooden figures, was worn and chipped- not from time- but from being well used. Livia kept everything extremely clean. Although it was easy to tell that no one had stayed in this room for a long time, there wasn't a dusty shelf or cobweb in sight, but floorboards still gave away the house's age. As soon as I stepped foot off of the bed, they creaked under my weight.

My feet brushed over the cold wood floors on their way to the window. The beach house that was trapped in my thoughts was out there somewhere and my eyes tried their best to pierce the darkness that stood between here and there. No luck. Staying mindful of each creaking board, I paced around the room, stopping only to pick up one of the wooden balls from the toy shelf, and tossed it back and forth between my hands. Staring at the worn surface of the ball, I toyed with the idea of making a solo trek to the house. The thought of being alone, sitting in the darkness of where my family used to live, was comforting. Would Nira have felt the same way?

A shallow gurgling sound behind me caught me off guard and the wooden ball plummeted to the dark oak floor, leaving behind a hollow thud that echoed through the dark, empty house. I stood silent for what felt like an eternity, just listening for stirrings from any room.

Why was I so on edge? Could be that I took Henry's ass out without even knowing what I was doing. Or that I had caused Livia serious pain without even leaving a mark. Or the fact that I'm pretty sure I did the same thing to Nira the day before she died. Or it could be that I've been told to keep it a secret from the only two people that I have left in this world. Maybe it was because I was still wondering if Aunt Jerry blamed me for what happened. Did she know what I could do? What was done to Nira because of me? Would she ever forgive me for what happened? Maybe it was because the person that I had spent my entire life looking up to, the person that kept me level and loved me more than anything, was gone. Nira was my world, and she was taken from me. How was I supposed to live through all the shit being flung at me without my sister there to hold my hand and tell me it would be alright because it had to be? Because we had each other. Now, the only part of her I had left was a slight blotch on my skin.

A rush of anger flooded through me. Without thinking, I picked up the wooden ball and slammed it into my arm where the bruise Nira had given me was starting to fade once again. A sleeping Josie began to toss back and forth after the first hit, a small whimper escaping her lips. Had I made her feel that? A panic settled over me as the taste of burning plastic quickly coated my tongue. The sparks that were now encasing my vision spurred me on, and I raced for the front door. No one else needed to be hurt tonight because I couldn't control my emotions.

The cold night air was a welcome shock as I ran the distance to mine and Nira's old childhood home. We hadn't done anything to shut the old beach house back up and several birds had taken this to their advantage. And by the sounds of it, had already taken to building nests in the living room. At least someone would make use of this place once we went back to Coranta. My legs ached from every tree trunk and hole I had collided with. Darkness is never a friend to the clumsy, and my legs would be the proof of that when daylight came. For now, the house was still pitch black and promising its own number of bumps and bruises. The moonlight that had guided our way before was now smothered by clouds. I awkwardly tried to vault myself over the window ledge that Henry had helped me with only hours ago. It seemed like a lifetime ago. I guess everything will seem like a lifetime ago when the person you think you are changes every couple of hours. A soft, red glow emanated from the hallway and sparked something in my brain.

"How did I forget about you!" Remembering the light from when we first peeked through the darkened windows, I rushed over the ledge and bolted down the short hallway before it could vanish again. A faint red light was shining up through the floorboards. Frantically I searched for something to pry the wood up with and quickly returned with a spoon from the kitchen. As hard as I tried, the boards wouldn't budge from their resting place and after several attempts and a very, very bent spoon, the stubborn side of me went to find something a bit more destructive. The pipe Henry had used before was still laying on the crumbling front porch.

"Sorry birdies, but if I'm not sleeping tonight, neither are you." With the first strike of metal on wood, the startled birds flew from the house all at once. Although Josie would certainly not agree, the assault on the old floor was just the therapy I needed. A large gap in the splintered floor was my prize. My feet were steady as I braced my legs under me, the first floorboard wedging little wooden spikes in my hands. The rusty nails screamed their frustration as I pulled them away one by one.

Below the boards, a metal box sat, covered in years of dust. Looking at the state of it, it was hard to believe that the little red bulb was able to produce light at all. The number panel on top gave no sign as to what that code might be. One thing was certain, whoever put this here knew that they wouldn't be returning for it any time soon. Why else would they have nailed it up?

A rustle of papers and the sound of something rolling from side to side with a gentle clink answered as I shook the box. Brute force had served me well so far, so I saw no reason to turn my back on it now. The sounds of chaos rumbled through the house with each slam of the pipe on the number pad. Unfortunately, by the end of my assault, all I had managed to do was knock off all but one of the numbered buttons and leave the metal box with several small craters. I, on the other hand, did not fare nearly as well. My head swam with exhaustion as my body yielded to the strength of my mysterious treasure.

The warm glow of light that snaked its way toward me did more to piss me off than lend any help. The coming light meant that I would have to face Henry and Josie and all the other lies that others had forced me to live.

CHAPTER TWENTY-THREE

HENRY

My heart was still trying to break its way out of my chest as I gripped the frame of the door. Through ragged breaths I spoke to an unconcerned Josie, "I don't know what you are talking about, but I know that my chest feels tight and I'm having a hard time breathing."

The look that Josie was throwing my way was a mixture of what I had been taught to recognize as affection and something else. Humor, maybe? But this was no joking matter. Minus the telltale tingle in my arm, this was a textbook heart attack. And she was laughing.

I exhaled as slowly as I could before continuing, "I realize that I'm new to understanding emotions, but I can't puzzle out why you think this is funny." I had woken that morning to check on them both to find Siana was gone. After a thorough search of the property, I had woken up Josie to inform her of my findings. Unfortunately, my current medical state had put a momentary halt to my search.

The cold floor sent a shock up my legs as I followed Josie. The hallway, although lit by rays of morning sun, still clung to the chilly night air. I entered the kitchen to find the kettle that had been my alarm clock earlier this morning had been moved from the old wood stove. Livia must have woken up early this morning and had already started her day.

"I'm not laughing at you having a heart attack, Henry, because you're not having a heart attack. You're scared because you don't know where someone you care deeply for is, but I can guarantee you she is just at the beach house." She took one of the many chipped mugs from the cabinet above the stove, like she had lived here all her life.

Thinking back on our past cases together, I could see a habit of making herself at ease with every situation. I'm now realizing what an accomplishment that had been. Her calm demeanor made my jaw clench as she worked on the three cups of tea in front of her. Pacing back and forth in front of the kitchen island only had my heart pounding harder in my hollowed out chest. The wooden stool scraped against the floor as I pulled it from under the counter. My fingers ached from gripping the edges of the stool tightly as a churning sensation went to work in my stomach. A strain pulled at the back of my eyes as I squeezed them shut, trying to calm the dizzying fog that overtook me.

"Do you remember the man that was brought in from G Borough? We had just finished a case and were at the station filling out the paperwork when they brought him in. His wife had jumped into the reservoir and couldn't be found." Josie's calm had shifted as she crossed her arms over her chest. "He was inconsolable. Remember how you had to restrain him?"

"Yeah. And wound up with a broken finger and a pretty sizable black eye for the trouble."

She didn't look at me while she continued.

"After the call came in that she had been found alive but badly hurt, the destruction that he was causing changed to this sickness that overwhelmed him."

The scene brought a tightness to my chest that had never been there before. I found it hard to think about the man now. The memory seemed fresher in my mind than it had, as if it had sharpened and was now cutting through my throat from the inside. A burning sensation gripped my lungs.

"He loved her. He was broken when he thought he had lost her, and he did the only thing that made sense to him. He made everything he touched as broken as him. And when they found her, his body was already so devastated from the destruction, its only recourse was to fall apart until he could be with her again. That's what emotions are, Henry. They break and heal us over and over again and if we're lucky enough, we find someone that urges those feelings to heal us when we are with them and shatter us when they're gone." A gentle smile graced her hopeful face. "I'm sure that when he was able to hold her in his arms again and see that they would make it through, every part of himself snapped back together." Eyes alight with hope, she took a deep breath and handed me a cup of tea.

The sad realization that the story didn't end the way she thought tugged at the edge of my mind. His wife's injuries had resulted in her death later the following day. We sat for a while with only the sound of spoons clinking on mugs to break the silence.

"I've known for a while that you love her." Josie had finished her first cup and was now staring at me through the steam rising off of the second. A soft and knowing smile disappeared as she took a long drink of her tea.

"Josie, I've never had access to what I felt before the last week. I'm much more aware of my body when she's around. Most of the time, I just feel like I'm going to be sick. But I don't want to be away from her."

"I think you should tell her."

"She just lost her sister. Even I understand she needs time to heal from that."

"What she needs is to know that the people around her care for her."

"The last thing that she needs right now is me telling her I feel nauseous every time I look at her."

"Wow. I would say that I could change my perfume, but I don't wear any."

If Josie was shocked by Siana's unexpected entrance, she didn't show it. The stool I had been sitting on just seconds before was still wrapping up its percussive fall as I hurried to leave the room.

"He was a lot less weird when he was a robot."

Siana's voice didn't carry the same bite that usually clung to her tone when insulting me.

The final click of the door shut out whatever response Josie was giving her. The tingling sensation creeping up my neck and face carried a fire with it.

CHAPTER TWENTY-FOUR

SIANA

I had arrived back at Livia's, finding Josie laughing hysterically and a flustered-looking Henry. My entrance had sent Henry fleeing down the hallway and Josie into action, checking me over and pouring me tea. Although the attention reminded me of how Aunt Jerry and Nira would fuss over me when I was littler, it had left a pit in my stomach.

"I'm going to go make sure he's alright. I think he's still in shock from the whole' not dying thing." Josie made her way toward the space where Henry had fled.

We had to go back to Coranta as soon as possible.

Henry would already be in trouble, but because of what happened last night, Josie had come up with a plan to have him admitted to the Med Borough. If everything worked out, we would have time to come up with a plan for keeping him from being sent to RightCorp or a rehabilitation center.

Livia had been driving up to the house this morning as I made my way back from mine. She had answered all of my questions about my family that she could. What my family was like and how we had all came to live here to flee the Overseeing families. Her eyes glazed over with tears as she told stories about all of us as kids playing on the beach and drawing shells in the sand.

"I'm sorry that we weren't able to find you before all of this happened. We looked for you as best as we could, but we couldn't risk being found again." Livia's eyes watered as she spoke.

"What I can't understand is why Aunt Jerry never reached out to you." It seemed like an innocent enough question, but the red that shaded my vision had to be coming from Livia.

"You must have known Aunt Jerry?" The red darkened, giving me tunnel vision.

Her gaze didn't shift from mine as she went on. "You lost so much the night you and your sister were taken."

"Taken?"

Livia released a slow breath, steadying herself before lowering to sit on the old couch. "Come sit with me." I moved to sit beside her, leaving space between us.

She stared at the space and went on. "Your father

loved your mother so much. By the time he lost her, he had already lost all hope in RightCorp. It was the final push he needed to get both you and your sister out. To get all of us out."

"Out of Coranta?"

"And away from RightCorp." The hairs on my arm tingled as she reached for my hand. Red stained the edge of my vision and pulsed with a heartbeat that didn't match my own.

We all thought he would die too, and in a way, he did. We didn't know it at the time, but he began taking Soterapine to ease the pain. Your aunt tried her best to help, but nothing seemed to work. She thought that you would all be safe, but I really don't think she saw how far gone he was. None of us did."

I got the feeling that she had paused to let me take everything in before delivering the worst of it.

"Your aunt went on a run to help another fraction being ravaged by the effects of Soterapine and returned to a house full of strangers. They took everyone, but your Aunt Jerry fought back and fiercely. RightCorp hauled you all away before anything could be done." A sour taste was lingering in the air as the red faded from my peripherals. "You've already lost so much, sweet girl, that I hate to cause you any more pain. But you need to know that the woman you grew up with was not your Aunt Jerry. She died the night you and your sister were taken."

RightCorp had taken my family from me. A family that I should have grown up with and loved. We should have been able to share memories instead of the lies that had raised me.

"That can't be right. Why would someone give up their life to pretend to be my aunt. Aunt Jerry isn't a bad guy. She's our aunt. She loves us." I took a breath when the panic began to rise again. Henry and Josie were too close. I couldn't lose myself and hurt them again. I couldn't. I pulled in another slow breath. "How do you know all of this? How did you get away from them?"

"I'm sorry, Siana. I'm so very sorry." The tears had escaped her eyes and were now falling unhindered over her sharp cheekbones.

"We hid. I couldn't stand the thought of them taking my son. I was scared. I couldn't risk my son."

Without another word, I closed the space and wrapped my arms around her. The feeling of loss was debilitating. For what seemed like a lifetime, we sat there wrapped up in each other's arms and crying. From the bottom of my heart, I hoped that she could sense what I was feeling. I couldn't possibly blame her for what had happened to us.

The blame rested firmly on RightCorp's shoulders. It was time to go home. Time to find a way to make them pay.

The drive back to Coranta had been slow.

With Josie focused on the road, there had been very little conversation. Henry had tried to take the wheel of his newly restored car as we had said our thank you's and goodbyes to Livia and her friend, who had fixed it. Turns out that the battery cable had just popped off when we hit the post. I couldn't help but chuckle at the sight of Henry, his face drawn down into an unmistakable pout as Josie took the keys from him, saying she didn't want him passing out at the wheel.

"You okay?" Henry leaned over and waved his hand in front of my face.

"Mmm hmm." The bumpy road was jostling us back and forth and turning us into a peculiar set of bobble heads. The smile I gave him was less than genuine. Running over all the information Livia had given me had left me zoned out since we left. Something was bothering me about her story. I had a sneaking suspicious that she wasn't telling me something important, but I just couldn't put my finger on what it was. Her heartache was real, I could feel it; but I could have sworn I felt something more sour. A regret that wasn't as cloudy as her pain. It was sharper, as if she weren't remembering it but living it.

As I stared out of the window, the landscape changed. The tall trees gave way to decomposing signs. A sinking feeling in the pit of my stomach accompanied the knowledge that we would be back in the city soon. A city filled with people, most void of feelings, but vulnerable none the less. Taking a deep breath, I looked at Henry. As long as I kept my feelings in check, there would be no risk of me hurting him again.

He caught me staring and smiled.

"Do you think she'll hit every pothole on the way back?" There was a hint of a tremble in his tone, probably from the bumpy ride. He must've been nervous about Josie's driving.

"Correct me if I'm wrong, but there is only one person here that has ever wrecked a car." My eyes caught his, and I hoped that he could see the humor there. He had never been good with jokes or sarcasm before. My own smile returned at the smirk he gave me.

"Well, if we are pointing fingers, there is only one person in this car that makes a habit of breaking things. And it's certainly not me." He angled his body toward mine.

"Well, if someone weren't the most annoying dire in the world, I wouldn't have to resort to violence all the time." A chuckle came from the front seat. Our focused driver was invested in our conversation. Speaking of interrupting conversations…

I looked at Josie in the mirror. "This morning, when I came back from the beach house, you two were pretty deep in conversation. What were you talking about?"

"Funny you should ask we were…"

Henry grabbed my hand to get my attention. "Talking about adjusting to being off of the Soterapine, among other things." With his hand still on mine, it was hard to focus on anything that he was saying. My head tingled as I felt a pull to him. I had always thought Henry was handsome enough, but now that he had a personality, or at least was growing one, something felt very different when he was so near. There was a strange mix of emotions that seemed to war against each other. Josie slowed the car as I inched a bit closer in the seat.

"We're here. Sit tight while I make sure we can make it in unnoticed." The door closed, and I found myself alone with Henry.

An overwhelming smell of spiced tea filled the car as the temperature began to rise. My heart pounded in my chest as Henry's eyes glazed over, a golden fog covering my own. The feelings hovering over me were a strange combination of longing and fear that threatened to suffocate us both. Henry closed his eyes and clutched at his heart.

"Henry." I grabbed at his shoulders and face–my fear rising. What if I really hurt him this time? I forced myself to focus on being as calm as I could. I thought about the sound of waves from the beach; the smell of dust falling from the cover of a book; the taste of freshly brewed tea on a cold night. Hands still on his face, I opened my eyes.

"What was that?" He looked as confused as I felt. It wasn't fair to keep putting his life in danger.

"Henry, I'm sorry. I should have told you as soon as I figured it out. I should have trusted you with it, but it was new and scary and I didn't know how you would react."

"Siana, I think I'm feeling the same way. All I know is that when I'm not around you, I feel sick and when I am with you, everything is brighter and I can sense things that I never have before. I'm learning how to be this new version of me one day at a time, and I have you to thank for it. I think I loved you even before I was allowed to. I think that's why I've always been pulled to you, and why now that pull is even stronger."

Before I could explain, Henry pulled me to him. His lips were on mine before I could take a breath. A slow warmth spread from our pressed lips, and I could feel his entire body shiver as he held me. The golden glow that had surrounded my vision was almost blinding now as

Henry pulled away to look at me, his expression full of love and hope. It felt as if a string was pulling me closer to him again. The kiss we had shared left a pleasant taste of candy behind.

An alarm went off in my brain. Something wasn't right. Before I could ask if he sense it too, the door behind him opened, and he was ripped away from me.

Two men pulled Henry toward the front of the car where Josie was being held back by two more. From the commotion, two imposing figures made their way through the chaos, ignoring both of my friends and blocking my view of the scene playing out in front of me.

"Henry! Josie!" Neither answered my call.

"Ms. Viteri, I'm so happy to see your safe return. Nira always spoke so highly of you." Ethan Rightley stood before me with a cocky air that screamed bad guy. How had no one seen this before? The Rightleys were scum, and I would make sure my sister's name never came out of this asshole's mouth again.

Elation pulsed through me as I stared at him. We had planned on spending the day figuring out how to get to him and now here he was. Tendrils of smoke poured from my vision as I focused on the feeling of rage bubbling up inside of me. I imagined Ethan's pants catching fire while he screamed in agony. The smell of burning flesh and hair fueling my anger. My vision began to darken around the edges as Ethan took a step forward, clearly in pain but smiling. A smile that held no kindness but victory.

I had shown him exactly what he wanted, that his plan to activate me had been successful. That by murdering Nira, he had forged himself a weapon. The pain I was sending down the connection with Ethan threatened to tear me apart as well. I didn't care. I would take the risk of burning if it meant that the person responsible for my sister's death burned with me.

Frigid fingers traced along my skin. Not realizing I had closed my eyes, I looked to find Ethan kneeling before me on the ground. Rhett Willulf standing behind him with an air of satisfaction making him glow ice blue. The cold continued to seep through my veins. Wait–this wasn't coming from me. Panic was all consuming as he stalked toward me. The air was solid as my feet stayed frozen in place. Turning to desperation, I looked behind him, hoping to find one of my friends racing to help me. In the distance, I could see Coranta. The empty gates we had left from were now teaming with trucks and guards in Right-Corp uniforms. A new panic reared its head. Josie and Henry were nowhere in sight. My body went into an icy shock as darkness obstructed my view. I could feel myself falling before being caught up in a warm embrace that made my frozen skin sting.

"Henry?" My heart and head were both pleading for it to be my friend holding me.

"I see your little game of Hide and Seek has expanded, Siana." Rhett's deep voice sounded far away as I continued to descend into darkness. The warmth of his cheek on mine left me repulsed and aching to flee.

He whispered in my ear, "And once again, it looks like I've found you." For the first time in my life, I was at an almost total loss for words.

Almost.

"Bastard."

The cold snapped through me, followed by a dark laugh. That laugh would no doubt play on repeat in my nightmares.

The darkness flooded my vision as I fell.

CHAPTER TWENTY-FIVE

RHETT

The image of Ethan kneeling on the ground in pain will forever be my favorite memory. On the drive over to the Rightley's estate, I couldn't help staring at the layer of dirt coating the knee of his dark dress pants. I took pleasure in these minor victories.

The body that was tossed in the backseat of his car was in no small way responsible for that. She and her friend were now somewhere in the Rightley's ridiculous house. They had been taken to a set of adjacent apartments as soon as we had arrived, while Ethan and I went straight to the study.

Dark furniture covered every corner of the room and

contrasted the white marble finishings echoed throughout the house. The shelves that lined two of the walls were filled with seemingly random knick knacks that were out of place in this morose setting. Of the entire property, this was the only place that felt honest. Too many times I had met here with Ethan.

Since first coming to Coranta, Ethan had given me more than a few dark tasks from this room. Tasks that had ended in adding to those shelves of which only one did I regret. A worn blue dog collar was propped on one of the many displays. Over the years, I had trained myself to ignore it anytime I was in this mausoleum. But today, it seemed to pulse. A painful reminder of another failure that I should have prevented.

Dark brown liquid swirled in the glass decanter as Ethan pulled at the airtight stopper. There was a sheen to his eye as he handed me a glass and poured. The clink of glass meeting glass was harsh on my ears. With his own already half gone, Ethan sat on the stiff leather couch, arm draped over the back and a look of victory plastered on his face—smug asshole. He was basking in a win that he had done nothing to earn.

My hand brushed over the letter that now rested in my pocket.

Wolf- He's taken the map of the continent and a squad car. Kindolf reported that they have yet to leave his house. What steps would you like us to take next?

My response had been quick, "Clear the gate." The more she knew about Hartlem and the rest of the continent, the easier it would be to train her for my purposes. I had needed her back in Coranta. Everything had been in place to keep her as far from RightCorp as possible and now, here she was, upstairs instead of hidden away. She shouldn't be here right now. I stared at the brown liquid with a scowl as I thought of the uncomfortable amount of time I had spent with Eklund to swap his pills.

Slowly decreasing the cop's intake of Soterapine was supposed to form a connection with her. Keep him close to her and have him report back with any changes until she could be moved. But his week-long nap had knocked that completely off schedule. Luckily, he hadn't short circuited on us. I knew firsthand what happened to a dire when their pills are cut off all at once. It's fucking terrifying.

"You seem to be very pleased with yourself." I glared over at my glass. It would remain out of my system. For as long as he had been offering them, I had been pouring his expensive bourbon in the plants around the room. He didn't tend to them. Even so, I couldn't believe he never saw how many of them died this way. I guess since someone else handled them, the self-centered prick didn't care.

"She's only been activated for a week and she just about knocked me out. Can you imagine how strong she will be with some training?" He tapped his fingers on the side of his drink as he spoke. "She is the leverage we need to finally get out from under Hartlem's blade." He lifted his gaze from his now empty glass. "She can win them their petty war and bring us peace. The Gifts can stay with my people."

He almost sounded noble as he crossed to the small

metal drink cart, filling his tumbler to the brim with the muddy fluid.

"Better be careful, Ethan," I spoke slowly while giving him my most menacing grin, "Someone might accuse you of being a philanthropist."

A cold glare was his response as he stalked his way over to his grim treasures and slammed his glass down. The shelf, though sturdy, shook. The items laid to rest there rattled like bones as liquid splattered on anything in its path.

"A society that does not know about the danger surrounding it is more productive. They aren't distracted by the terror of, 'What if?'" He pulled a steel gray handkerchief from his pocket and used it to dust off the dirt that still clung to his pants. "If I can give them a small portion of what they already think they owe me back to them, they will rejoice in it, work twice as hard to please me, and scramble to fight for me when the time comes." The crooked smirk returned as he took the same handkerchief to wipe at the liquor coated item in front of him.

He continued, "I will sacrifice as many of these mannequins as I want if it means taking back what should have belonged to me."

I caught the dark gray and now brown stained square of fabric Ethan threw to me. The grisly token earning his attention now smeared with muddy streaks. A single tea rose crushed between two planes of glass.

CHAPTER TWENTY-SIX

SIANA

A whirl of unfamiliar colors and shapes crowded my vision as I slowly propped myself up on the soft ground. What I had expected to be gritty, unforgiving dirt was a mess of soft linen sheets and blankets. From the feel of them, very expensive linen sheets and blankets.

Where was I? Panic squeezed at my lungs and pushed the air into my throat. I swallowed as hard as I could to force the air back down and breathe. A searing pain in my chest accompanied the breath that followed. Legs kicking and arms flailing, I fought my way out of my soft prison. Cold slab met my feet as I threw myself off of the unfamiliar bed.

"If you don't calm down, you're going to send the entire house into a coma." The lilting voice came from a dark corner of the room and added to that already growing terror that was trapped and clawing at my insides.

"Where am I?" What I had meant to be a demand for answers sounded more like a plea for help. The creak of a heavy wooden door was my only answer.

"You're awake!" Josie's speed seemed almost inhuman as she threw herself at me. We both landed on the bed that I had just escaped, bouncing with the force of impact. Another door creaked open and closed while my friend hugged me. This time, no one entered.

"Are you alright?" She held me at arm's length to make a thorough assessment of my body. Every part of me was aching. The headache that was pulsing behind my eyes seemed to be radiating through the rest of my body, spreading like acid and burning each place it touched. Which was a stark difference to how I had felt just before. What the fuck had they done to me?

"I remember Ethan and Rhett. They did something to me." Flashes of the ordeal cascaded through my mind. I had almost taken Ethan down, but Rhett had somehow stopped me. Checking my fingers for signs of frostbite, a chill skittered down my spine and wrapped its way around the room. Josie's teeth had begun to chatter.

"Leave it to the Rightley's to have real air conditioning in their house." She tugged at the periwinkle blanket that was trapped under us and, after freeing it, bundled us both up together.

I gave a slow glance around the room. The house was more homey than I had expected. The paintings around the room were of beautiful landscapes: an open field covered in purple blooms, a waterfall cascading down a sparkling stone wall, and canopies of lush green leaves which hid several strange looking animals. A table and stool were perched near a window, each covered in chips and dull stains. What I had thought had been a cold concrete slab turned out to be a beautifully worn hardwood floor–the color reminded me of chocolate or coffee. My stomach followed that train of thought with a growl.

"I'm starving, and it feels like someone took a frozen hammer to my skull. What's going on, Josie?"

"They haven't told me much of anything since we got here except that they were waiting for you to wake up to talk to us together." She spoke quickly, as if she couldn't get the words out and away from her fast enough. "When they were carting us off, I overheard them talking to Henry."

The pause that followed was jarring.

"They arrested him for Nira's murder."

"That doesn't make any sense!" I was off of the bed again in an instant. The cold had left the room, and the air had seemed to have gone with it. "Henry would never do something like that!"

"I know that and you know that. But they know he was off of his medication. They think that the sudden drop in his Soterapine levels may have caused him to have a mental break." I glared. The malice in the look wasn't meant for her. "It sounded like total bullshit to me, too. Don't worry." She didn't move from her place on the bed. Instead, she picked at the embroidery lining the blanket.

"Tell me."

She looked up at me with tears already falling down her face and into her long curls.

"They are going to start him on the Soterapine again. He will rot away in some facility as an empty shell and when they tell him why, he'll think he belongs there."

"No. We won't let that happen to him."

The sound of footsteps in the hallway set us both on alert.

"Did you hear the woman that was talking to me when you came in?" She gave me a suspicious look before glancing around the room.

"You and I were the only ones here before I went to the bathroom. If someone was here, they would have to be pretty good at hiding." We both inched a bit closer together. "What did she say to you?"

"That if I didn't calm down, I was going to hurt everyone."

"Josie, I have to tell you something." I chewed on my lip as I thought about how crazy I was going to sound every time I had this talk with someone. How do you even start to explain that you are genetically altered and have government issued super powers?

I let out every puff of air in my lungs before taking in another deep breath and diving right in. I told her everything: from what happened the night before Nira died, to the twists and turns of Livia's story, to the creepy comment from the corner of the room earlier. And I did more than that. I showed her how it worked. I didn't hold back. There was no need to. Josie was my best friend, and I knew without a doubt that I could trust her with my life.

Josie was still staring at me with wonder in her eyes when Ethan Rightley himself came to collect us. As we followed him through the house, I realized that I had been right. The house was as uninviting and harsh as the Right-Corp buildings. The white marble that covered nearly every surface was blinding. The room we had just left was more than a little out of place here. Josie held my hand as we made it to a grand staircase leading down to an imposing entryway. The large glass doors were stunning and let in all the light of the day outside. It should have made the space warmer, welcoming even, but it only shined light on how empty and void of life it was. We walked further along the balcony before passing the stairs. Another set of glass doors greeted us further ahead. These, however, were embellished with wood and glass, throwing rays of colored light cascading over the floor. Ethan stepped to the side to usher us through, an oddly gentleman like gesture for a cold-blooded murderer.

My jaw dropped as we entered the room. Books covered the space haphazardly. Shelves were packed two rows deep with books on everything from romance, classical literature, medical journals, to home repair. The dark wood floors continued throughout, but here they held a touch of warmth. Had Nira ever been in this room? No. She would have insisted that I came to see it. A full wall of windows let in more light and gave a perfect view of the gardens outside, including Nira's. Splashes of colored light fluttered around the room as the doors closed behind us. Of course, my paradise would belong to this asshole.

"Please, come sit with me." He gestured to a cerulean set of furniture placed in front of a large open fireplace.

There was no grate in front to protect the treasures here from floating embers. Josie must have seen me looking and came to the same conclusion.

"You know, if you don't properly protect the things around you, you're going to lose them." I don't think she had meant to make a statement, but it came out that way, nonetheless.

"Yes, well, it's never really been my job to take care of the things around me. Just to make sure that they stay around me. I have other people to take care of them."

"Where is Henry?" I didn't want to sit here and talk about proper fire safety with this man. I'm pretty sure he already knew enough about it. All I cared about was helping my friend out of whatever cold cell this monster had locked him in.

"Henry is at the precinct being questioned. He will remain there until we have the evidence to convict him."

"Or the proof that he didn't do it." My eyes didn't falter as I continued to stand and stare him down. Judging by the way he stared back, he had done this before.

"Siana, why don't you sit down so Mr. Rightley can explain what's going on," Josie's face softened as she flashed him a smile, "It really seems like he's just trying to help."

Shock hit me. Had Livia been right? Had my best friend already decided to side with the villain?

No.

Absolutely not. Josie had a plan, and I needed to follow until I figured out what it was. It had better be really good though if I was going to be made to play nice with this prick.

"Thank you, Mrs. Rutledge. Or is it Miss Rutledge?" He snaked his arm down his chair to grab his drink, a slimy smile hinting at his face.

"Miss. So, Mr. Rightley…"

"Ethan, please."

My gag reflexes were not strong enough for this exchange.

"Ethan, could you tell us what evidence you have that Henry did this?" Josie seemed unfazed by the flirting. If I didn't know better, I would think that she was enjoying it. It was a good thing that I knew better.

"I can't give you any information on an ongoing investigation, but the chief of police and my attorney are working to gather everything we need to proceed. I want to make sure that something like this won't happen again." Leaning forward, he set his glass down on the table that separated the three of us. His eyes were firmly locked on Josie.

"Understandable. Thank you so much for looking out for us. But may I ask you what we are doing here—in your home?"

He turned his attention back to me.

"Your house was completely destroyed by the fire. Nira was a valued and highly respected employee of the Rightley estate." He stood and crossed to the large window, no doubt looking down on my sister's garden for dramatic effect. Asshole.

"I would like to show you my condolences for your loss by offering you both a place here." He turned back, probably expecting to see the gratitude shining on my face. He wouldn't get it no matter how tightly Josie was squeezing my hand. I'm sure he assumed the scowl on my face was just an overwhelming emotion due to his kindness.

"It pains me to think that you were staying with your sister's killer this whole time." If we didn't get out of here soon, I was going to lose it and I wouldn't have to wait for my abilities to take hold of him. I was going to jump off of this sofa and smash his ugly ass head in with a book. Josie could sense it too and placed herself in between.

"That is a very kind offer, Ethan, but what would we do here? We have to contribute and we have been away from work for too long already."

"Our library hasn't had an attendant in many years. I haven't had the need to see to it and as you can see, it has fallen a bit into disrepair. Siana, you will be my in-house librarian. And Josie, since Henry will no longer be needing your services, you will work at the RightCorp facility. We always need talented emotional interpreters for our dires there."

Before he could make it back to us, the doors to the room opened and Rhett walked in, a look of pure disgust on his face. My breathing became quick and shallow as I stared wide eyed at him. I had found it hard to believe before that so many were frightened of him. Not anymore. Sitting up straight, I fought the urge to run. He was a predator who possessed the same abilities as me. Only he knew how to use them. The sense shift that he so expertly forced on me outside of Coranta's walls hit my memory like a cold snap.

The sound of heavy breathing echoed throughout the room and the bright colors turned dark. I pushed the feeling away, trying to steady myself. When I looked up, Josie and Ethan were both breathing heavily with their eyes firmly closed. Rhett, although breathing a bit faster, seemed mostly unfazed.

"You'd better rein that in before you give your friend a heart attack." A fresh terror ran through me as I turned to find Josie, eyes wide but slowly realizing what was happening. With a click of the latch, Ethan and Rhett left. The base of their voices carried back to my ears as they retreated down the hall. With every step that took them further away, I breathed a bit easier.

"What was that? Are you alright?" Josie put her arm around my shoulder and pulled me in. Our foreheads rested against each other.

"Ethan Rightley may be the person that wanted Nira dead, but I'm pretty sure that Rhett Willulf was the one that set the fire." Anger bubbled up, but I wouldn't let it drown me.

"When we got back to Coranta, he did something to me. He made me feel like I was actually frozen. Not just frozen with fear, but as if he had actually plunged me into an icy lake, kind of frozen. And I don't think it's the first time he's done it either." Josie didn't say a word as I continued.

"I know it shouldn't be crazy, knowing what we know now, but it still feels weird to say it. I think that he can control the temperature. Like he can make things deadly cold or…"

"Or blazing hot. Hot enough to start a fire without leaving any evidence behind."

"Exactly." It came out as nearly a whisper.

"He may be dangerous, but I think that Rightley is who we really need to watch out for." She stared at the door they had just exited, pure hatred on her face.

"What, no Ethan?" I had meant it as a joke, but it sounded harsher than I had intended.

"Give me some credit," Josie smirked at me. "He's a narcissistic sociopath."

I let out a laugh.

"Now you're just making shit up. That's not a thing." Since I had known Josie, she was always talking about different words for different kinds of people. It had never once made sense to me. You were either a selfish, unfeeling, dire or you were a regular human with regular human emotions. At least, that's how it used to be. I guess since I knew that was the farthest thing from the truth.

"It is a thing, and a vicious one at that. He is nothing short of in love with himself. He will eat it up if we can get him to believe that we worship the ground he walks on."

"Uh." That was going to be a stretch for me, for sure.

"And," She continued despite my interruption, "he will take actual pleasure in the thought of inflicting pain. Whether it be emotional or physical." She took my hands and looked me in the eye. I knew this tactic of hers.

"This ability of yours, we can use it against him if we can get it in check. We will have to work on your emotional response to things, of course. If he sees that he gets to you, he will keep using it against you." For being someone who was so sweet and soft spoken, she sure knew how to rally the troops.

Whatever plan she had, I was ready to follow. "So, what do we do now?"

"We wait."

I wasn't ready to follow that one. "What do you mean we wait?"

"He has made his first mistake. He is so sure of himself that he has let us into his home. We have full access to his darkest secrets. We just have to bide our time until he slips up or we uncover some dirt on him. Waiting will also give us time to hone that gift of yours."

"Don't call it that. I didn't ask for it and I don't want it. It's the reason Nira is gone."

The room seemed to darken as I realized what I had said. Had I even known that was true before now? The threads that I had been picking at on the couch were now coming out in long strands as I focused my energy on its arm, anything to avoid looking at my own.

"Siana, I know you're hurting. I know that you will never fully recover from losing her, and I don't think that you should." Her voice was quiet as she glanced at me with pain in her eyes.

I swallowed the lump in my throat just enough to whisper, "I don't deserve to heal because it was my fault." She slowly made her way to kneel on the floor in front of me, placing each of her hands on my face.

"Look at me. That is not what I meant. You are not responsible for what happened to Nira. What I meant is that you should always hold on to her memory. Don't let them take her from you completely. Live with what happened and use it to make you stronger. Use it to take back her memory.

"The Rightleys are morons to think that they could plunge people in the fire and not be forging them. They knew what they were creating. Now, you're going to show them how strong they made their blade."

CHAPTER TWENTY-SEVEN

HENRY

I had sometimes seen small children, the ones that didn't belong to a dire parent, holding hands and twirling around: laughing so hard when they inevitably let go of each other and fell to the ground. When I asked Josie about it she had said that it was sometimes fun to be dizzy and unsure of your footing. That sometimes a minor loss of control made people happy. This wasn't one of those times.

I had been in this room so many times that I had lost count. It always smelled sterile, clean. Its small dimensions had never bothered me before, but now it left my head spinning. The stone gray metal table in the center of the room was unblemished and shined unnaturally. The harsh light above reflecting off of it and into my eyes. I closed them and pressed my forehead on the surface, hoping that the cold would ease back the bile that was threatening to overtake me. A door opened.

"Alright, Eklund, this is how it's going to go. I'm going to talk and you are going to sit there, like a good little puppet, and listen. Yes?"

Oh great. All I needed was to be pushed over the edge by this jerk. My head was a leaden weight that wouldn't budge from the table in front of me.

"Where are Siana and Josie?" To my surprise, the question came out clearly, despite my current position.

"You have bigger problems to worry about than those two. Besides, they are safe and sound at Rightley Manor." The smugness in his voice was hard to miss. Even if I couldn't see his expression, I knew he was smiling down at me. But he was insane if he thought I would sit here and listen while Siana and Josie were with Ethan Rightley, unprotected. The screeching of metal on concrete jolted me upright as Willulf dragged the only other chair in the room around to the side of the table. The sound and quick movement sent electricity flicking down the sides of my neck and chasing the path of my spine.

"So what exactly have you convinced my chief that I am guilty of? I'm sure she will know that, whatever it is, it isn't true. In fact, does she even know that you have me here?"

I had him. No way Chief Sheridan knew what was going on. She was a dire as well. She lived off of facts and numbers and no matter how charming this guy thought he was, he couldn't convince her I had done anything. She would see right through him.

"Oh, you mean Prue. She and I actually go way back. Old family friend, you know how that goes." He picked at invisible lint on his jacket sleeve.

"I'll have you know that she is such a good friend that I bet she would go along with just about anything I say." He flashed me a toothy smile. My wrists burned as they strained against the metal encasing them. What I wouldn't give to knock one of those pretty teeth right out of that toxic mouth. Get a hold of yourself, Henry. Think. What would Josie do in this situation?

"I believe that you're trying to intimidate me, correct? Josie has taught me this one before. I believe she said that intimidation is mostly used by men who are overcompensating for something. Whatever that means." Keeping the smile off of my own face was a struggle as he faltered.

"You think you're being smart, don't you?" He leaned forward. The chair slid back as he pushed it away from the table.

"I'm sure that I don't know what you mean. I'm a dire after all. Some of these things are lost on me." He sat back in his chair, a look of triumph re-plastered to his face. My throat tightened and burned. The struggle to keep myself from reacting to his smugness was creating needles that pierced through my body.

"Stop staring at me like that."

"Why, Eklund? Does it bother you?"

"I don't understand what you mean." I knew exactly what he meant.

He reached for the brown leather briefcase that had

been resting on the table, a familiar rattle emitting from it as he moved to open it.

"It's funny you should mention being a dire, Officer Eklund." He grinned as he tossed something at me. I don't know why he thought I would be able to catch it with my hands cuffed in front of me. I managed to get them up just in time to knock the item even farther across the room and send it colliding with the gray brick wall. The small white pill bottle busted open on contact and spilled its contents all over the interrogation room. The small orange pills skittered around the room like rain on a windshield until finally the last one halted by my right foot.

"I hope there was a point to that, because Mary isn't going to appreciate having to clean up after you." I doubted he cared, but I actually did feel bad that she would have to clean this mess.

"Those are your Soterapine, Eklund. Even if you hadn't slept for a week, the batch you've been getting would have had you feeling like a real boy in no time."

"Am I supposed to understand that reference? Or anything you're saying, for that matter?" I tried to keep my tone steady, but I felt my gut churn and twist.

"You don't lie to me and I won't lie to you." In an instant, his mannerisms changed completely. He went from the cocky predator lawyer to something else altogether. "I'm done with the banter. You are going to help me and I am going to help you. Because murder charges don't just disappear into thin air, my friend."

"What murder charges?" The metal of the handcuffs chaffed my skin as I began to wring my hands. My head was full of smog that spun itself into a toxic haze. I already knew the answer to that. Please don't let Siana think I could have done this. Surely she had seen enough of the actual me to understand the kind of man that I was. Hurting her like that would be the last thing that I would ever do. Even before I was able to think straight, I never would have hurt her like that. I would never hurt anyone.

"I had nothing to do with Nira's death."

"It looks like we finally agree on something. Now we just have to agree on what you need to do next."

"What's that?" I asked, shifting uneasily in my chair, my foot accidentally crushing the pill under it and leaving a smear of rust colored dust behind.

"I need you to go to jail for Nira's murder, anyway."

Sheridan marched me out of the precinct while a crowd of people gathered to stare.

"I know that it's a lot to take in, but what you are doing is important." She pushed my head down as I lowered myself into the police cruiser that had been waiting just outside.

"I always had a feeling we would have you in the end." Taking all the information that had been piled on me in the last few hours was dizzying, but my mind cleared enough to snag on what she said.

"You had a feeling?" She winked at me before closing the door. She had been working with Rhett Willulf for who knows how long. And now, apparently, so did I.

As the car pulled away, I stared out the window, shrinking back as people looked on in shock. A dire had murdered someone. Something that had never happened before. As far as they knew, I was now being transported to a detainment facility to await my murder trial. Little did they know, I would be sitting back and twiddling my thumbs while Siana and Josie survived in the viper's den, with only Willulf to protect them. A scratching metallic noise sounded from the front seat of the car, followed by a familiar voice.

"Take him straight to detainment 4. Don't stop for any reason. Do you understand?" Rhett's voice shut off abruptly, followed again by the loud static. Had he tricked me into confessing to Nira's murder? My heart sped up in time with the car as it raced away down the uneven road.

The driver didn't slow or falter as he picked up the radio and answered.

"Understood, Wolf."

"Wolf?"

The officer didn't respond. A sinking feeling in my stomach was accompanied by a terrifying thought. I may have just made a tremendous error in judgment.

CHAPTER TWENTY-EIGHT

SIANA

Sitting at a table with a Rightley would have been an honor a month ago. One of those things that you dream about but know you would never be worthy of. A month ago, I still viewed them as the saviors of Coranta. Yeah, they had also been responsible for creating the people I had once viewed as mindless zombies–but I could always look past that. Now, as I sat across from not one but two of them, I held nothing but disgust for them. They may as well be consuming human flesh. It wouldn't surprise me. If anything Livia had said was right, they had about as much regard for human life as a zombie would.

"Your home is beautiful. Thank you again for being so generous and letting us stay here while everything is being sorted out." Josie was good at putting on a show.

"And how are you enjoying your stay with us, Siana?" Melissa Rightley was as dangerous as her brother. But where he was cold and calculating, she was unpredictable—two sides of the same stunning coin. Her rod straight blonde hair fell down to her waist. The light shining on her pale skin showed off every shadow mapped across her body, while the veins under her skin wove delicate patterns over her arms. At first I had thought she was covered in tattoos. Did she ever leave this house? The dark green eyes she had focused on me were piercing. Ethan was manipulative and charming, but Melissa Rightley just creeped me the fuck out.

I popped a potato into my mouth. "Great, thanks." Focusing on stuffing myself full of food was a great alternative to having to talk to her any more than I had to.

"Siana's Aunt Jerry is an amazing cook, but I have to admit that this is even better." She had meant to take the focus off of me. Tears welled in my eyes as I gripped the cloth hanging off the side of the table. I hadn't told Josie about her yet. The thought of telling her about the woman who had tricked Nira and I for so long made me want to hide in a dark closet, clutching my knees to my chest. It felt too raw to share, even with my best friend. Melissa pushed the contents of her plate around, playing with her food as if it were a board game she was strategically setting up.

My head felt tight as I tried to avoid Melissa's expressionless stare as she went on. "Deanna is wonderful.

My parents always missed her cooking while she was with you and your sister." Ethan narrowed his eyes at her. His own fork scraped heavily across his plate as he pierced a piece of meat. She returned a single shoulder shrug at me in response. "I can see why."

Now I had a name to put to the traitor's face. Something about it suited her better than 'Aunt Jerry'.

"Who's Deanna?" The river of blood pounding in my ears nearly drowned out Josie's question.

"She's here?" I straightened in my seat as the wooden chair scraped at every inch of my exposed skin. My ears pricked, waiting for a sound that would signal her approach from the shadows. The food that had just before been an escape now taunted me and left a gritty and bitter taste in my mouth. My heart pounded as I searched the large room. The door across the table from me seemed to vibrate. Was she on the other side, listening, waiting to make her grand entrance? To say what a stupid girl I had been, to not notice the truth.

I felt a tug like thousands of tiny strings pulling at my brain as the room began to pulse and distort. A shift was happening.

My bare feet were cold as I padded across the kitchen floor toward the smoking stove. Searing hot water was boiling over the charred gray pot and had already put out the burner flames. In my hurry to reach up and remove the pot of lemons from the stove, I splashed some of the scalding water on my arms and hands. Holding tight to the pot handle, not wanting to spill even more, I moved it to the island, my teeth grinding together to fight the pain.

Aunt Jerry had promised that she would make a recipe that Nira had been begging for. Something that she used to make all the time before we moved to Coranta. The heavy pot teetered on the edge of the island before crashing to the ground and creating a sea of bitter lava that I just escaped by launching myself on one of the high stools.

"Siana, what are you doing?" Aunt Jerry had rushed into the kitchen after hearing the crash.

"I wanted to help with Nira's surprise. The water was bubbling over and I thought I could help. I didn't mean to ruin it." Tears streamed down as I buried my face in her arm.

"Oh, oh, oh. There now, my sweet girl. You haven't ruined anything." The circles she traced on my back with her palm were warm and loving.

"We can go get more lemons and start again. It's alright. I think I made that batch wrong anyway, so really, you just saved us some time." She took my chin in her hands and smiled down at me.

"Besides, this floor needed a good cleaning." She held me close to her chest again as she sang a lullaby. The out of tune humming still managing to soothe me to sleep.

I gasped for breath at the same time as Josie and Ethan did.

"Are you alright?" My friend was gripping my arm, her head still facing the ground as she tried to steady her surroundings.

"I'm so sorry. I don't know what happened." My eyes widened as I searched the room for any sign of my old home. The pungent smell of lemons still permeated the surrounding air. Both Josie and Ethan scanned their hands and arms while the other dinner host starred down the table at me–a look of pure delight in her eyes.

"You're very strong, Siana. I can't help but wonder at the kind of things that were done to make you this strong." She wasn't looking at me anymore as she spoke. Instead, she kept her eyes down.

"I think it's time we have a talk. Since my sister can't find it in her mood today to behave, we will move to the library for the rest of our discussion. As you can imagine, there are many things we need to go over and much that you need explanations for." My breath seemed far away as it escaped me in slow, hollow bursts. I only managed a nod before standing to follow him out of the room.

"Make sure Miss Rutledge makes it back to her room. I'm sure she is looking forward to a good night's rest." There was no movement behind me as I turned to check on Josie one more time.

"My mouth tastes like batteries." She looked up at me with sad eyes. "And I can still feel the burns on my hands. I can smell the burnt hair on my arms. Your arms. Siana, how…" A hard hand guided me back out of the room. My footsteps felt sluggish as we ascended the grand staircase to the library.

The library doors made a hollow click as Ethan closed us off to the rest of the house.

"Can Josie and I see my sister's garden tomorrow?" I looked for any sign of remorse in Ethan's eyes. Anything to show that he cared about the woman he had spent so much time with and then betrayed. Nothing.

"Tomorrow I will show Mrs. Rutledge around the RightCorp building where she will work from now on. There are quite a few security measures that we have to go over. It will likely take most of the day." He took my glass from my hand, placing it down beside his own on the wooden serving cart.

"Rhett will escort you through your new duties tomorrow and prepare you for your visits to RightCorp."

"And Henry? What is going to happen to him?" I looked him dead in the eye, but he didn't shirk away like I had hoped.

"Do you know what happens to a dire who stops their medication?" He spoke to me as if I were a child. He still thought I believed the lie he was about to tell me.

I snapped at him, "I know the dires can live without the Soterapine."

"That's good. You are a step closer to knowing how our world works then." He smiled at me like he pitied me, and I hated him all the more for it.

"There is a fraction called Renbrough far North East of here. The Overseeing family in charge of that fraction of the continent thought the people would be safer if they knew the truth. As soon as they discovered Soterapine wasn't needed to survive, they cut their communities off from it. It only took a matter of days for them to tear each other to pieces. Being cut off from one's emotions for your entire life, it can be jarring when they all rush in on you. They were confused. They didn't understand what was happening. I'm sure you've been terrified before as a child, but with time and experience, you learned how to cope. Without that practice, they destroyed anything that felt like a threat to them.

"Henry was always around your family. It's natural that he would have felt something toward Nira. She was a remarkable woman, after all." He smiled and gazed out the window. My chest and ears burned. Whether it was from hearing him talk about Nira as if he loved her or as if Henry did, I wasn't sure. Both seemed to stir up something uncomfortable.

"I wouldn't be surprised if he started behaving the same way towards you after Nira died."

The kiss.

"We know he was there the night of the fire, before the it started. We interviewed several of your neighbors who had to be taken for medical attention. They said they saw him go into the house an hour before the fire."

Why wouldn't he have told me about going?

"Medical attention? I didn't realize the fire had spread that much?" The front of my dress was damp as I wiped my sweaty palms over it for the billionth time tonight. "Were many others hurt?" Thinking about how many children lived so close to us left me unsure if I wanted to know the answer.

"The fire was contained to your home. Thankfully, there was only one casualty from the blaze that Mr. Eklund started."

My brows drew together as I looked up at him. Was he pausing for dramatic effect? His eyes narrowed on me like I should already have the answer to the question. I had tried my hardest to not think about that night. About the feeling of her hand in mine as she lay there unmoving. About the smell of burnt hair and flesh that wrapped around and suffocated us. About Henry or the sounds that echoed through the lonely night air afterward. About imagining Nira call out for me just as I let myself fall into nothingness.

Oh. Oh no.

I had shifted.

I whispered to myself, "I hurt them."

Though I did not mean it for him, Ethan twisted the knife further, "Yes. Anyone within a block from your house blacked out from the force of what you did."

"Are they alright now? Did I..." I couldn't finish the sentence.

"Did you kill anyone? No. Just some minor bumps and bruises from falling." He walked to the glass decanter and refilled his drink.

"But you could have." His voice was full of thinly veiled excitement. A promise that someday, I would. Tendrils of nausea curled their way up my throat. I would never use this thing to take someone's life. Never.

"What do you want with me?"

"There is a war going on beyond our continent. It's one that has been raging for almost a century. The short of it is that Hartlem protects us. That's why we send them the Gifts. They shelter us from the storm that threatens to overtake us every day and the people of Coranta live in peace, not knowing how close they come every day to being slaughtered."

"Why don't we protect ourselves? Coranta could fight back like Hartlem does?"

"Weak men will always turn to violence when they know they are cornered. Powerful men will turn to science. Dirations were created to sustain the people when they were forced to send all of their resources to the war. Hartlem blocked us off from the rest of the world to protect their supply chain. And today, we are still sending them resources that belong to our people."

I wondered if he had rehearsed his speech in front of a mirror, practicing each expression to be sure he got it just right.

"I've been to Hartlem. There's nothing there but boarded-up buildings and sand."

"You've been to Hartlem's port at the edge of our continent. Hartlem is a much larger place across the sea. Coranta and the other fractions were created to produce for them. To keep their war going. It doesn't have to be that way anymore. I believe we can take back what belongs to the people and save them."

"You mean everyone but the people like me. The ones that you trade to them." I squeezed the book I had been holding to my chest.

"Sacrifice is sometimes necessary to make sure the many can thrive. Because of what you can do, you can stop anyone else from having to pay for Hartlem's mistakes. Our people are depending on you, Siana."

"Our people?"

"When you are the thing that stands between them and destruction, they become your responsibility."

"What can I do?"

"Your abilities are no accident. They were cultivated in your bloodline by RightCorp to be used for Coranta. With some training, what happened in the dining room tonight could be used on a much grander scale to help

Hartlem stop their war."

"What you mean to say is that they could use me as a weapon. I thought you said violence was for weak men."

"That's why we made you. This wouldn't be violent, it would be peaceful. If you work hard and master the task, no one would have to feel an ounce of pain at all. You can stop anyone from having to suffer ever again. All you have to do is focus and do as I say." Shadows now engulfed the room, the fire being long since extinguished. The smell of the charred wood still lingered on the dark fabric of the seat, and when he came to sit beside me, the smell of it fanned out around him. As he placed his hand on mine, I fought the urge to shake him off. This man repulsed me. He was a murderer. But would I be able to let others continue to pay for my vengeance? I wanted to make him suffer for what he had done to Nira, and someday I would. But for now, I would play his game because he was right about one thing. The people of Coranta shouldn't have to suffer.

"How much of it do you think is true?" Josie had already filled me in on the weird workings of Melissa Rightley as soon as I returned to our shared room. The moon was casting a serene glow across the hardwood floor. Every part of me ached to crawl into bed and sleep. But not this bed. Even with its pillowy mattress and buttery soft blankets, I longed for the familiarity of my own bed.

"I'm not sure. A lot of what he said makes sense, and he sounded genuine for most of it. What do you think about it? Would a narcissisy tell the truth about something like that?"

"It's narcissist and absolutely. Especially if they thought they could use the information to manipulate you." Her reflection seemed to stare back at her as she folded her arms and scrunched her face at the cold window. "It is hard to believe that a war, started decades ago, would still be going. It makes you wonder. What kind of things must Hartlem's enemies possess that they would need so much from us to fight back?"

I continued her train of thought, "and why would RightCorp need to engineer people to fight them?"

"Siana, what you did at dinner tonight was scary. If that's what they expect you to do in Hartlem—" she didn't finish the thought but simply held out her hand for me to take, the warmth of the gesture making me long for times we had curled up on her couch and laughed about nothing. Somehow, facing the truth behind what she wasn't saying left the memory feeling like it belonged to someone else.

"I don't know what else to do though, Josie. It feels like I'm betraying Nira staying here while he breathes in another room, but I'm worried about what could happen to everyone else if I don't go along with him. I mean, how do we even know if what he says is true? We don't have proof of anything."

"Then we get proof. Whether it's proof of what he did to Nira or proof of this war, we find it and do whatever we have to do to make things right. No matter what, we do what's right."

I hugged her as tight as I could. "Please be careful when you are with him tomorrow. I would be lost without you. With everything that's..." my breath tightened around the words as what felt like splinters lined my throat, "I won't survive losing you, too."

"Don't say it like that. I'm not going anywhere and neither are you." We both stood and looked in the gilded mirror that sat across from the window. The braid she had put in my hair was messy and imperfect. She hadn't had a sibling to practice on when she was growing up. But that didn't matter. When it came to the important stuff, she didn't need any practice. It came naturally to her.

"We are going to help Henry. We haven't lost him. I'm sure Chief Sheridan has already cleared everything up and sent him to the Med Borough. He's probably there right now."

I stared out the window, trying not to think about the ugly questions that Ethan had rooted in my mind.

CHAPTER TWENTY-NINE

RHETT

I needed to be back at the detainment facility; I knew that, but I also needed Ethan to think that he still had me under his thumb for just a bit longer. With my car parked just outside the tall white pillars that guarded the ridiculously pretentious entryway, I followed the steps up and let myself in as I had done almost every day for the past five years. The Rightley's mansion and sprawling grounds were too large for them. Taking pride in what you own is one thing, but taking more than what you are owed is something else all together.

Years of wading through mountains of shit were finally about to pay off. The look on that bastard's face when he realizes I'm the one taking his place—priceless. This was the reason I kept coming back. Shutting the large glass door behind me, I made my way toward the stairs. A new thought brought a smile to my face as my foot hit the first step toward Ethan's study and I would be lying if I said that the thought of a certain brown haired firecracker didn't send a welcome pulse through me. Although the last time I saw her had probably left her with some not so welcoming feelings toward me.

Henry was right for worrying about Siana and Josie. Being at the Rightley Estate put them at Ethan's discretion. He would do whatever it took to make sure Siana went to Hartlem, whether she wanted to or not. Luckily, I had someone who wanted to take down the Rightleys' legacy as much as I did. Maybe more.

"Mr. Willulf, has anyone ever told you it's rude to come into someone's home unannounced?" The melodic voice had come from a dark space cast in shadow by the grand staircase.

"Ms. Rightley, has anyone ever told you it's rude to lurk in dark corners?" A pale hand reached out through the wrought iron banister and clasped hold of my ankle.

"Speak to me like that again, Rhett Willulf and I will make sure that you fear every dark corner for the rest of your life." Someone cleared their throat on the landing above us.

"I'm growing tired of your games, Melissa, and frankly, I don't have time for them. I'm going to be nice and give you two choices; One, you go to your apartments and stay there until you can do something useful." Ethan didn't bother with niceties around me anymore. I had long since been privy to the disappointment she had been to him. "Or two, you can go see Dr. Hawthorne at the lab. He has been needing to test out some new treatments before trying them on our new friends." The nails digging into my skin had nothing to do with me. I could feel the fear radiating from her, but she wouldn't let him see it.

"You're no fun anymore." She rounded the banister and slowly ascended the stairs, reminding me of a child dragging their feet to keep from having to do a chore. I could feel how much restraint she was using to keep her steps slow and steady. She continued on without another word.

"She's been trying to get under my skin since my guests arrived." My eyes trailed down the hallway where Melissa had just vanished from. Making my way past him, I walked to the study door and turned the ornate gold handle. It was locked. He had never locked it before.

"We can talk in here today." He turned and headed towards the house's grand library. Had he just waited for me to try the door, knowing he had locked it? I fucking hated this asshole.

"You will watch Siana today. Keep her docile and compliant but do not let her out of your sight. You can show her what she needs to get done in the library while she's here, but your primary job is to assess her abilities. Push her as far as you can and keep her away from my sister. They aren't compatible yet."

"And what do you have on your schedule today?" If he was leaving his prize for Hartlem, there had to be a good reason.

"Miss Rutledge and I will go to the lab." He stated it as if he was talking about running to the store, or going to fetch the paper. I knew better.

"The tests that you mentioned before?" I leaned back on the wooden posts encasing the library doors. I had learned long ago to make my body do the exact opposite of what I wanted to do, which right now was run at him, head on, and slam his head on the hard wooden bookshelves repeatedly until he was a crumpled up bloody mess incapable of letting another word escape his mouth. Instead, I leaned back, folded my arms, and gritted my teeth. My only tell was a slight pop in my jaw as I bit down on the words that I would soon be able to say. "What would be the point of testing her? She doesn't have the genetics to be activated? Any data that the doctor collected from her would be tainted and unreliable." He stalked forward toward the open window, looking down his nose at something out on the grounds.

"What I do with her is not your concern. Just like the first girl was none of your concern." He turned, still composed. "Someday, when you return to your fraction, you'll understand that sacrificing the few for the many is necessary to thrive." He smiled as if he had just given me a precious gift in the form of his sage advice. A tight-lipped smile was all I could muster. "I know you would never question me intentionally. For now, he's only going to run some preliminary tests to see if she would take to being an amplifier." The smugness radiating off of him was nauseating. "The sister is powerful and with her friend as an amplifier, we'll be able to solidify the deal with Hartlem. Everyone loves a gift with purchase." He chuckled under his breath. Leave it to Ethan to laugh at his own joke.

"If you know how powerful Siana is, why are you keeping her here? There would only be so much that I could do to protect you once she knows how to use her senses. And on top of that, I'm not always here to keep you from harm. I know you trust in Hawthorne's dampening serum, but it can't block everything."

The hard soles of Ethan's dark brown shoes punctuated each slow step he took toward the drink cart.

"It couldn't block everything." He didn't bother to mask his satisfaction as he took a sip of his dark amber drink. "I know why you are so invested in them. It must be hard knowing that this one became more than you, despite having to go through the same testing. It would please her father to see what she has attained."

I grit my teeth at what he was insinuating. My father would not—was not. But Ethan was wrong. I wasn't invested because of what she became. It's because I remembered what they both had gone through to get there. She may not remember, but I would never forget.

He raised a hand to dismiss me. "The girls are walking the grounds right now. Send me, Ms. Rutledge, when you find them. I would like to leave immediately."

The vision from before continued to claw at my brain. We were too close for me to ruin everything by doing something stupid right now. Satisfying, but stupid. Getting out of this room was becoming more of a necessity, and I knew Josie would be safe, at least for now.

CHAPTER THIRTY

SIANA

It would be easy to forget the outside world in a place like this. The lush green grass covered the entire property like a luxurious blanket embroidered with flowers. Symmetrical patches of plants wove in and out as far as the eye could see. Several small columned buildings popped up around the edges of each separate garden. The garden sheds came off a bit ostentatious, but what were the Rightley's if not ostentatious? We had come outside under the pretense of getting fresh air and exercise, but it was easier to plan without the walls listening. Turns out Melissa made a habit of being a massive creeper, hiding in corners and waiting to scare the unsuspecting. The disembodied voice in my room yesterday had been hers.

My whole body shivered as I remembered the way she had pulled that memory from me at dinner. It was more than a bit unsettling.

"So we have a plan, then?" Josie said as she locked her fingers with mine.

"You will go with the narcissisy to butter him up and get on his good side. Find out anything you can about what RightCorp is doing to everyone."

"While you stay here and convince Rhett that you are sick so you can snoop around for information about Hartlem and these abilities." She took a heavy breath. "Are you nervous?"

"I am. But we can do this together." A tingling sensation lingered in the back of my head as we hugged. The smell of fresh cut grass and jasmine surrounded us as I sifted through a sense shift. A calm bubble seemed to close shut as warmth spread out between us. Maybe this thing I had wasn't a curse after all.

"Thank you." Josie's breathing steadied as she raised her head from mine.

"I think I'm ready to face the narcissisy. Are you ready for tall, dark, and scary?"

I let out an annoyed groan. "Maybe if you would stop calling him that, I would be."

"It would probably take more than ten seconds to make that change." She gave me a knowing look that was completely lost on me. With an exasperated sigh, she turned me to face the house, and a fast approaching Rhett Willulf.

"For the millionth time, I don't believe you." Rhett's eyes narrowed, one eyebrow arched as he crossed his arms and leaned against the stone building. "And if you keep lying to me, I'm going to make you pay for it." He kicked his ankle across the other lazily–never taking his eyes off of me as he made his challenge.

"Seriously, I…"

"No, you don't. You don't have a headache, your stomach is fine, and you don't actually think Melissa could have poisoned your pancakes this morning at breakfast." He laughed darkly as he continued. "You do, however, keep getting quite flustered every time you look at me, which is why you're pacing back and forth and avoiding eye contact." Pushing himself off the wall, he planted himself directly in my path.

"What the hell? Do you make it a habit to piss off everyone you meet, or am I just really lucky?"

"I don't piss you off." He didn't budge.

"You did some kind of weird mind freeze ray thing to me which landed me here. So, yeah, you piss me off."

"You want to be. But you're not."

Of course I was. How could I not be? And the fact that he was telling me what I felt pissed me off even more. Shoving past him, my feet thudded heavily on the hard packed earth that separated the gardens from the surrounding woods. My legs ached from wandering all over the grounds. Trying to lose my babysitter had been exhausting, and now I just wanted a place where I could sit down and ignore him. The headache I had lied about was threatening to make a real appearance.

"Are you alright?" He was so close behind me, his

voice sent a chill down my spine. I turned on my heel and met him head on before quickly losing my balance and falling to the ground with a hard thud. He towered over me. The heat in my cheeks creeped up the side of my face and set a blaze to my ears.

He offered his hand and a grin. "You don't need to be embarrassed."

"Stop pretending like you know me. Or that you know what I'm feeling. You don't know me!"

Finally, he took a step back, placing his hands in his pockets. His eyes stared off into the distance as he chewed on his bottom lip before crouching down to look at me.

"We aren't going to get anywhere like this. If we can just get past the fake 'I hate you' bit, things will be much easier." He gave a slow glance behind him before continuing.

"I know where you went when you left Coranta and who you met."

A tightness in my stomach was my response.

Eyes focused on the trees just beyond a row of shrubs, I kept a steady tone as I repeated the lie we had told Ethan Rightley.

"I was overwhelmed and needed to get away from people. Josie and Henry came to find me. It wasn't their fault that they missed their work. They were just trying to find me."

His eyes locked with mine, but his expression was gentle: a weird tactic from his usual intimidation.

I went on. "We didn't meet with anyone. We didn't mean to miss working, and Henry didn't hurt my sister."

Henry.

A tingle in my leg had me pushing myself to sit upright on the ground. A steady beat pulsing in my ears made it feel like I was sitting in a tunnel as smoke swirled just on the edge of my vision. "I don't believe that Henry killed Nira."

Rhett stared at me, eyebrows drawn, hands still in pockets. "And you believe that I did."

"I've seen what you can do. I've felt it. You could have set that fire without leaving a trace of evidence."

The feeling of sandpaper being drawn down my throat was not far off from what I was experiencing as Rhett stared down at me. I narrowed my eyes at him. He wasn't going to scare me off. I could feel a gentle pull at my mind before a wide grin tugged at his face.

"Let me get this straight. You think that I set your house on fire — with my mind?"

A sinking feeling overtook me as I held my breath. I had definitely thought it was a possibility until he said it like that.

He lowered himself to sit beside me. "Can you set a fire with your mind?"

"If I could, you would be far crispier than you are now."

He laughed. "My abilities are a similar, if not watered down, version of yours. Where you seem to be able to access all the senses, I can only affect physical responses to those around me. For instance, when your heart races or you get a chill down your spine, I can sense that. I can project any physical response I've ever experienced and some sights, if they had enough of an impact on me. I cannot, however, set things on fire with my mind." I thought of all the things I had felt around him. My eyes widened and my shirt snagged on a root as I went to pull away from him. The dirt under me stuck to the backs of my legs and sweaty palms. He looked me over with a broad smile, which left me staring at a mouth full of perfect teeth.

"Stop that right now." The dirt chaffed my legs with the pressure of my arms wrapped around them.

"It's not something that I enjoy doing." He lowered his head, gaze following to search for my eyes. "Most of the time, anyway." His eyebrow shot up again, the corner of his mouth followed.

Why are you looking at his mouth, Siana!

He let out a slow breath and continued, "I've learned to shut it off. Most days, I have enough trouble deciphering my own mess."

He began to slowly drag his fingers through the dirt until the hard soil became a small mound that he could manipulate.

"You, on the other hand, are a bit different." He drew swirls in the earth as he spoke. "The shift is linked to all of your senses. You can take in or project anything that you or anyone else is feeling. You can also force memories, but eventually you should be able to relay any scene you can imagine. Right now, the worst you can do without help is overwhelm someone with your own senses. Which, without any training, will mostly end in them blacking out. Their brain struggles to understand the multiple signals and shuts it down as a defense." The swirls now covered the ground in front of him. The urge to inch closer to him was overpowering as the smell of sand, salt, and water enveloped me. Was he remembering the ocean?

"How do you know so much about this thing?" A tremble in the words that came out betrayed me. Something coiled around my memory. I was right on the edge of remembering something important before it was beyond reach again.

"There are a number of answers to that question that I would love to give you. For now, just know that I did everything in my power to keep Nira safe."

My eyes wandered to the swirls that he had stopped painting in the dirt. They had become a wall of seashells.

"Why are you working for the Rightley's?" Keeping my eyes down and on the shells, the words came out strong and assertive. "If you know where I was and who I met, then you also know that I know who you really are." Ok, so maybe I wasn't as smooth as I had thought, but the point came across. "Your family are Overseers for a different fraction of the continent."

He worked a spot on the back of his right hand as I continued.

"There's probably a house just like this one with your name all over it. You are Ethan Rightley in sheep's clothing." My face was a mask of stone intimidation as our eyes locked.

Got him.

His booming laughter caught me off guard. The dirt sprinkled back down to the ground as he rose and patted it off of his pants and hands. Now free of earth, he ran them through his dark hair before taking one of my own and hoisting me unceremoniously from my seat. He hadn't killed Nira. I could feel it; sense it. But that didn't mean that he couldn't have stopped it. The strange feeling

I had had in the car before Henry had kissed me was back. A warring between emotions that seemed alien to me. Henry. My nails scraped against his skin as I ripped my hand from his. His face soured as he looked at me.

"Let's get started on accessing your skills." He led me to another section of the property; a garden, not flourishing like those we had passed to get there, but showing subtle signs of neglect and decay. He didn't need to tell me where we were.

She was everywhere my eyes looked.

Withering jasmine crept its way up the stone benches lining the pathway while cerulean delphiniums cascaded over the slightly overgrown grass and in the center of it all, several shrubs sat barren. Nothing more than a skeleton of empty stems. The brown and withered petals laid scattered around its base. Squeezing the hem of my dress did nothing to stop the shaking in my hands as I pulled at the memory of flowers strewn across a messy kitchen island. The smell hitting me hard enough to make me gasp—tea roses. This was Nira's garden.

"You need to learn to block your emotional responses if you are going to wield your abilities." The dark rumble of his voice was unwelcome in this space. Rubbing my left arm, I looked for the bruise. It still hurt. The garden started to spin as my breathing quickened, blood rushing to my ears and fingertips. Pulling every bit of my energy, I pushed it out toward the man standing in my sister's sanctuary.

Rhett's knees gave out, and he slammed onto the ground in front of me. Focusing all of my energy on the night I lost Nira, I let him feel all of it. Every aching heartbeat, every nauseating smell, every dark shadow that tunneled my vision and threatened to pull me under. Before the world snapped back, an arm closed around my waist.

"You did this to her, you son of a bitch!" His usual composure was gone, leaving behind the animal that lurked from just below the surface.

"Ethan Rightley did this to her and to you and to more people than you could imagine." The garden shifted to a sea of red as I imagined him burning. He clenched his jaw as I felt him mentally push back. I let all of my anger lash out as I screamed.

"You're his beast. Don't think that everyone doesn't know you do all his dirty work. What was your plan, Rhett? Bring me here to break me down, make me cry in your arms like a good little girl while you prep me to be sold to Hartlem?"

There was no assault, no physical pain, no fire running up my arms. He wasn't fighting back.

"Fuck you!" My chest and lungs ached as my legs carried me back to the mansion. The sun was still high in the sky when I reached the imposing house. Josie and Ethan would still be gone for a while. It may have not been the way I had planned it, but Rhett Willulf was no longer hounding me. Which meant that my search for answers on the Rightley's and Hartlem could begin—just as soon as I visited the drink cart in the library. The overseer of Coranta may be scum, but he had a decent taste in booze. Knowing my day with his lap dog wasn't over, I was going to need some liquid courage.

Much to my dismay, Rhett took less time than I had expected to recover from the scene in the garden. Which meant searching for answers would have to wait until tomorrow.

The rest of the day inched by while working on cataloging the library. It was obvious the only spaces truly taken care of here were the sitting area next to the fireplace and the drinking cart. The rest of the room, though clean, was in disarray.

Okay, maybe not to the naked eye, but to me it was chaos.

There was no order to the conglomeration of texts strewn about the shelves. The slightly smooth pages of each book called to me to sit down and dive into their world and it would have been a welcome escape from my own if not for the reminder every fifteen minutes that I should be practicing using my sense shifts. After the fifth or sixth time, there seemed to be no avoiding it. I took my time crossing to the armchair that Ethan usually reserved for himself. Immediately regretting my choice of seat, but not wanting to budge, I focused on the disgust I felt and sent it to him.

"Ready to work?"

Leaning forward, the only thing I was willing to give away was a smile.

The silver tray holding the now cold tea rattled as I brought my feet up to rest on the table. It had been brought to us earlier 'at the request of Ms. Rightley' and there was no way I was touching it. Knowing whose hands had most likely prepared it brought on a wave of nausea. Plus, I didn't trust Melissa and odds are she would poison Rhett too if she felt like having a laugh. On that thought, "Why don't you have a nice cup of tea before we start?"

He ignored the prod and moved to the window instead. "Which sense flows out with the least amount of effort?" He wouldn't be giving me the rise that I was suddenly so desperate for. Damn. I would have to think of another way to rile him up enough to get out of my hair.

"Smell."

"That's interesting. Almost every other sense shifter that I have heard of focused mainly on touch or physical responses."

"Oh no. Is poor Rhett not as special as he thought?" Sarcasm dripped from every syllable.

He stormed over to me, grabbing the arms of the chair and entrapping me in the space. My heart slammed in my chest, but I wouldn't shrink away. Sitting up as straight as his arms would allow, I steadied my breath.

His deep languid voice rattled through me, "If you're going to act like a child, Siana, I'm going to treat you like one. There are people who are depending on you to learn this shit, and fast. You've done great on your own so far, I will give you that, but if you don't stop acting like a tantrum throwing child, they are going to be sorely let down." My strong facade broke as I let out a slow, uneven breath and shrunk back into my chair.

"Asshole."

"True." He sat, closing his eyes and slowly ringing his hands together. He took a deep, intentional breath and opened his eyes. "I know you don't trust me yet, but I swear, I had nothing to do with the fire that took Nira away from you."

I looked away. I already felt this was true, but hearing him say it out loud made my eyes sting.

"There is so much that you don't know about the world around you and if it were possible, I would tell you everything. You deserve to know everything." He took a sugar cube from the tea tray. As he went on, little showers a white dust fell to the table between us.

"Ethan wasn't lying when he told you that the people of Coranta are in trouble. The war that Hartlem shields the continent from is real and brutal."

A flash of pure chaos split my vision. I couldn't raise my voice above a whisper even if I had wanted to. My throat was raw with tears that weren't mine.

"What was that?"

"Hopefully, a sign that you can trust me. I have been shown what's coming. No matter what he says, Ethan won't be able to block us off from the rest of the world forever. What is out there will come here and everyone needs to be prepared. There are people relying on you. People that would give anything to see you succeed, and hopefully, I can take you to them sooner rather than later."

"I thought you worked for him. Don't you want what he wants? Isn't that why you knocked me out and brought me here in the first place? To train me and trade me off to Hartlem." The accusation and rage I had meant to show were empty as I picked at the arm of the chair.

"I am sorry for your part in all of this."

Yet again, he didn't say no.

"We should get back to training." He shifted forward in his seat and crossed his arms over his wide knees.

"Since smell is your strongest sense, let's focus on shifting that to me." His quick change left me feeling confused and brushed off. Whether intentional or not, it pissed me off. Much to Rhett's displeasure, I took my lesson very seriously, focusing on the more unpleasant smells trapped in my memory. The boroughs of Coranta had plenty of noxious ones to choose from, and I wanted to make sure that he sampled them all.

CHAPTER THIRTY-ONE

HENRY

The Sector. They were a silent terrorist organization that worked to bring down the tenants of the Rightley's Coranta. Everyone works. Everyone Strives. Everyone Gives, So Many Survive. Never thinking much about it seemed normal. Everyone in the boroughs followed these rules, and being a hard working dire, I upheld them. They were what kept everyone thriving in the city, so how could they be wrong? All police officers are briefed about them when they begin work in their designated borough, and I had been no exception. We learned that the Sector was calculating and ruthless and they would stop at nothing to upend the way of life that RightCorp had produced.

Every call that had resulted in someone being carted off to a rehabilitation facility or RightCorp had been because of them and their influence. And now I knew why. The people of Coranta weren't surviving. They were headed off a cliff without even a sign to warn them they inched toward the fall. The Sector was hanging over the edge, trying to catch anyone who went over.

One slow breath after another was my new focus as I stared around the room. I had never felt the need to imagine what the rehabilitation might have looked like, but when we arrived in front of the imposing gray building, my body had frozen. The rusty metal that made up the fence surrounding our entrance into the facility had been battered by time and neglect. The spots where the fence had completely fallen still would have been too dangerous to cross through because of the jagged spears of metal left there to decay. Where Coranta was a city of organized patchwork, the rehabilitation center looked like it had been abandoned long ago. The inside was another story. Livia had greeted me warmly just inside, ushering me to a large room full of warmth from the many windows as well as the many people who were waiting there. Smiling faces beamed at me and hands shook mine as food passed in front of me. It was hard to take it all in while a constant feeling of panic for Siana and Josie still swirled in my chest.

After living a week with the Sector, it was clear to see that everything I had been told to believe was wrong. Coranta had manipulated even my own feelings. My ears felt hot as the anger tightened in my throat. I glared down at a spot on the worn wooden table where someone had carved a delicate tree. My fingers traced along the worn lines where the edges had been smoothed out over time. The tree would never survive in the world. Its thin trunk stretched skyward, where a heavy top full of blossoms spilled down around it. The weight of the beautiful blooms would surely snap the very thing that supported them, but here it held in place, the only threat to its existence was time.

The glow from the morning sun was starting to warm the large space as movement continued to build around me. The cafeteria and kitchen were where I spent most of my time since I had arrived. There was always someone around. Even if I didn't speak to anyone, they were close by, and that usually eased my frayed nerves a bit.

"How are you coping with your detox?" Livia passed a basket full of rolls across the table toward me. My mouth ached at the warm, savory smell that wafted from the golden mounds. Without hesitation, I lifted one to my lips. Had food always tasted like this? The RightCorp really had kept so much from us.

"I'm fairly sure I slept through the worst of it." I mumbled as another roll joined the first.

"Those girls really are a wonder." She poured water from a pitcher into a blue plastic cup and handed it to me. My stomach flipped as the ice cold water met the warm rolls. Gulping it down was a convenient excuse to not have to talk about Siana at the moment. Livia had filled me in on everything that she failed to inform us of at the beach house. Like how she was Rhett Willulf's mother, and he was actually one leader of the Sector. Or that Siana could manipulate how people felt or viewed their world. Without Josie, it was difficult to decipher everything I was feeling. Even though Livia had told me she had no control over her abilities before, the thought that I had escaped being controlled by one group just to be manipulated by another was nauseating.

Hands still coated in butter, I ran them through my hair. I immediately recoiled at my mistake as Livia let out a warm chuckle and slid a towel to me.

"It may not seem like it now, but you really are very lucky to have her, Henry. If you take the time to get to know some of the people around you, you'll understand why." The cafeteria of what Coranta had thought was still a detainment and rehabilitation facility had filled with people as we talked. Looking around, I noticed they were almost all in their late twenties or younger.

"They're almost all dires from Renbrough. A fraction forced to endure the plunge into humanity that you did, but with no one to ease their transition. They were all children when it happened and for their parents, it was too much. They were overwhelmed and scared, not knowing what was happening. They tore each other apart to free themselves. Luckily, the ones you see here, the children, took longer to succumb. They were stronger than the people who had brought them into this world, and they fought it. And now, they fight to protect. To protect the people who don't know that they need it, yet."

The fear that had set in when I started my transition had been overwhelming, but to be a child and go through that was unthinkable. My body felt weak as I imagined them wandering around in a cold city with no-one to guide them. I looked around the room, half expecting to see sad eyes looking back at me. Instead, what was there were smiling faces and warm eyes. People who had lived through the worse and somehow came out of it.

I looked back to Livia. "And you have people in the city helping you. Like Sheridan?"

"Yes, among others. They keep to themselves and live like dires, either to facilitate moving people here or for gathering supplies."

"All the people I've arrested for not contributing. Where are they?"

"Most are here or in Willulf district. Some very unlucky ones were sent to the RightCorp lab. We've only ever had one person return after being sent there."

I thought of what the old man Siana had helped said. "He pleaded not to go back, saying that we didn't know what they did."

"Sam. He was one of ours. He volunteered to go to RightCorp. Sheridan arranged for him to be taken in to collect information." Livia reached out to squeeze my hand. The warmth of it was comforting while also making the knot in my throat worse.

My voice caught as I asked, "If it's so bad, why would he agree to that? Who would do that to themselves?" I couldn't imagine a purpose that would make me walk willingly into that place.

"The Viteris weren't the first to be activated. Hartlem has been receiving sense shifters as protection since they were first discovered. But it takes a strong emotional trigger to activate the part of the brain that the chemicals had affected."

"That doesn't explain why he would go in. It seems like you already knew what you needed to about the activation. Why would you let him willingly walk in there?"

"We didn't know who they were targeting. Sam agreed to get us that list somehow. He spent the better part of five years doing it." She pulled her shawl tight around her shoulders before placing several more rolls onto the plate in front of me. "He offered to help so that no one else's family would be torn apart by the Rightleys."

The rolls turned sour in my mouth as I struggled to swallow. I had helped send him back there. "Were you able to get him out again?"

Tears pooled at the corners of her eyes while she spoke, but a soft smile lingered on her mouth. "We got him back. He is resting with his family, a grandson and their dog, somewhere where the Rightleys can't hurt them anymore."

The tension that had been coiling its way through my limbs relaxed, knowing that he was safe. "So, why are you sending so many of them into the city when there is nothing that can be done?"

"We aren't. We don't control them here. They are free to live as they choose. We just offer them a safe place to do it. The people that are here from Renbrough are happy to stay and plan until we are ready to make our move." The sunlight had now filtered into the entire room and the bustle of people, some of whom sat down with us, was making it harder to hear her. Livia gave a warm smile to each of them, greeting everyone who sat down by name before continuing. "Most of them understand what leaving would mean and the risks. But the ones that come from Coranta, most of the time, they are leaving to pull someone else out."

"I still don't understand how. How have you been able to keep all of this away from Ethan and RightCorp? You're taking people that they have sent to their own rehabilitation facilities. You have taken their facilities. What happens when the people don't come back?"

"Henry, RightCorp rehab facilities have never been what they say. They started out as a center for their genetic testing and then they became holding areas for people that didn't fit into Coranta's system. But one thing that they never were was a place for people to be helped and then sent home. They aren't expecting for anyone to come back. They expect them to be carted off to Willulf district, where they will be burned, bled or broken because that's what we have always done before."

A sour feeling pinched at my insides as images of what I imagined she could mean rolled through my head. "Your family are the Overseers there. How could you let that happen?"

"Hopefully you can take comfort in the fact that that is no longer the case. The people who die now and are sent to Willulf are remembered, celebrated, and put to rest with their families."

She had meant it to ease my worry, but had unknowingly made it so much worse. My heart ached for poor Sam all over again.

Leaving my appetite behind, I made for my room. My feet picking up the pace as the distance between me and Livia grew.

Dire Mistakes

My next training session was in half an hour and the butter in my hair needed washing out before then. After a quick shower, I made for the large open space they called the ring. It was the only place in the building void of all character. A large empty domed shaped room that would have held two courthouses in it and was just as cold. The purpose was to be clear of any sense stimuli for training, but it felt wrong. It felt too much like being dire again.

Today, there were at least a few handfuls of people to buffer the lonely feeling the room gave. At least fifty Sector members surrounded the circular room and as I moved toward the center, a tingle at the top of my spine was my only warning that what they called a "sense shift" was happening.

Warm water splashed on my face, followed by the scent of floral soap. Laughter filled my ears as I rubbed my eyes with the back of my soft pajama sleeve, a slight sting from the soap leaving my eyes blurry. My fingers curled around a mug settled at the bottom of the sink to scoop up the soapy water, but before I could dump it over her, it had slipped from my hand. My heart thrummed in my chest as the sound of shattering glass sliced through our laughter, replaced by a hiss of pain and tears. Red brimmed my vision as blood trickled from her cut foot. I hadn't meant to hurt her.

"No, no, no! I'm so sorry." The words echoed fifty times over all around me, pulling me and everyone else out of the shift.

Continuing forward through the crowd, I wiped my

hands on the back of my pants, body trembling as I tried to shake off the feeling of being inside someone else's head. As the other Sector members paired off into smaller groups, I clenched my fists and struggled to slow my breathing. She caught my gaze as I moved closer. It was hard to put everything that happened aside and focus when I knew how much pain she had caused.

"Are you ready, Henry?" She smiled, just as sweet and warm as ever. But now I knew what had been hiding under all of it.

"Do I even have a choice, Nira?"

CHAPTER THIRTY-TWO

SIANA

The soft feel of the blankets would have been a soothing way to wake up in normal circumstance. Breath held, I pulled the blanket slowly away from my face, fully expecting to see Melissa's eyes staring back at me or Rhett bringing in a pile of food, way too big for any normal human and expecting me to eat it all before training. Both had happened more times than I could count in the short time I had been forced to call this place home.

My body instinctively curled in on itself at the first touch of the cold floor, but as I looked around the empty room, my muscles eased. No Melissa and no Rhett. Also, no Josie, but I had already expected that. She had been coming back late and leaving early every day since she had first gone to RightCorp. My heart palpitated at the thought of her being there with Ethan, but I knew the information she was getting would be invaluable as we finalized our plans against him.

I still had no proof that he had hurt Nira except for the queasy feeling I got in my gut when I thought of him. For a moment, I had begun to think that he really did care about Coranta. He seemed so genuine when speaking about the people, almost as if he felt like each person really was his to protect. Searching the mansion for information about my family had been a bust so far, but what I did find was just as telling. The house was full of rooms with endless amounts of empty beds that no one slept in and closets of clothes that no one wore. Clothes that showed no sign of wear, perfectly sewn for whoever had once owned them.

The people of Coranta did well to patch and reuse things with expert skill, but the clothes in these rooms would be enough to clothe an entire borough, if not more. That was proof enough to tell me that, although Ethan claimed everything he did was to protect them from the war in Hartlem, he didn't actually care about the people. He followed in a long line of Rightley's who thrived off of what others had sacrificed for them—people like Henry.

The door to my bedroom was silent as I opened it into the hallway. I still couldn't get used to how still this house was. Every door in my house on Echo Street squeaked, every floorboard creaked, and every sound of the city flowed in through every window. Until coming here, I thought I had loved silence. A calm place to read a book had been a constant search for me, but here, the silence was suffocating.

The library doors were open wide as I stepped inside. I felt a familiar pull toward something in the space. I wasn't alone. The person I was sensing was warm and inviting. It was strange how Rhett could feel so different that how he presented himself.

The thump of a log being placed in the unlit fireplace made me jump as Rhett stood to grab the matches on the mantel. Despite the cold, I wanted the fire to stay out. I thought of Henry again.

"Are you the one building a case against him?" I said

"Case against who?" Rhett cast me a sideways glance as he continued to light the fire. "Oh right, the cop. I hope you trust that I would never hurt someone that you care about. Even if they are a pain in the ass dire, who doesn't know how to follow simple instructions."

"You know, you're very good at not actually answering any of my questions."

"Yes."

The legs of the low couch scraped across the floor as I dropped into my usual spot. My face grimaced at the thought of having a usual spot in this place.

"Yes, you're building a case against him or yes, you know you're not good at answering my questions." I glared at him.

I rubbed my shoulder to my ear as the rasp of the matches striking the hard stone sent a shiver down my body. The smoke built in the fireplace as the paper he had placed there to help ignite the wood shriveled up against the growing flames. He placed the matches back with a satisfying rattle as they met the mantle. Hands tucked in pockets, he turned toward me, not taking a step forward but leaning instead, silently, against the exposed brick.

"Well?"

He smirked, "Yes."

My frustration bubbled up again. "You keep telling me to trust you, but you're not telling me why? You're not telling me anything." He stared at me without a word as I continued. "I want to believe you, but I'm not an idiot. I don't know you. Yeah, you may be a very different person than the monster you became for the Rightley's, but you could just as easily be exactly that."

"True. So let's do something about that." He smiled.

He stood and crossed to the door, already heading out before I questioned him. He was all business again, which meant time for training.

My hand curled around the smooth banister as we made our way down to the kitchens. Even the stairs here, covered in carpet, dampened the sound of our descent. How could anyone live in this place without going completely mad? My eyes darted around the room on instinct. Melissa was probably somewhere nearby watching. A hard chill ran down my entire body at the thought.

Rhett continued on through the heavy kitchen door. Several of the Rightley's staff were moving about the space. It was a welcome change of scene from our usual training sessions. He greeted several before we moved to a space out of earshot, and he directed the conversation to me again in hushed tones.

"Ethan is taking you to RightCorp tomorrow to meet

Dr. Hawthorne. Even I don't know everything that they do in that place, but I know that it won't be pleasant. And I don't know what things they may try to get out of you. They know you went to the port for Hartlem and came back with that box. They want what's in it and they may very well think that you know how to get it."

"Are they dense? I trashed that thing and it still wouldn't open." I stared at him. "What do they think is in it, anyway?"

"The Viteris did important research for the Right-Corp before they disappeared. Whatever is in that box could very well change everything for them. At least, they think it could."

Pots and pans clanked in a large metal sink accompanying the sound of more and more staff coming in and out of doors. The light flowing in from the open window and door combined with the movement of bodies added a warmth to the space that had been missing upstairs.

In true Rhett fashion, he changed the subject without warning. "There are three people here that don't belong. Find them."

"Um, ok?" I moved around the room, passing closely by each staff member to glean any signs of them being out of place. After staring awkwardly at the third dire, an averagely tall man with slicked back blond hair and the same bland look that was plastered on everyone's face, Rhett cleared his throat behind me.

"What are you doing, Sia?"

I quickly returned to where he stood. "First off, don't call me that. It's weird. Second, I'm trying to find these people that don't belong."

"First off, I enjoy calling you Sia. Second, don't say that so loud. Always expect that Ethan is listening."

I sneered, "Or Melissa."

"Third," the tone of his voice changed as the muscle in his jaw clenched, "why are you using your eyes?"

Red covered my face and chest as embarrassment flooded through me, but I refused to lower my eyes. A million quips died on my tongue as my senses reached out to him. A repulsion that wasn't mine slithered its way through my chest and stomach before I realized he was staring at something behind me. I heard her voice before I saw her.

"We don't need you in here right now, Deanna. Please report to Ms. Rightley upstairs."

The rapid breaths that escaped my lips made my jaw shake as I turned to see her. She smiled. "Yes, Mr. Willulf. I was just coming to see if Siana would like any bread. It's her favorite. Siana, would you like some bread?"

A fog swirled around my eyes, but it was Rhett who spoke. "No, she wouldn't. Thank you, Deanna."

"Of course." And without another word, she left.

Rhett's hand rested on my shoulder. "I'm sorry."

"She didn't ask about Nira." I spoke to myself, but Rhett still answered.

"She knows. She just doesn't have the choice to care." He didn't have to spell it out for me. I knew what he meant. They had pumped her full of Soterapine.

A bitter taste that I didn't recognize lingered on my tongue as I looked around the room. "Is that coming from you?"

He leaned down to whisper in my ear, "We are not

the only ones here affected by the Rightley's influence."

I didn't look at him, but instead scanned the room. This was what he had meant. I needed to focus on the senses of the surrounding people. I closed my eyes, blocking out thoughts of my fake aunt and pulling everything else in. The bitter taste intensified and a green haze filled my vision. Whoever I was sensing was letting the memory they were focusing on fade. I pulled at the feeling until a pressure built in my ears. I could hear the rushing of water. My hands grasped at my throat as spots built behind my now closed eyelids. Something tugged at my jeans as I took an unwanted gulp of acrid fluid. Was I drowning? Another pull came, this time at my shirt.

I couldn't be drowning because I was still in the Rightley's kitchen. The breath that I forced into my lungs caught but was followed by another and another. My eyelids felt stuck together as I pulled them open. A blurry Rhett knelt at my feet, clasping his chest with one hand and the hem of my shirt with the other. Looking around the room, I found I was the only one still standing. Most of the dires were looking around the room, confused and visibly shaking, but three sets of eyes were fixed solely on me.

The man with the slicked back hair broke his stare first. Without a word, he stood, tears rolling down his face, and walked out of the still open door. No one followed.

Rhett's hand was warm in mine as we crossed the hard stone floor to the pantry. Shelves lined the space, filled to bursting with bags of grain, cans of fruits and vegetables, and an entire shelf dedicated to fresh food from the gardens. There was no way the Rightleys needed all of this for themselves.

Rhett's face was still pale when I turned to him. "What happened to him? The man that I sensed."

"The real question is what happened to everyone else?" His brows furrowed as he stared straight at me, now holding both of my hands in his. "The dires here have way too much Soterapine in them to be affected that strongly by a sense shift."

Sounds from the kitchens filtered back in through the door as the people on the other side had gone back to their work like nothing had happened.

"If you're looking for actual answers, you should already know that I'm not the one to ask." My heart was pounding in my chest as I looked down at our still joined hands. "Are you going to let me go anytime soon?"

"Deanna must have triggered something. But even so, to have that kind of power could only mean—" a sad pang stung my eyes before he continued. "Did you and Nira ever talk about your life before Port Hartlem?" His expression was impossible to read, and I was having a difficult time tapping into his senses after what had just happened in the kitchen.

"No. Not really, but we were so little then and I don't think we were there for very long before... everything."

"You were there for three seasons before the Rigthleys found you and Nira. And before that—" The smell of ammonia and blood were trickling into the space as my lungs constricted.

"Rhett, you have to calm down. Whatever you're feeling, whatever you're remembering, it's making it hard for me to breathe."

His grip tightened for just a second before he took a deep breath and spoke. "What can you feel from me right now?"

I closed my eyes, but I was drained from what had just happened in the kitchen. The smell of beach sand and warm sun brushed up against my mind as he moved closer. My head pulsed as I strained to hold on to whatever he was pushing out to me. The door to the pantry opened, letting the light from the kitchen spill inside. As the door clicked shut again, my eyes re-adjusted to the dark faster than my hands did to the cold now seeping into them. Rhett pulled his hands away and shoved them into his pockets.

The man who had entered the pantry with us was now shuffling back and forth. "Sir."

"Get out. You can't be in here with her." Rhett looked down at me. "It's not safe."

My heart sank. Just when I thought I was getting to the human beneath the monster, he grew claws again. But before we left the room, for a split second, I thought I could sense something almost like hope.

CHAPTER THIRTY-THREE

RHETT

"Is she ready?" Melissa sat cross-legged on her four-poster bed, staring at me with hopeful eyes. She'd been waiting for this for as long as I had. Enduring all of her family's cruelties had shaped her, but not how one might imagine. Her scary loner persona was just to trick her brother. She carried many scars from the years of testing. First by her father and then, when he died, her brother. Some were visible, and some were not, but both were branded into her. It would have been impossible for anyone to walk away from years of trauma completely unscathed. It was improbable that she could emerge from that heinous facility still in possession of an ounce of heart or empathy, and yet, there she was. Sitting on her bed with youthful hope radiating from every inch of her being.

"She'll be able to fight." My gaze fell as I gripped the edge of the desk. Melissa's face blocked my view of the floor. I hadn't heard her move.

"You know that's not what I asked."

"No, she's not ready for everything we are going to ask of her. She's not ready to know she's been treated like a pawn and, with the help of her own sister, no less." Arms crossed against my chest I avoided her eyes.

"It's not your fault she's here."

"How? How is it not my fault? I should have done something the second I realized who Nira was. Because I was so obsessed with bringing down Ethan, I let them be broken by him. I did to them what they had refused to do to me." The gentle back and forth of her thumb as she hugged my arm made me shrink away. I didn't deserve forgiveness, and it wasn't hers to give.

She let go of my arm but kept my hand in hers, continuing to try to soothe me. She had gone through just as much for far longer and still had it in her to worry about how I felt. "Does she remember anything? Nira at least remembered some details."

They did something to her. Something different from me, and Nira, and the others. The thought of whatever horrors they inflicted on her to give her the ability to do what she did in the kitchen broke my heart for her all over again.

"I can't feel any of it from her and I don't want to. She's already gone through enough because of the testing. She doesn't need to relive the past as well."

"But so have you. If she knew at least some of her past, the parts with you in it, she might have a better understanding of why she has these abilities and why you want to help her."

I let out a slow breath. "I would rather she hate me than remember." I stared at Melissa down the bridge of my nose as she placed both hands on the sides of my face. I never had a sister, but I imagined Melissa was as close as it got.

She spoke quietly, "She is going to be hurt and she will blame you for it." Air puffed out of my mouth as my stomach tightened. I ran my hands through my hair and gripped the back of my neck. She had said what I had been thinking and hearing it out loud felt like a punch to the gut.

"Whether or not she knows it yet, she cares for you. She cares for everyone. She has a gigantic heart, and she wants to trust that someone will take care of her. Show her that after it's all over, she can trust you to be that person. That is what will get her through this with the least amount of scars." She smacked both of my cheeks with a grin. "Now, we just have to figure out a way to show her and lucky for you, I happen to know that Ethan got the box back today, unopened. He's been skulking over it in his study."

"If she couldn't get into it then, what makes you think she will be able to now?"

She shrugged her shoulders before wrapping her arms around me. "Just give her the opportunity and don't push her."

I squeezed her tight and made my way to Ethan's study.

CHAPTER THIRTY-FOUR

SIANA

Most nights, sitting alone in the warm library after dinner was my greatest comfort. Working every day with Rhett was taxing on every level, but at least on most days he would leave long before Ethan and Josie came back from RightCorp. Most nights, I went to bed knowing that I wouldn't see my friend until the next morning and since Josie was insistent that we focus on honing my skills every morning before she left again; I was slowly feeling like I was losing her, too. When I did see her, she had become so focused on what I could do. She had even stopped talking about Nira or Henry in exchange for telling me all about the great Dr. Hawthorne. She had become convinced that working on my sense shifts would be our greatest asset.

When she had arrived in time to have dinner alone in our room, I felt elated. It was as if I had a part of myself back as she insisted we take the night to just be us. We laughed as we told stories about growing up in E Borough. About the time we had first met after she had been assigned to Henry. It felt so good to have my friend back. As we settled in for the night, the conversation weaved its way out of my memory and back to the real world.

"Dr. Hawthorne has everything ready for you. I'm so excited for you to meet him." Josie combed through her hair. "He said that if everything goes right, you should be ready to go to Hartlem in a week or so. He just has to finish the preparations for the barrier."

My fingers traced the edges of the bright starburst pattern lining the carpet. Josie hadn't told me much about the barrier except that it would be a way to block the continent off permanently from the war raging on the other side of Hartlem. Building the barricade meant that coming home wouldn't be an option for me. Another perk Ethan had forgotten to mention.

"I know you have been feeling unsure of everything." Her reflection smiled at me. She gave me a knowing look that Aunt Jerry had perfected, and it made my stomach coil. "So I told Ethan that I was worried you may have reservations—" My eyes narrowed at her in the mirror while she continued to brush her curly hair.

"Why would you tell him that?"

"I told him because of the barrier. And because he

just wants to help."

"When has he ever wanted to help? Do you really think for one second that he cares for anyone in Coranta? Do you think he will take everyone off of Soterapine once the barriers are up?" I was on my feet, heat coating my cheeks, ears, and chest–hands clasped in fists at my sides.

"I don't have all the answers, Siana—" She twisted in her chair to face me, brush still in hand, "but what I do know is that no one, including Ethan, wants what happened to Nira to happen to anyone else. Poor Henry is going to rot away in a cell for a crime that he didn't even know that he was committing. That's what happens when a dires go off of their meds too fast." We stared at each other as I sat on the edge of the bed, my legs buckling from exhaustion.

She rose and crossed the room and wrapped me in her arms. "Everyone has been given so much more than they should have to deal with, especially you. I just wanted you to know that you won't be doing it all alone." She pulled back to look at me with a wide smile. "I'm going to Hartlem with you. Dr. Hawthorne wants to see you tomorrow because he has been training me to be your amplifier."

Unpleasant flashbacks to our first Rightley dinner came to mind as I shifted back and forth on my feet.

"Are you sure that's what you want? What if we can't get back?" Her hands felt icy in mine.

"Everyone gives so the many survive." She squeezed my hands before crawling into bed behind me. An uneasy feeling had clawed its way into my chest. Was I being selfish? The warm fireplace in the library flashed in my head as I thought of the books there. Did they have libraries in Hartlem?

"You're right." I said before standing and placing the robe draped across the foot of the bed around my shoulders.

"Where are you going?"

"The library. There is a section that I didn't get to finish cataloging before dinner. If I'm going to RightCorp with you tomorrow, I should really finish it tonight."

The fuzzy robe did little to comfort or give warmth as I made my way to the hallway. Feet taking me as quickly and quietly as possible, I made for the library–the moonlight finally making her entrance and shining silver light through the windows to guide my way.

With my arms and legs tucked in, I curled toward the back of the couch, holding my newest book. The house was always quiet by this time, except for the occasional Melissa sighting. I walked the other way when I saw her, no matter the time of day. What she could do was terrifying. And thanks to me, Josie would hold that same power.

I tried to focus on the book in front of me instead. My eyes scanned over the page, taking nothing in. They were straining to make sense of the blur of letters, the only light coming from a small bronze lamp. The book was rough, its spine cracked long ago, leaving a split in the cover along the edge. Several pages had been folded in at the corners to mark where the previous reader had left it. I pulled the cord on the lamp and sat, flipping through them, wondering about the person who bought it when it was brand new. What it must have been like to walk into a store full of books that had never been read before and every time you went, there was some different adventure to become a part of.

Hushed voices outside of the library made my ears twitch. The dark room seemed longer than usual as I made my way to the glass door. Sinking down into a crawl, my hands padded on the hardwood. My body hugged the wooden frame as I peeked through the door's stained glass. Although distorted, I could just make out the forms of two men—Rhett and Ethan.

"You're welcome to stay here for the night. No need to crash that pretty car of yours into one of my fountains on the way home." A round of sloppy laughter accompanied Ethan's offer. The door to the study closed and the click of a key in the lock followed.

"That would probably be for the best, thank you." Rhett had a slight drawl to his words, but compared to Ethan, didn't seem as bad. As soon as the thought left me, the blob that was Rhett lost its footing and fell into the blob that was Ethan.

"Sorry. Sorry."

He didn't sound that sorry.

"I should get off my feet before I crash my pretty self into you again." Footsteps faded down the hall. Adrenaline coursed through me, leaving no chance for going back to my room to sleep, but my mind was too scattered to focus on reading. Instead, I turned my lack of focus to the lie that brought me to the library in the first place. Cataloging books. After an hour, the hairs on the back of my arms stood up. My ears tingled, focusing on any sign of movement. I didn't need to hear anything. I could sense that someone was coming.

The breath that escaped my lungs came out in quick bursts as I rushed to a dark corner of the room. The library doors opened and closed, leaving me in the dark library with Rhett. He held a silver box in his hands along with a large envelope. Halting just long enough to shut the doors, he moved to the desk in the corner of the library before walking back out in silence.

I knew that box from the broken and battered top I had given it. Rhett had the box that I had found in my family's home, the light still glowing red. My fingers tingled as I rubbed my hands together, itching to grab it and run. Opening it may have been impossible for me, but leaving it in the hands of these people, the people responsible for it needing to be hidden in the first place, was unacceptable.

Rhett's footsteps stopped. Had he known I was here? Moving to peer out of the room again, I watched him check the door to the study. He took something out of his pocket and a small click followed. He had the key. My palms were damp against the cold floor. My pulse quickened as he turned and headed back my way. Heart racing, I crossed back to the smoke coated couch. If he was sensing me, this wouldn't work, but the last thing I wanted was for him to think I was spying on him. I had a better chance of getting that box back if he suspected nothing. The door brushed open just as I shut my eyes, curled up on the couch where I spent so many hours training and reading. With any luck, he would buy that I just fell asleep here. Trying to calm my mind, I thought of the gentle purple of lavender, the warm sweetness of spiced cinnamon tea, the fuzzy cloud-like feeling of the robe wrapped around me. If nothing else, my training was going well because I started to doze despite the adrenaline that had been rushing through me seconds before. The door to the library closed before his footsteps circled the room for what felt like an eternity.

A gentle pull tugged at my mind before arms wrapped around me, not picking me up, but adjusting my body so that he was sitting with me, my head resting in his lap. The calm mindset that had just moments ago been pulling me under quickly left my body as his hand brushed through my long hair. His hand traced down the side of my face as my heart fluttered furiously. A wild bird trapped in a too small cage. I didn't move. I felt his body shift as he leaned down, his lips just grazing my ear.

"If you don't breathe at some point, you're going to find yourself actually passed out." As he pulled back away from my ear, our eyes met.

"Has anyone ever told you that you're a huge asshole?"

"Besides you?" He stroked a lock of hair out of my face and smiled. "No one has ever had the guts to say it to my face."

"You're not as scary as you pretend to be, you know that?" He cocked his head to the side and bit his lip. Reaching down to my hand, he held it, interlocking his fingers with mine. His gaze drifted back to my own.

He smirked down at me. "Which must be the reason that you are still laying in my lap, despite hating me so much."

The hard floor did nothing to cushion my fall as I

rolled away from him as fast as I could. My legs shook as I bounded back up to stand a suitable distance away. He laughed before gesturing toward the things he had brought from the study.

"The box and papers are for you. It's important that you understand a few things before heading to RightCorp tomorrow."

"You knew I was here the entire time? I didn't feel you pull me?" He returned with the box and papers in hand, placing them gently on the table in front of me.

"It was more of a gentle nudge. Besides, I don't need to sense shift to know when you're near." He shoved his hands in his pockets before walking to the glass doors. "I'll be back in an hour to put everything back." And with that, he left.

I tried to push him from my thoughts as the contents of the table called to me. The box had proved to be as stubborn as me and the pulsing red light celebrated that it was still locked. If we were at Henry's house, he could bust this one open like he had the other. My stomach flip-flopped as I thought of him. I couldn't erase the feeling that I was missing something important. Not wanting to waste any more time, I picked up the loose pages. There were several envelopes from Hartlem addressed to the Rightley's. Strange, none of them were addressed to Ethan.

The end of the year is unacceptable. You have had over two decades to find a solution. You will need to move up your deadline for delivery if you want to stay in good standing. Despite our past transactions, we will discontinue all efforts to shield the Continent if the timeline isn't sped up. We will con-

sent to your "barrier", but you shouldn't expect a high survival rate if these assets fail. My men will arrive for both in one month. There is no need for further correspondence.

Did they just refer to me as an asset? And Nira? The papers were heavy in my hands as I read the words again. It would seem like the date for my hand off was fast approaching and had been planned. All I wanted to do was to bring down the Rightley's but found myself trapped in a cage to help Coranta survive something so much worse. How did my world turn so utterly hopeless in a month? Flipping through the stack of papers left me with more questions than answers. A letter from the infamous Dr. Hawthorne caught my eye.

Mr. Rightley,

The girl has been transitioned and is ready for the amplification procedure. She needs to be in contact during a full sense shift which, according to Mr. Willulf's report, should be possible now. Regarding Mr. Viteri's lock box—it is RightCorp issue however, the override codes will not work because of the entry pads corruption. This model has a vial behind the pad that will render the contents useless if we force it open. The destruction done to the pad may have already set it off, but there is no way to tell from the outside. Mr. Viteri's original code will need to be recovered. Correspondence with Recreor has revealed that it may have something to do with his offspring, but more specific information couldn't be accessed. However, it was confirmed that the elixir we suspected he made could be in the box. I don't have to tell you what kind of upper hand this could afford anyone with access. -Hawthorne

The box resting on the table became a blur as tears flooded my eyes. I knew that the box I found in the beach house belonged to someone in my family, but knowing that my father had filled it left me even more determined to see its contents.

Turning the box, I looked for any clues that I hadn't seen before and found nothing. They had reconstructed the battered pad on the front with much effort, but it still showed signs of where I pummeled it.

What had my dad been working on that RightCorp would want to get their hands on it so badly? Whatever it was, the thought that I had messed up their victory with my tantrum was even more satisfying. I had unwittingly given myself more time to open it.

The code had to do with me and Nira. Our birthdays would be too obvious. Not only that, but they wouldn't fit the four-digit lock. Four numbers that had to do with me and Nira. Something that he would have been able to remember and that someone he trusted could guess. If not birthdays and not age, then what?

I pulled my hands down my cheeks in frustration. Movement in the hall made my ears twitch. My spine straightened, each vertebra aligned with the one below it. My body was rigid as I waited for any sign that someone might be outside the door. After a few moments of silence, I took a slow and deliberate breath — the silver mystery in front of me regaining my attention, although my body was still on edge.

It was good that Henry hadn't been able to work on this box. If he had, everything inside would have been lost, if I hadn't destroyed it all already. The things we had found before had started us down this path. No, that wasn't true, was it? It was the old man in the library. It felt like such a long time ago that I had found his letter for Wolf. I couldn't help but wonder if he came to me on purpose for help. Me, number 78. It seemed like a bit much for all of it to be a coincidence.

Hold on a second… The box almost fell from my hands in my hurry to snatch it up. The heartbeat pulsing in my ears was deafening. Resting the box on my lap, I wiped my hands off on my shirt. My fingers trembled as I reached for the number pad. The red light flashed with each number entered. 7- red light, 7- red light, 7-red light. My entire body felt charged as I held my breath and entered the last number with shaking hands. 8.

A gentle whirring followed by a click sounded inside of the box. Was this the self-destruct mechanism that Hawthorne had mentioned? I stood, debating whether I should toss the box out of the window. Would whatever vial of unimaginable stuff remain inside the box or would it blow up in my hands? A fog clouded my vision as my heart tried to escape up my throat. I made for the window with the smell of acid in my nose, a high-pitched ringing in my ears and copper on my tongue. The doors to the library flew open. Standing there looking just as terrified as I felt was Rhett. He had me by the shoulders before I had a chance to throw the box.

"Are you hurt? What happened?" He looked me up and down, a desperate hurry to his search.

"Here, look!" I lifted the box to his eye level, nearly hitting him in the chin.

His eyes rested on the box for only a moment before locking with mine. He slowly pushed the box down and out of his face. As he did, a faint green light twitched.

"I did it. I unlocked it." I staggered back to the couch with my well-earned treasure as Rhett eyed the empty room.

"I could feel your terror. Hopefully, you didn't wake up the rest of the house."

"I thought I made it self destruct."

Rhett paced behind my seat without another word — obviously still worked up.

"I wasn't sure if it was going to blow up or something."

The lid squeaked as I opened it, giving away its age. How long had it been since anyone had looked inside? My stomach fluttered at the thought of my dad holding it and placing secrets inside for me to find one day. I took a deep breath and looked inside. Foam slots with four glass vials laid on one side of the box and papers, words concealed by a black liquid, the other. My entire body sank. I had set it off after all.

"Some of it may still be salvageable," Rhett said as he rounded the back of the couch to sit with me. "I think I know why RightCorp wanted this box so badly. If I'm right, and your father pulled it off, those vials contain a solution that would act as an amped up Soterapine to anyone with abilities."

"What would be the point of that? Unless my dad just wanted a bunch of super robots." I smiled. Rhett didn't.

"Exactly. If someone with abilities has their emotions

stripped away, then they could be used to control anyone so long as they were given a logical reason for it."

"But I thought you said that emotions and memories are what make it work. If someone is on Soterapine, they have no emotional connection to anything."

"Once someone was activated, it wouldn't matter. Everything that they had experienced up until then would guide their powers. In fact, they wouldn't even require an emotional connection to something to pass it on. Anything they had seen, read about, or imagined until that point could be sense shifted on a large scale."

"Why would my dad have anything to do with something like that? He and my family ran from Right-Corp. They wanted nothing to do with them. So why create this special potion that would feel right at home on their shelves?"

"The answer to that is probably on one of these papers. If we can decipher anything past this goop. From what we do know, I bet my fraction of the continent that one of those vials of liquid reverses the other."

Although each vial was coated in the nasty security substance, two of them revealed patches of yellow underneath. I thrust my hand in the box, fishing for anything that might not have been ruined when I bludgeoned it.

"Ow!" Both mine and Rhett's voice echoed through the room as a piece of glass coated in the black goop sliced through my palm. He grabbed the box to set aside as I inspected my bleeding hand.

"Let me see it." He spoke softly as he pulled it toward him. The cut was deep, and spots of blood already dotted his gray sleeping pants. A curious sheen wrapped itself around the room as he led me to the now extinguished fireplace.

Taking a bottle from the drink cart, he turned to me. "I have to clean that. Try your best not to yell out."

A generous pour of the clear liquid puddled in my hand before falling to the floor in murky red drops. I braced for the pain to come–it didn't. Rhett wrapped my hand with a rag from the same cart and stared at me, his eyebrows pinched together and his mouth slightly open. He reached for me and I stared at his hand as he rested it on my arm. He walked back to inspect the box, never taking his eyes off of me until picking it up.

"The vial under the lid is still intact. Whatever that black stuff is, it came from one of the vials your father placed there." He was right. Of the four slots that housed vials of liquid, only three were unbroken; one black and two of them yellow. I looked down at my now wrapped hand. Whatever the black liquid was, it must have entered my bloodstream through my cut. Fascinating.

I started for the door, but Rhett stood blocking my way.

"Move." What was the purpose of him standing there? I didn't need him to help me.

"Siana, something is not right. I can't sense anything from you right now." His eyes narrowed as he waited for an answer.

"I need to get by. Stand aside or I'll make you."

"I don't think so. Come sit down. The serum must have gotten in your cut." He grabbed my hands to pull me so I kicked him in the kneecap as hard as I could. He had to understand I had something I needed to do. His eyes watered, but he didn't go down like I wanted. Never having been in a fight before, I wasn't expecting it when he swept my legs out from under me and carried me to the couch. Not wanting to be held up any longer, I bit him on the shoulder, causing him to drop me. I rolled off the couch, my head hitting the table hard. Warm liquid streamed down my face as I shoved my palm upward toward his nose. His grunt was confirmation I had made an impact. As I walked past him, he grabbed me by the waist.

"If you continue to try to stop me, I'm going to have to actually hurt you, Mr. Willulf." He let me go. The clink of glass was all the warning I got before he tackled me to the ground. Pinned beneath him, I narrowed my eyes as I tried to push myself from the floor. I need to inflict more physical pain to achieve the desired goal. Cutting myself on the vial had hurt and it could have been worse. My vision tunneled in black. The sheen that had been making everything glow seemed to pool itself until it found its target on his hand. I thought about the feel of the glass cutting through skin, the blood that flowed down, the sting of the chemicals entering my wound. Rhett dropped the vial and pulled back his hand–blood running from it and splashing down on me. I smiled.

Before I could make my way out from under him, he grabbed the dropped vial and forced its contents into my mouth. Bursts of light flashed in front of my eyes and I tasted–cotton candy? The weird glow that had been covering the room was gone and in its place were the feelings of pure disgust and rage. I stared at Rhett's hand in horror.

"I'm so sorry. I didn't mean to… well, I meant to, but I wouldn't have meant to." We sat in silence, our heavy breathing the only sound besides the sporadic branches that scraped against the walls outside.

"No one can ever know that we found this." Rhett grabbed my hand in his, still clenching his other in a tight fist to stave the blood flow.

I sat, in absolute horror, at what my father created.

CHAPTER THIRTY-FIVE

SIANA

The drive to the RightCorp building was too short. My head ached from where it had bounced on the hard glass while I tried to catch up on sleep in the car. Last night's scene with Rhett left me with a too many questions. It would have been impossible to sleep even if it hadn't been for the poison that my father invented nearly making me butcher someone that I—didn't hate all the time anymore.

We met shortly this morning before breakfast to discuss what needed to be done while I was at the lab with Josie and Dr. Hawthorne. He and Ethan were taking a trip to the courthouse to make sure everything was ready for Hartlem's arrival, which would be in five days. I had never felt more sick, and I had tasted Josie's cooking before. This was so much worse.

Among the things I was supposed to look out for was another serum. I had my fill of brain altering chemicals the night before, but apparently this one would block whatever senses someone may send out. Hope swirled around in my head. If it could keep the people I cared about from being hurt, I would turn the entire RightCorp building over to find it.

"The people in Coranta can live in peace because of what happens behind these doors." Josie turned to me and smiled. The car stopped, and we both scooted out. The marble arches no longer held the same wonder and inspiration that they once had. Now, their words encouraged me in a different way.

The halls of the great marble building were cold and sterile. There wasn't a speck of dust or character to be seen. Just like the courthouse, this place could be the setting for one of the horror novels I read. As my feet clacked down the never-ending marble floor, I couldn't help but wish I was back at the library, going through musty boxes full of attic treasures.

Bile rose in my stomach and this time it didn't stay. My muscles locked up at the sight in front of me. Behind a wall of glass, a woman lay tilted up on a med borough style bed. The torn shirt she wore clung to her body in dark purple strips, showing off her arms. Arms that were covered in deep cuts and burns. My stomach clenched painfully at the sight of the rest of her body. Further down on one of her legs, the skin was peeled off.

"Was she in some kind of accident? Who's helping her heal?" My eyes never left the woman.

"The doctors here at RightCorp are healing her. They have been working on several remedies for wounds that a soldier could incur during a fight." The fascination in her voice scared me, and I took a step away.

"They did that to her, didn't they?"

"The things that RightCorp has provided to Hartlem has kept all the Continent safe. Everyone has to give, Siana."

I took another involuntary step back as she tracked my move with her head.

"Come on. Like you said before, they're just dires. Nothing more than people puppets. Besides, they're happy to do it."

"They don't understand what happiness is. They aren't allowed to." My eyes fought to stay focused on Josie and not wander back to the woman who was now smiling at us through the glass.

The stranger that was taking the place of my best friend mirrored the woman's smile.

"Dr. Hawthorne created a medication that inhibits their pain receptors." She turned and continued down the hall without me, a gentle bounce to her step.

"What have they done to you?" I quickened my pace, not sure if I actually wanted to catch up.

For the past week, I had suspected there was something wrong with my friend. I had just assumed it was the stress. Maybe she was acting strange to help me deal with the fact that I was being traded off to protect everyone else. That she was trying to protect me by making it easier for me to do the right thing. I couldn't have been more wrong.

As we continued down the levels, the hallways became more and more dark as one thing became even more obvious. RightCorp needed to be destroyed, along with anyone who had helped build them up. I wasn't sure if I could stomach another floor of horrors.

"Why aren't we using the elevator?"

"It's broken." I knew the real answer without having to ask her. He wanted me to see this. He wanted me to see what he could do and what he would continue to do if I didn't play along with his game. My gut twisted, and the hairs stood up all over my body. I had spent my life in Coranta fighting against an unfair system. I thought the worst thing in life was people being punished for not giving. But somewhere out there in the world, the horrors I saw in this building were being used against people. People without the luxury of not feeling pain.

Josie placed her hand in mine and moved me away from the glass. She rubbed my arm, though the gesture left me no warmer than before.

"Do you remember that story you told me about the time you and Nira camped out in your backyard? You had just read some book about camping and wanted to try it out. Your Aunt Jerry had argued with you about it for hours, but you were so set on it."

She sounded like my Josie again, the laughter and kindness returning to her as she smiled at me. The cold tremble that had been permeating my body left me as the pull of the memory cleared my head.

"We took a blanket from the house and hung it from that big tree in the backyard to make a tent." A smile tugged at my mouth before a pin prick shot through my heart — that same tree now looked over my sister's grave. My mind moved away from the pain and towards the memory.

"You kept hearing all of these strange sounds in the dark outside of that horrible yellow blanket that barely touched the ground."

Not sure where she was going with this, but elated to have my friend back for a moment, I added, "We eventually got to sleep by singing some of Aunt Jerry's really bad songs."

Another slap in the face. A sweet memory now stained by time.

The click of my nails scraping against each other had her looking down at my hands. The dirt under my nails was almost gone from picking at them. The stiff fabric of my pants scratched at the palms of my hands as I trailed them down to stop myself from fidgeting. She stared at me through empty eyes.

"But when you woke up, it was so cold. The blanket that you had hung from the tree had fallen and Nira was gone."

"Why are we talking about this? What's going on with you?"

I felt the strings snap into place, as if hundreds of tiny waiting wires had just pulled themselves taught on my brain. A sob caught in my throat as I fought the urge to cry out.

Dire Mistakes

The brown dirt under my legs gripped the brittle yellow grass as I pulled it out in clumps. Anything to distract me from the clatter of my teeth. I should have thought about it being so cold. The characters in my book didn't say anything about the cold, but we were in too deep now. If we gave in, Aunt Jerry would never let me live it down. Thankfully, the wind wasn't too bad right now or it would have ripped our sad yellow tent down. Movement to my left caught my attention. Nira was walking from the house with a pile of treats in her arms.

"Skootch over, I'm coming in with rations to save the day," she said.

"Well, it's a good thing I brought our medicine then." I held up a thermos filled to the brim with hot tea. We played and joked for hours while huddled together, her arms wrapped around me to keep me warm as everything else faded away. Eventually, sleep took hold and a dark blanket surrounded me as I nodded off.

I woke up with a start, my teeth chattering so loudly I was afraid I would wake Nira. The sky had gotten dark, the air frigid, and the sounds around us became more and more frightening. My eyes scanned the darkness, but my sister wasn't there. The soft yellow blanket had fallen from the tree and was now laid over me in a damp pile. Everywhere it touched me, it plunged the cold even further into my bones.

If I were a dire, I could be braver than this.

The ground shifted beneath me as my vision cleared. A shuddering cry came hurdling out as I fought the urge to hide and instead stood there fighting off the chill encasing my body.

Something moved to my left.

"Nira?"

A dire, covered in brightly colored tubes and wires, was now crouching down on the floor, his teeth clashing together. I focused and felt the pull again. Before I could stop the shift, the dires in each room began to drop, each with a grotesque thud that echoed down the hall. The white coats in each room made quick scratches on clipboards.

I banged on the glass in front of me.

"Help them!"

"This is how we help them, Sia." Her voice was full of hollow triumph as she placed her hand on my shoulder. My jagged nails scratched her wrist as I swatted her away. She didn't flinch.

"If we go to Hartlem, this all stops. RightCorp won't need to continue these experiments to support a war that isn't ours. The many will survive."

The shift I had been forced into fell as the wires broke their grip on me — the tears I had been fighting to contain fell with it.

How many times had these bastards repeated those words to her?

CHAPTER THIRTY-SIX

HENRY

The longer I stayed at the Sector's headquarters, the more enraged I became. Nira had taken to guiding me around any chance she had between plotting and training. Turns out, she had been an integral part of their group since the day she "died". She was offering her sister for the greater good. Her sister who very well may have used me to trek across the continent to find her answers.

The more I learned about their abilities, the more I wondered if she had used them so I wouldn't leave her on her own to search for answers. I should have known that it wasn't love. Josie said that love is supposed to be pure and uplifting, but when I was around her, my body felt like it was going to burst and fall apart. I could feel it even now when I thought of her. Deep down, I still wanted to be near her, despite everything that she did to me. Closing my eyes, I took a deep breath to steady myself. I could almost smell her. Black tea and syrup.

"You're going to crash into someone if you keep daydreaming." Nira's voice chimed in my ear.

"Oh. Right. Sorry." I broke off quickly, hoping to seem busy enough to not need her around. She didn't take the hint.

"You were feeling some pretty powerful emotions just then. Can I ask what they were about?"

"I would rather you didn't. I don't have time for it. The great and mighty Wolf will be here soon. Livia's asked me to take over for her in the kitchen while she is in her meeting." I stopped and turned to look at her. "Shouldn't you be there with them—making plans?"

Her hands were warm on mine. "If you need to talk to someone, I will be here for you. You're the closest thing to family that I have in this place. I want to be there if you need me."

My shoulders relaxed, and I took a step toward her. I pulled her in for a hug, feeling more at ease than I had since I arrived. After a moment, she pulled back and held me at arm's length, a warm smile spreading from her mouth to her eyes. I knew without a doubt that my expression matched hers.

"I'll let you get back to work. If you need me, you know where to find me."

She patted my arm gently and took the hallway leading to the group's meeting room. I smiled after her. This feeling was new. It wasn't as chaotic as when I was around Siana. Nira had made me feel protected. As I walked down the hall toward the kitchen, my muscles tightened again as I balled my hands into fists inside my pockets.

I had fallen for it again.

CHAPTER THIRTY-SEVEN

RHETT

"As we speak, Siana is in RightCorp."

The roll I had torn apart and stuffed in my mouth was delicious. The thing I missed the most while I was living in Coranta was Mom's cooking.

"She's strong, and she's mastered her abilities. I don't think she will have a problem with the skill part. The part that worries me is whether she will want to help when all is said and done. How will she know she can trust us?" I tore apart another roll.

Nira didn't look away while speaking. "She'll trust me. It'll be hard for her to understand right away, but I know she will help me get the barricade up."

I had to admit, Nira was good at being a leader. While working at the Rightleys, she had always been soft-spoken and demure, but now she was confident. Finding a purpose had made her strong.

My mom passed me her plate full of rolls with a sad grin. "I know you want to tell her, but there's no way of knowing what tests they will put her through at the lab. If she says the wrong thing, it could alert them. We need Hartlem's men and Ethan in the same place for everything to work." She stroked my cheek. "You have a beautiful heart, son. I know it hurts you to keep her in the dark, but it's what has to be done. In a few days, it will all be over."

"She's a good person. She has the biggest heart of anyone that I know. She's going to understand why we had to keep her in the dark for just a little while." Nira said while avoiding my gaze.

We had been going over everything for an hour when the smell of hot buttered rolls and stew wafted through the room. Henry carried in a tray with enough food piled on for the four of us. He had taken his sweet time finding his way here after sending for him half an hour ago. At least he brought food with him.

"Thank you for taking time out of your busy schedule to join us." I wondered if he understood sarcasm yet.

"Of course, I love being summoned by our valiant leader." Apparently he did.

"We will hold your murder trial on the same day Hartlem is sending men for Siana." I grabbed the bowl of stew from the tray, the fragrant steam rising. I took a bite, a warm blanket spreading out the second the savory goodness hit my stomach. I let out a grateful sigh before continuing.

Henry stood behind Nira, hands shoved in his pockets and muscles tense as he glared down at me. It was normal for dires to go through a range of emotions when transitioning. He was still working through the anger stage.

"Why am I having to go through with a trial? It doesn't make any sense." He scoffed as he pulled a chair out between Nira and mom.

I finished my meal without looking back at him. "It makes sense because a dire murderer is big news. Everyone will expect a huge turnout to watch, which means when the entire Sector shows up at the Courthouse, no one will suspect a thing." A small spot now marked my shirt where the stew had dripped on it.

"That's great. So you want me to play pretend as your little puppet." He bit the inside of his cheek. "Am I right?"

Nira answered, "The Rightleys are a plague on this continent. They take whatever they want under the guise of keeping everyone safe. You, more than anyone, understand the horrible things done to 'protect us'."

A catch in her voice made me look up. She went on.

"You pulled me from those flames, Henry. If you hadn't, I wouldn't be sitting here. Had you still been on Soterapine, you wouldn't have considered going in a burning building to save one person. They take away the dires' humanity and it's not right. You can help us make it right."

"If you have so many people on your side, why haven't you just taken over Coranta by force yet?"

"Because they have Hartlem on their side. They may fight their own war, but the Rightleys have been making sure that they stayed on top for almost a century. They would let the fighting spill over in a heartbeat before they lost their advantage."

Henry's expression softened as he raked his hand over the stubble on his face. His hard features softened, leaving behind a disheveled man with shadows beneath his eyes. As much as I disliked him, in that moment, I pitied him more.

"We'll use the trial to overthrow Ethan and take control of Coranta. Hartlem needs to see that we are a legitimate power, and recognize the Willulf family as controlling overseers of all the continent." I leaned forward and rested my forearms on the table.

"And what makes you think they will side with you?"

"Ethan wants to cut them off and shut them out of Coranta. They are so desperate for a weapon that will win their war for them they will risk it."

"So you give them Siana and they keep the technology to keep winning their war. The barrier becomes nothing more than Ethan's fever dream, and you become the continent's newest savior for freeing all the dires. The great and mighty Willulf Overseer, just like your father, right?" Henry scoffed, crossing his hands over his chest and shaking his head.

A snake coiled in my stomach, one that I was all too familiar with. The images of what my family had built flashed in my head. I had long since learned to master my shifts, but the thought of what I had seen my father do, what I had done, made me sick. My blood boiled while a bead of sweat rolled down Henry's forehead.

"We give them both of us." Nira held out her hand to

Henry. "She and I pool our strength to raise Ethan's barrier, only we leave one entrance we retain full control of."

"And the dires?"

"They stay under for now." I said. Henry released Nira's hand and stood with his fists planted on the table across from me. Both ladies were at his sides, speaking softly and rubbing his arms as if he were a child.

"And this is exactly why. A newly freed dire is unstable. We can't risk them burning Coranta to the ground because they get their newfound feelings hurt."

"Rhett." My mother scolded me.

"He needs to understand. Yes, our goal is to create a free continent, but for that to work, we need to continue on like normal for now." He leaned further over the table.

"How long?" The rage in his eyes seeped into his voice.

"A year. Maybe two. However long it takes to assure Hartlem that we can run things. We will release everyone, but slowly and in stages. They will have a choice to go wherever they want when the time is right. But not now. Not yet."

CHAPTER THIRTY-EIGHT

SIANA

Days of what Hawthorne referred to as R&D had proved maddening. The crushing pain in my chest seemed to intensify every time I stepped under the marble arches lording over the entrance. I wasn't sure how much more I had to give. The RightCorp was evil. The things that I had witnessed this past week were unimaginable, and they played in my mind every time I closed my eyes. Did Hartlem know about or even care that these people suffered for the sake of their war?

"Sit down, Ms. Viteri." Hawthorne scuttled around in front of a row of sterile chrome counters. "Josie, could you please let the lab assistants know we will begin the barrier test in five minutes?"

She nodded her head and left the cramped white

walled room, the heavy metal door slamming behind her.

"I didn't realize that you and my best friend were on a first name basis." The stiff plastic covering the arm of the chair let out harsh screeching sounds as I moved around. Dr. Hawthorne's shoulders rose as a chill sent his body shaking like a wet dog.

"Josie has proved to be a most valuable lab assistant."

The sound of metal and glass gently knocking together piqued my interest. The chair cried out again with the full weight of my body pushing off against it. My footsteps clopped against the spotless tile floor as I made my way over to him. The meeting with Hartlem was tomorrow. Josie would come with me to Hartlem, and we would be far away from all of this. Channeling my inner cat, I looked the good doctor in the eye before swatting several tubes of liquid on to the floor.

"Oh no. Those weren't important, were they?"

"Ms. Viteri, I would suggest that you sit back down before drastic measures must be taken." The vitriol in his voice matched Ethan's.

I didn't move. Instead, my eyes shifted to a tray with several shiny metal tools. If they had ever been used, they didn't show it. Their surfaces reflected the harsh light of the room while their sharp edges gleamed. Feeling the satisfaction rolling off of him was enough to make me act stupid. The ear-splitting clank of metal on tile rang out through the room and brought a genuine smile to my face. His face burned red hot as he grabbed his ears, cursing. Nothing could be done to me. They needed me to end their dependence on our neighbor across the water. I was untouchable. I all but skipped back to the medical grade plastic chair, my heart fluttering. I had learned by now that the Doctor hated irritating sounds and I had become quite good at getting snippets of information by putting him on edge. I slowly trailed my fingers down the arm of the chair.

"So now that we're besties too, do I get to call you by your first name?"

Only the sound of scraping metal answered me.

"Ok, let me guess. Hm, is it Carl? No. Kevin? No. I've got it! Hubert!"

Still nothing.

"That's it. So, can I call you Hubie for short? I just feel like we've already been through so much together that we really are in nickname territory." My arms and legs stretched as I tried to look as bored as possible. The chair gave another satisfying plastic squeal as my body stretched.

"What do you say we save making friendship bracelets until Ethan gets here, though? I would hate for him to be jealous because he missed out? I turned in the chair to rest on my side. My cheek propped in my right hand as I gave an innocent look at the doctor. He had moved to stand at the table beside me.

The deadly look that filled Hawthorne's face rattled me as my heart dropped. His eyes narrowed on me as the corners of his mouth tugged downward. I imagined a dog snarling just before attacking. The sharp points of the multiple syringes were the teeth he would use to tear me apart. The brightly colored tubes of fluid looked toxic and probably were. My throat tightened as I tried to swallow.

The door to the room swung open, and my heart slammed in my chest. I let out a startled gasp as Josie spoke to Hawthorne. "It's done."

My head snapped back to the needles.

"You're just in time. Please proceed with the injections."

I panicked as she sat in the chair beside me and reached for the first one. This sick bastard was going to have my best friend do it. My head swiveled, frantically looking for a way out before I heard the clink of metal on metal. My eyes widened, looking at the empty syringe on the table. Josie had already picked up the next. This one looked like an oil slick. Without hesitation, she stuck it into her waiting arm.

"Stop!" My hand darted out to grab her, but it was too late. The contents of both were now coursing through her.

"What the hell was that?" I spoke through clenched teeth, wishing more than anything that I had my father's elixir with me right now. The thought of what I would let myself do to this man sent a chill down my spine and bile up my throat. He didn't answer my question.

"Ms. Viteri, I would like you to focus on this sensation." He brought a small metal device down on my bare leg. My body rocked forward, teeth clenched as pain rippled up my body. The smell of bleach flooded my nostrils and my jaw locked. The pain stopped as suddenly as it had begun and I inhaled as deeply as I could. A dark tunnel clouded my vision. Black clouds seemed to circle my brain as I reached out.

"Josie!" Everywhere ached as I found her hands and

brought them to my chest. "Josie, what's happening?"

It wasn't her that answered me.

"What's happening is that I gave you very painful stimuli to create an essential memory. One that our friend has now amplified and, if my positing is correct, sent to every person within a measurable range. And because of the formula that she injected, she can continue the sense shift without the need to keep you active."

"Why aren't you on the floor, then?" I held her in my arms, hoping to protect her from any other atrocities they might inflict upon her. His eyes moved to a small box resting on a counter beside the door. He straightened in his chair, shoulders back and chin up as if he was accepting an award.

"I've created a serum that nullifies your specific abilities as they are." The giddy tone in his voice sent white hot rage shooting through me.

"We will need it while the actual barrier is being constructed." He rose to collect something from a far table. "You've already had the pleasure of trying out the support system for my barrier pods. Thanks to that technology, we can sustain life for quite some time. This method will work for a while, but eventually, she will expire."

I held Josie out at arm's length. A small drop of blood had fallen from her nose onto her white lab coat. The barrier wouldn't be some kind of stone wall. It was human–it was Josie. They would use me to charge her and leave her there at the border-nothing more than a battery to them.

No matter how much I wanted to do the right thing, I couldn't let them continue to do this to her. Ethan Rightley and his Doctor had done something vile to my best friend, and I would not let them hurt her anymore. As soon as I had an opportunity, I would take Josie and run.

On the drive back to the manor, I tried to come up with a plan. It seemed only fitting that I end all of this the way that they had started it. I would set their home on fire and leave them to pick up the pieces.

Josie still had said nothing since the lab. She had emerged from her trance with the help of a small dose of the doctor's serum, and I had helped myself to the box as we had made our way out. It now sat heavy in my pocket. This was what Rhett had asked me to find, but I would have to lie when he asked for it. I needed it if I was going to get me and Josie out.

My feet slammed against each step as I made my way up the stairs, pulling Josie along behind me. She followed at my pace, keeping her stiff hands cradled in mine.

"I hope you understand now what is needed of you." Ethan's voice cut through my focus. He stood in the open doorway of his study, his arms crossed across his puffed up chest and a devious smile on his disgusting face. My fingers curled into tight balls and a slow breath escaped my pursed lips. Just a few more hours and we would be gone. And with any luck, so would he.

"How could I not?"

"Tomorrow is a big day for me, and I would like to go over a few things with you before I turn in for the night." He didn't wait for a response before walking back into the room, leaving the heavy wooden doors wide open for us to follow. I tried to steady my breathing as the tremor in my chin continued to intensify. Looking down to make sure my pounding heart wasn't actually visible beneath my shirt, I tugged at the hem. Did he already know about my plan to escape with Josie? Keeping my composure now more important than ever, I grasped Josie's hands in mine and forced my feet to follow Ethan through the cavernous doorway with as much bravado as I could muster.

Something about this room felt wrong. The hairs on the back of my neck and arms stood up and as a tingle ran up my spine. Something told me I should run.

"You can leave us, Josie."

Without a word, she released my hand and left, closing the heavy wooden doors behind her.

"Sit."

He gestured to a dark brown chair beside him. My feet turned to lead at the thought of taking me so close to him. His wicked grin fell as a shadow took over his features. The images of all the dires trapped in his despicable labs flashed through my mind, a reminder of what he was willing to do to get his way.

Each of my vertebrae stacked one by one as my body straightened with false confidence. The chair was just as cold and stiff as it looked, reminding me of Dr. Hawthorne's testing chair. I didn't make a move to see if it made the same sounds. A darkness seemed to linger in every corner of the room despite the glow of the amber lamps donning each table.

He didn't sit but instead leered down at me. His piercing eyes seemed to burn a hole in the pocket that held the serum. Did he know what was there or what I planned to do with it? My hand itched to cover it, but not wanting to give myself away, I held my body as still and calm as possible. He lowered himself to the arm of the couch, not once taking his eyes off of me.

"There are many people that will be hurt if you don't do what you're told. Do you understand me?" He leaned forward to grab the drink on the table beside me. When he straightened, his normally charming smile was plastered back on his face, almost concealing the murder that remained in his gaze.

"Dr. Hawthorne told you about the barricade that you will help make before going to Hartlem. He also told me about your antics in the lab today." The smile still held on his lips, but the promise of pain dripped from every syllable that escaped them. "That will be your last act of defiance. You will give a demonstration to our guests tomorrow before leaving Coranta."

He took a slow sip of his drink as he stood. "Your range is quite impressive. Even exceeding what the Dr. thought you would be able to accomplish. I have no doubt that you will make a good impression for me." He made his way to the door.

"Was anyone hurt?" My voice was small.

He didn't slow or respond until he made it to the doors, "Less than will be if you don't do as you're told tomorrow." He left the doors gaping wide as he crossed the landing, making his way to his room, shoulders high and triumph in every step.

I did my best to push away the thoughts of what I might have done. If I hurt someone, it was because of them. They used me. They had been in control of it — but not for much longer.

Ethan was desperate for his plan to work. Why else

would he feel the need to threaten me, which also told me he had no idea what I was about to do? I wanted to be sure that he was out of earshot before I left, not wanting him to see me going down to the kitchen. My eyes wandered around the room. The shelves were filled with a hodge-podge of things that didn't seem to fit with his psycho nature. They were displayed like priceless artifacts or treasures. Each item had a small golden plaque stamped with a number and nothing else.

My nails caught on the fabric of my pants as they raked up and down nervously. My chest rose and fell unevenly as I settled back down in my seat to wait. The item that had been placed at the center of the table across from my chair caught my eye. A single tea rose crushed, frozen in time by glass. The air froze inside my chest. My hands trembled as I stood, feet pulling me toward the familiar flower and gold plaque emblazoned with the number 77.

Disgust rolled through my body as a torrent of emotion blasted out.

Without another second of hesitation, I slammed the trapped rose against the table's edge. Glass shattered and spread across the floor in a wave as the floral notes hit my nose. With rose in hand, I squeezed the dead stem as a small knick barely registered in my head. My hand opened, and I focused my sights on the flower, not sure if it was a thorn or glass that had left a small red droplet on my palm. There would be no waiting for the right moment. The fire in my heart was ready to spread now.

Every step seemed to propel ever faster toward the kitchen. There was a chance that many people would suffer if I didn't succeed tonight. But more would continue to suffer at the hands of RightCorp if I didn't try. The war that was raging could be held off as long as they continued to receive supplies. We could do that. We had always done that without knowing, so there was no reason it couldn't continue. And if we destroyed the labs, they couldn't make anymore Soterapine to keep the people prisoners.

The pots clanked loudly as I pulled a large pan from the rack hanging above the island. I lit the burner and placed it on the now burning stove with a soaked rag and Nira's rose in the center. Hopefully, the water would give us enough time for me to grab Josie and get out before anything caught fire. Rushing to spread every flammable item across the counters, I didn't hear the approaching footsteps until they were right behind me.

I spun toward the all too familiar woman and a loud gasp threw my body into a coughing fit. The once calming smell of lemons filled me with repulsion as she rubbed my back in gentle circles, trying to stop me from choking on my spit. My hand flew out and with a satisfying smack as I batted hers away.

"Don't touch me!" The demand came out so much louder than I had intended. I struggled to pull in a breath.

"Can I help you with something?" She grabbed for my hands, but I kept them glued to my sides.

"I don't have time for you right now."

"If you're hungry, I can make you something." She looked behind me at the mess I had made, moving to the counter to clean it up.

"I'm fine. Please, just go away." She was hollow. They must have been pumping her full of the same stuff

Josie was on. Not a trace of who I thought was my Aunt Jerry remained. The cracks I had been holding together inside me split open into wide chasms as I was faced with yet another person who had been ripped from me.

The now familiar mist made my vision blurry as I inhaled lemon and smoke. My body shook as every emotion consumed me and I slipped into a sense shift.

Deanna fell to the floor, her body rigid while her face contorted in pain. Her breathing was ragged as her eyes pleaded for help. My knees took on a splitting pain as I threw myself on the floor beside her. A popping sensation in my head caught me off guard as she went limp.

The stove had begun to smoke as the water evaporated from the rag. I still needed to go find Josie before the water was completely gone and it caught fire. A heaviness settled in my stomach as I stared down at Deanna. I hadn't realized until now that others besides the Rightleys would still be in the house. I had to stop Ethan and Melissa. To make them pay for all the pain and suffering that they and their family had caused all of Coranta. But could I sacrifice the dires here to do it?

Her eyes fluttered open and locked in on mine.

"Sia. I'm so sorry." She sobbed frantically as something clicked on her face. Her body shook as she scurried across the floor to grab at my leg. "Nira is gone. I'm so sorry. I never thought they would hurt you. I didn't know. Please forgive me, I didn't know." She was shaking uncontrollably and staring at me with pure fear in her watery eyes. What had happened? The hollow dire that had just moments before offered me food was now full of terror and raw emotion. The rage in me felt hot enough to catch fire all on its own.

"Get off of me. You helped them! You work for them and you helped them kill Nira."

She pushed away from me like I had hit her full in the face. Pulling herself from the floor, she looked toward the stove. Before I could stop her, she grabbed my makeshift fire starter and flung it into the sink with an earsplitting crash.

"You can't!" She turned on the faucet and swung around to cut off the flame on the stove.

"You've already done enough damage, Deanna. If you are at all sorry for what you did to Nira, you will get out of my way." My teeth stung from the force of them grinding together. I knew if I opened my mouth fully, I would scream at her. "What's wrong? Are you worried that your precious Rightleys might get hurt?"

Sadness welled in her eyes. "I know you will never forgive me, but please, you have to trust me."

My laugh fell flat on the floor. "Trust the person who lied to me my whole life and helped the people that took everything from me, including my entire family. Tell me, did you help them kill my dad and my aunt? My real aunt. Or did you just stand back and enjoy the show?"

She held her hands out in defense. At least she wasn't completely delusional in thinking that I wouldn't sling a skillet at her head if I felt the urge. "RightCorp and the Rightleys have done more than their fair share of horrible things, but it was to keep us all safe. You don't understand what has happened to the rest of the continent."

"I know all about the war that the Rightley's claim to protect us from."

Her voice was desperate. "No. I don't just mean Hartlem. There is a reason the Rightley's attorney is so feared. The horrendous things that happen in the other Fractions would turn your insides."

My feet shuffled back and forth as I took in her words. "The Rightleys deserve to pay." I turned to leave. I needed to get my friend and get out. Now that we didn't have a diversion, we would have to move fast.

"He knew you would try to leave." Her voice was becoming increasingly shrill as she went on. "You won't find her."

"What did he do with Josie?"

"Please, Siana, please. Everything hurts and I can't breathe." Full heart wrenching sobs were pouring from her now. "He's going to kill me. He will kill me." She turned and ran to the door that separated the kitchen from the gardens outside.

"We have to grab Josie first."

"No! We don't have time. We need to go now." Her voice was carrying, sending my nerves on edge. If she didn't calm down, my plan would be ruined.

"Aunt Jer— Deanna, you have you be quiet." She gripped at my arms, her nails digging into my skin. The terror present in her eyes was unsettling.

"We have to run. We have to run. We have to run." Her repetitious plea was cut off as shouting sounded from outside of the kitchen door. I rushed forward to block it with anything that I could find. A thud sounded behind me. I turned, expecting to find Deanna moving some heavy object to help me block out whoever was trying to get in. The loud thud had been her falling to the floor. She had fainted — again.

The pounding on the kitchen door was reverberating off of the tiled kitchen walls. The noise was deafening and sent all the hairs on the back of my neck standing straight up. She had been right. I had to get out of here now.

The beating on the door drowned out the sound of Deanna's limp body dragging across the floor. I pulled her into the waiting pantry. Hopefully, if they found her here, they would think I knocked her out instead of thinking she had helped me. Maybe that would save her from Ethan's wrath.

Without another thought for the woman who used to be my family, I rushed toward the exit and barreled outside. The icy chill of the air hit my face, sending my adrenaline into overdrive as I took a sharp breath in. The estate was even more imposing at night as darkness wrapped its way around the grounds. My feet pounded across the hard earth as I made my escape into the night. A decent swath of the grounds was already behind me before the sound of the Rightley's shouting orders at their staff spurred me on over the pounding of blood in my ears. I didn't stop, but focused on the sound as I ran. Using as much energy as I could spare, I tried to send out a shift.

The feeling of connecting with them was nauseating. I could feel four of them, all dires. The ground spun as I put all of myself into sending every bit of panic down the invisible line connecting us. Heavy footsteps were making their way in my direction as I pushed more of my own senses through.

What would Ethan do if he caught me now? Damn it, Deanna. If she hadn't gotten in my way, I could be sitting back with Josie, watching while the Rightley manor went up in flames. Josie. What would he do with her now? As long as I was gone, he wouldn't be able to use her up to hold his barrier. But what did that mean for her? My eyes blurred with tears, making the already dark grounds even more dangerous. The burning in my lungs was becoming unbearable as I struggled to pull in enough air to stop my head from spinning. I took a chance and threw my gaze behind me. Although I could feel each of them, the night hid the men hunting me from view just as well as it hid the bushes that lined the edge of the property that led to a large section of trees.

As I tumbled headfirst to packed earth, I could hear heavy footsteps making their way in my direction. My hands and knees scraped across the uneven ground as I crawled under the line of shrubs. Every inch of my body was crying out in pain as the smell of ammonia coated my nostrils and the bone dry inside of my mouth. I threw my head to the ground and covered my ears as a metallic buzz rang out in my head. The sense shift threatened to tear me apart as each connection pulled tight.

Spots burst into my vision as the pain became more and more unbearable. I tried to pull back from the excruciating feelings that were now pulsing between myself and the dires.

Without warning, a loud popping sound knocked the breath out of me as each connection snapped. I stayed there, crouched on all fours, and listened. Silence. Not even the sound of Ethan's orders reached me.

Waiting any longer wasn't an option. He would, no doubt, send more of his men after me, and another shift might not be possible so soon. I had to find a place to hide that was out of the elements. Somewhere Ethan Rightley would never think to find me.

There was only one place I could think of to go.

CHAPTER THIRTY-NINE

RHETT

"Rhett!" Melissa's frantic shouting pierced through my sleeping mind. "Rhett!"

As I rushed down the stairs that separated us, the sleepy haze that had been covering my eyes dissipated.

"What's happening? Is Siana alright?"

"She tried to set the house on fire."

"Not great timing, but I can't say that I'm not proud of her."

A panic that I had never heard from her laced her every word. "She did something to the dires. We sent a group after her and when they didn't come back, we found them wandering the grounds—"

"Wait, you sent them after her, as in she's gone?" I

didn't wait for her answer as I made my way to the door.

"Rhett, listen to me for a second! She pulled them out of it somehow."

"I'm not following you and I honestly don't care right now. She's out there by herself, and I'm not going to stand around while you talk about your dire problems."

I took off down the steps to the driveway, the gravel digging into my bare feet. Melissa's voice caught me just before I stepped into the tree line.

She shouted after me, "They aren't dires anymore."

I tore through the trees.

"Siana!" I paused only long enough to listen, but was greeted with only silence. "Siana! Can you hear me?"

What would happen if she wasn't found? If she tried to take down Ethan by herself, then something truly terrible must have happened. She wouldn't risk anyone's life for less. A familiar wave of fear brushed at the edge of my mind. She was out here, and I could sense her. My head was foggy as I searched the darkness for her. We needed her for our plans to work, but if I found her and all she wanted was to run, then we would run.

"Siana!"

"Rhett!" I could hear the tears in her voice when she called my name. A feeling of relief washed over me as I took off further into the trees, the darkness surrounding them engulfing us both.

She crashed into me.

I could sense every emotion pouring out of her as she held tight to me. "It's alright. I found you. I'm here. Whatever you need, whatever you want, I'll do it. Just tell me what you want."

The darkness still surrounded us as she pulled back slightly from her hold around my shoulders, her cheek brushing mine. My heart pounded in my chest, and I knew she could feel it too.

A snapping of branches sounded behind us as an eerie glow lit up Siana's features. Her long brown hair, though pulled back, was wild where it had been tugged out of the elastic. Cuts lined her face, legs, and arms from where the branches had held her back and an angry sore where something had scorched her leg was highlighted by the bouncing light. Every part of me shattered as she froze, a look of confusion and betrayal on her face.

"Why is Melissa Rightley with you?" The accusation in her voice was a knife through me.

"You don't understand yet." And I didn't have the time to tell her before I felt a pull at my mind. Melissa was forcing me into a shift. The memory of my bed, warm and comforting, surrounded me as Siana's eyes, just moments before glowing with betrayal, softened and closed. Reaching out, I caught her up in my arms before her body could slam into the unforgiving ground.

"She's going to think it was me who did this to her." Since I had gotten to know the real Melissa, there hadn't been a single moment where I thought badly of her, until now.

"It had to be done and we don't have time to waste."

"If Ethan did this to her, I will kill him. And if you stood by and let him hurt her—"

"I don't know why she ran, but we can't protect one person while everyone else suffers. People will continue to suffer far worse fates if we don't follow the plan. This will be our last shot to get to Hartlem. After the barrier goes up, that's it. We won't have another chance."

Her body was limp as I held her in my arms. Melissa knelt beside her, knowing better than to lay a finger on her. Her heartache was as clear as my own as we stared down at the woman that didn't have a choice but to save us. I stared down at her hands—the same hands that, twenty years ago, held on to mine and refused to let go. She and Nira had pulled me from our nightmare. They had refused to leave me behind.

Her voice cracked as she spoke again. "If Ethan did do something to her, he won't touch her again. No one will. But, Rhett, she has to go back. It's only for one more night."

I knew that Melissa was right. She had to go back, but she wouldn't go alone. I made a promise on the night my mother and I hid in the shadows. I made a promise to find them and keep them safe and up until now, I hadn't kept that promise.

Ethan's car was already waiting as we made our way back to the driveway, Siana still fast asleep. The door opened, an invitation to place her inside that I refused to take.

I glared at my car instead. "Open the door." Melissa followed my orders without looking to her brother for approval. Loose strands of hair fell over Siana's face as I laid her gently down on the passenger seat and buckled her in.

Ethan had just stepped out of his car. "Take her back immediately."

"I swear, I won't leave her side." The promise was for me, but Ethan nodded his head to his sister.

I closed the door and watched as Melissa drove away from me, taking everything I cared about with her.

"If I didn't know any better, Mr. Willulf, I would think you had feelings for our little friend."

I couldn't stop the hatred that poured from my face and I ached to destroy the smile that crept its way up his. His voice dripped with satisfaction. "Everyone gives, so the many survive."

"Everyone but you, Ethan."

"Now you've got it. You might make a decent overseer for the Willulf fraction soon enough." He looked me up and down. "Thank you for returning my property."

As he drove away, he tossed a charred flower out of the window.

CHAPTER FORTY

RHETT

"You look horrible."

I stared at Melissa. She knew very well why I looked horrible. After they had driven away, I made the trek back to Siana. The ground outside her window was less than luxurious, but I would be damned if I was going to trust anyone to keep her safe in that house. More than once last night, I had felt sorrow coming from Melissa, followed by pity.

Hartlem's men had arrived early this morning, and I had had little time to make myself look presentable.

"They want a demonstration before they agree to let us put up the barrier. And since my brother had locked Josie away somewhere, he's informed me I'll be assisting." She rubbed her arm where a new cloth wrapping rested, most likely to cover a new batch of injection sights.

My heart ached for her. She continued to give. But I still couldn't bring myself to forgive her for last night. I fixed my eyes on the door as Melissa spoke. My mind kept replaying the scene from a month ago when I had stepped out into the hallway and back into her life. I longed for the life that my mother had told me about. From when we were younger; drawing shapes in the sand, playing hide and seek between our houses, reading stories with our families.

"And then we can put on our party hats and fly to the moon." Melissa raised her voice.

"What?"

Melissa looked at me with determination in her eyes, "I get it and I know where you keep going, but we need you to focus. So, after we show Hartlem what Siana can do, Ethan will tell them where Josie is…"

"Which is when we lock down the courthouse and offer them Nira and the continued Gifts as well, but only if they recognize our new leadership."

We had gone over the plan so many times now that I probably talked about it in my sleep.

"And they take Ethan to the other side of the barrier before it goes up." Melissa added. That part was new. She twisted at the hem of her shirt and I could feel the fog that surrounded her mind.

"He's done terrible things to me and to everyone else, but if we spare him, show him what mercy looks like, maybe he can change on the other side."

It was a nice thought. It wouldn't happen, but I understood why she needed to try it. No matter how horrible of a human they were, the urge to save the ones we love from themselves was always there.

I looked down at my watch, twisting the strap around my wrist. "Henry is being transferred in half an hour. We should probably get ready."

She took a deep breath and pulled me in, wrapping me in a hug that I didn't return.

"Good luck, friend." She pulled back at arm's length. "Years of planning, and we are almost at the end." She gave a sad smile and turned, walking out of the door.

CHAPTER FORTY-ONE

HENRY

The meeting room at the courthouse was just as unwelcoming as the one at the precinct. At least the furniture was more comfortable. Sheridan sat across from me, blocking my way to escape. I had to get to Siana. My heart flip-flopped inside my chest at the thought of seeing her. My knuckles cracked one by one against the palm of my hand as I paced back and forth in front of the plain white door. The carpet lining the floor held an imprint from where I had worn it down. As I turned for the hundredth time, the door swung wide. The splitting pain in my forehead was nothing compared to the annoyance the voice that entered gave me. The door slammed shut again as Rhett approached the chief.

"Slight change of plans. Ethan has hid Josie, which means Melissa will have to help with the demonstration. We need to hold until he tells Hartlem's men where to find her." He said without acknowledging I was in the room.

"Is she alright? Does anyone have any idea whether he's hurt her?"

"He won't hurt her right now. He's using her as a bargaining chip to make sure Siana does what he wants." For the first time, he looked at me and the look in his eyes said we were thinking the same thing. We would do anything to make sure she wasn't hurt.

"Were you able to get Hawthorne's serum?" Sheridan asked.

"No. Everyone will just have to be prepared for whatever she may send out." He continued, "Ethan and Hartlem's men will definitely have taken the serum, so whatever happens, they aren't going to be fazed."

"So, what's our signal to attack?" I leaned against the wall opposite him so he couldn't avoid my gaze.

"You are."

My head bounced back and forth between the two of them, knowing that whatever plan he was about to give, I would not like my part in it.

CHAPTER FORTY-TWO

SIANA

"Your antics last night were stupid but expected." Ethan looked out of the darkly tinted car windows as the courthouse came into view.

"What have you done with Josie?" My voice sounded foreign in my own ears.

"She is with Dr. Hawthorne, who has instructions to dispose of her if you do not cooperate." He crossed one leg over the other and peered at me over his clasped hands.

"Once you are well on your way, she will be

brought to the barrier location."

"Why are you doing this? All of these people suffering—doesn't it bother you?" He couldn't be that heartless.

"They can't suffer if they don't understand the concept." I could hear the air of superiority in his voice. The smug way one side of his mouth curled up. "They will continue to serve my family along with the rest of the continent and without the reasoning to complain, they will do so willingly."

My face contorted to one of pure hatred and disgust. The three vials I had hidden in my shirt were calling to me as the car door opened and a hand reached in to help me out. Each step up toward the courthouse held a promise.

"Looks like your fan club showed up early." I stared at the many people waiting to get inside.

I could hear the amusement in his voice when he answered. "Although that would usually be the case, today they are here to see the cop."

My eyebrows drew together as I glared at him, my feet faltering, almost missing a step.

"It just so happens that his murder trial for the death of your sweet sister is today. Too bad you won't be around to celebrate when he's found guilty."

Acid built in my stomach as I fought to keep my composure. We finally entered the main hall where men, all in uniform, surrounded the cavernous entry space.

"Let's get this over with so we can get out of here. These people of yours make me feel uneasy."

"Of course Robertson, we are just waiting on—" before Ethan could finish, Melissa made her way down the stairs, "my sister. She is an amplifier."

"You would part with your own sister. The Director said you were heartless."

"She isn't strong enough for what you need. She's only here for the demonstration. Your amplifier will be in transit as soon as you are to the border."

"Enough, just show us what she can do." Robertson already looked bored.

My eyes narrowed on Melissa. She had been the first to force me into a shift. The things Dr. Hawthorne had done to Josie were because of her and her brother. The image of her with Rhett had played on repeat in my mind, and another wave of nausea rolled over me.

"Now, Siana." Ethan growled at me. I felt the pull before I had a chance to prepare myself. My feet shifted back and forth as I focused on the memory. My vision tunneled as I was led to the sharp pain the doctor had subjected me to. I fought the sickness bubbling in my stomach as the smell of burnt hair and ammonia circled the space. The entire room was a grotesque sea of convulsions. Ethan, Melissa, and Hartlem's men were, however, left completely unfazed. I pulled myself back out before Melissa could even let me go and the hairs on my neck stood up as I fought the urge to fold into myself.

"And how far is her range?" Robertson asked.

"On her own, minimal. But we estimate that with an amplifier she can affect anyone within five miles, maybe more overtime." Ethan glowed as if he had done it all himself. Whispers around the hall grew as people began to realize what had happened to them. "We will send you the amplifier once this one is in place."

The two men deciding my future were deep in conversation when the doors to the main courtroom flew open.

"Henry." My heart soared to see him.

He stared at me for only a second before yelling, "RENBROUGH!"

Chaos erupted throughout the large foyer as people emerged from every corner of the space. My hands placed firmly over my ears were hardly a barrier to the deafening sound that bounced off of the cold hard walls and rang out from every direction. Ethan's grip on my arm was painful as he forced me into someone else's waiting hands. "Get her to the car. Now."

Melissa didn't say a word as she held on to both of my arms. She was gentler than her brother, but the touch made my skin crawl all the same.

"SIANA!" Rhett's voice was strained. As I looked up to see the fighting that had broken out on the second floor landing, I saw him standing in front of several men, all of them on their knees and shaking. The memory of the icy grip that had held me when we had first returned from Port Hartlem turned my insides molten. I may not have known what was happening, but I knew exactly what those men were feeling. My senses still felt raw from the demonstration, but I shifted through as best as I could. As I sent the memory of sitting in front of the fireplace in the library to them, one by one, each man stood and rushed at him. A strange feeling coiled around my heart as I watched them disappear farther back into the shadows, only to be covered by more fighting.

Dread washed over me and somehow I could hear my heart slamming inside my chest over the earsplitting noise that was sending vibrations through the building. Melissa's grip was like a vice on my arms as she had stopped trying to drag me outside and was instead staring up at the place where Rhett had been. Before I could try anything, she whipped my body around to face hers, the usual cold features replaced by ones of concern.

"Siana, you are going to—" Bodies slammed into both of us, the force knocking myself and Melissa to the floor. My hands and legs collided with the hard floor as I struggled to crawl away and stand. My feet refused to stay underneath me as they slid on the now wet surface. Blood had pooled around a body that was now laid at the bottom of the enormous staircase.

Panic raced through my blood at the sight. The man lying there couldn't have been much older than me, possibly in his early thirties but now dead all the same. I stared at the blood now smeared across my own hands before someone else's, too big to be Melissa's, grabbed mine.

"Henry." Tears sprung to my eyes at the sight of him. The sound of fighting continued as we ran toward the main courtroom.

"We have to get you to a safe place until the Sector gains control."

"The Sector? What the hell is going on?"

A loud crash sounded from behind us as metal canisters smashed through the courthouse windows, leaving shards of sword like glass coating the once pristine marble floor.

"Now isn't the right time. You just have to trust me, please. Rhett—"

"You're working with Rhett?"

"I'm helping the people of Coranta and if that means helping Willulf, then that's what I'll do." There was a pain in his eyes when he looked at me again. Without another word, he pushed me behind the large wooden doors of the courtroom and began barricading them.

"Rhett Willulf is working with the Rightleys."

Another crash sounded from the other side of the door, this time much closer.

"No, Siana. You don't understand what he's done—"

"No, Henry, you don't understand what he's done. He gave me to them. He's handed me over to them on a silver platter more than once."

"I know. And it's not fair. The sacrifices that you have made have never been your choice." My heart plummeted down as a thunderous boom shook the massive doors. The sound echoed over and over as whoever was on the other side continued their onslaught. They were trying to get in. Trying to get to me.

"We have to get you out of here until the fighting is over."

My ears rang as I brought my hands over my ears. The sound coming from the other room was deafening as he rushed me to the far side of the courtroom, a door on the side of the judge's bench our target. My feet slid as we rounded a large polished table at the front of the room, just as the door ahead of us opened.

Everything stopped.

The vibrations from the battle outside still made their way up my body, but the sound of crashing and screams were drowned out by the rushing in my ears. The heaviness that overwhelmed me threatened to pull me down with it as I stared. I checked for the pull that always accompanied a forced shift and I wavered in place as a ripple of dizziness started pulsing its way through me, but no pull. She was real.

"Siana."

"Nira." I didn't dare move as she rushed toward me. Her arms encased me as a shuddering sob left my body.

"Are you really here? Please, let this be real. Please. Please."

"I'm so sorry, Sia."

I gripped her tighter as an earth-shattering explosion sent fragments of the door behind us flying like knives through the open space. Another uproar followed from the spectator balcony above as people from all sides poured into the room.

The thought of losing her again had my head spinning. Even now, as I held her, I could feel Ethan closing in on us. I let the red haze of the shift encircle my vision and pulled it in to myself. I thought of the feeling of the burn on my skin left there by Dr. Hawthorne. I thought of the heat that had rolled off of our home as Nira had laid on the ground. I thought of every moment of my life that wasn't my own and every ounce of pain that had been inflicted upon me and the people that I loved more than anything in this world. Even without an amplifier, I could feel the tendrils of my shift branching out. Grasping at everyone in the room. I could feel the panic rolling off of them as heat blistered through their unmarked veins. All of them.

"Siana, stop. Please." Nira was gritting through clenched teeth as I realized I had no control over who I was targeting. I pulled the shift back as fast as I could, not yet realizing the damage I had unwittingly done.

In front of me stood Ethan Rightley, a look of pure malice plastered on his untouched face. The blocking serum running through him and his men had left them unaffected by my shift and closing in on us. Forced to his knees on the balcony above me, knelt Rhett, blood trailing down a gash marring the side of his face. Ethan glared up at him. "I always knew there was something wrong with you. Really, you've done me a favor." He turned to the man beside him. "Tell Dr. Hawthorne that Willulf fraction will be ready for his transfer sooner that we expected. He will be delighted to have more material for his tests."

Ethan's voice grated at the insides of my ears and sent white hot hatred coursing through me as he narrowed his sights on us.

"Nira, my love. How wonderful to see you again."

"Don't." Nira's voice was defiant but strained. The urge to barrel forward and ring his neck was sickeningly strong. With a small whimper, Nira placed her arm on mine, her palm sticky with sweat. My hand went over hers as she swallowed hard. A feeling of pain shocked my senses. I looked down at her hand. My heart thundered in my chest as I saw what I had thought was sweat. A piece of the heavy door had pierced her side and blood was already coating the front of her worn, gray shirt.

"It looks like our reunion is going to be rather short-lived." Ethan's voice shredded my insides as a thought passed over me.

All the sounds of fighting had stopped. The Sector had failed. No one was coming to save me or Nira or Henry. No one was going to save Josie. No one was going to stop this man that was now stalking toward me and the people I loved.

No one but me.

On the balcony above, Rhett was fighting as hard as his wounds would allow him and more, an animal cornered and scared of what might happen next.

"Siana, hide! Hide and I swear, I will find you again!"

He stopped fighting, his movements becoming deadly still as I fixed my sights on him.

"If you don't want me to kill you when that happens, you'll save her this time."

Not a threat, but a promise.

Nira's blood had soaked through the fabric of my jeans. Not again. I wouldn't lose her again, and I wouldn't let Ethan or Hartlem use her. Not when I had the answer to save her this time. My father's legacy sat heavy against my heart.

"Looks like it's time for a change of plans, then." Reaching into my shirt, I pulled out all three vials and passed two to Henry.

"You need to take the blue one now. The yellow one is for me." My hands were steady as I pulled the stopper on the shadow black vial. Henry, confused, held the yellow back out for me.

"Not yet." I pushed it back into his hand. "After I've done what it takes to keep everyone safe. If it makes sense, if I can still live with what I've done," a tear streaked down my face, "that's when it's time to bring me back." Henry reached for me, and I took a step back.

"I don't understand. What are you asking me to do?"

Panic laced his voice as the footsteps behind me came even closer.

"No one deserves to live like this. Like you had to. I hated the dires with every fiber of my being, but the horrible things that I've seen—someone has to save them. I can save them, Henry."

"What do you need?"

"Right now, I need you to take that." I pointed to the blue vial. "And remember that it's still me."

He downed it in one quick gulp, and I followed.

"No, Siana!" Rhett's voice cracked as a purple cloud encased my vision. It was as if everything I had ever experienced, good and bad, was trying to fight for dominance behind my eyes. Strong arms surrounded me before…

CHAPTER FORTY-THREE

HENRY

She swallowed the vial in one quick movement. Her eyes immediately pleaded for help as she grasped at her throat, falling to the ground, convulsing just as Rightley and his men approached us.

"The Director won't be happy with damaged assets." They had already started walking away from Siana's crumpled form as if she were a bit of trash under their feet.

"Get ready to double your shipments for the next couple of months to make up for this." I rose. She didn't deserve this, to be treated as if she were only worth what they could use her for. My feet felt heavy and my head pounded as I stalked toward them with deadly focus. A hand on my shoulder stopped me.

"Siana."

I grabbed her shoulders, checking every inch of her I could see to make sure she was alright. She grabbed both hands and placed them gently at my sides before stepping around me, giving me a clear view of Nira. The chunk of wood that had caused the damage to her side was visible on the floor beside her, but the wound was gone.

I rushed back to Siana's side. The smile she threw Melissa Rightley's way sent a shudder down my spine before Melissa screamed and clawed at her head, as if trying to pull something from her own brain.

"Interesting." The voice didn't sound like it belonged to Siana anymore.

All around the courthouse, people dropped, their bodies rigid with whatever she was doing to them. Something tried to pull at my mind as I stared, legs trembling and fighting a powerful warning in my brain to run. An unearthly heat crept over the courthouse, followed by a blanket of silence.

Siana popped her jaw and opened her eyes.

"What just happened?" The disbelief was written clearly all over the face of the man from Hartlem.

"Any dire within range has had the Soterapine blocked out of their system and everyone else is just taking a nice little nap so we can chat."

The rage building in Ethan was clear for everyone to see. He had just lost his army of drones.

"Calm down, Ethan, before you hurt yourself. Now, gentlemen, I would very much like to speak to Mr. Hartlem about a new arrangement. So, if you would please, take me to him." Something about her sweet demeanor seemed hollow. Her words, although cordial, dripped with an unseen threat. A threat that the men in front of her were not taking seriously.

Ethan fumed as his words hissed out between clenched teeth. "You will not speak to anyone. You have no voice here."

"Our arrangement is with the Rightley's and I think you'll find it in your best interest to do what you're told, sweetheart."

She smiled.

Ethan's anger had finally hit its peak as he began screaming.

"You're a stupid, stupid girl, Siana! Your friend is dead, do you hear me?" Ethan's face was blood red and the vein in his forehead pulsed. I stepped forward to stop the assault I knew was coming. A wet snap cut through the hall as Ethan's body went limp, his head folded grotesquely to one side: the force of it so much that it ripped the skin on his neck. His body stayed upright for only a beat too long before it fell to the ground with a sickening thud. Siana didn't look at his now lifeless body as she side-stepped around him to close the space between her and the beast of a man.

"I think you'll find it in your best interest to do as you're told– sweetheart." She gave him a closed lipped smile before walking past him to the car waiting at the bottom of the courthouse steps. I silently followed.

"Get in, Henry. We have a stop to make before we head to Hartlem." Her voice was flat. My eyes rested on the vial gripped in the palm of my hand.

"Where are we going?" I knew Siana was in there,

but after what I had just seen, I found myself occupying the seat furthest from her. If she noticed, she didn't show it. Her face was unreadable as she turned her gaze from the courthouse to me.

"I think I need to see my doctor." The smile on her face was wicked as she looked back out the window in silence.

CHAPTER FORTY-FOUR

RHETT

Melissa had been frantic since she woke me up on the balcony floor. She had been shouting things about Siana murdering Ethan before running off with Henry. According to her, Siana had put everyone to sleep and snapped his neck without touching him. I took a deep breath, rubbing at my temples. She had taken her father's serum. Which meant she was no longer Siana. The carnage we found at RightCorp made this even more apparent.

"It's as if she did something to the Soterapine in all the dires as she moved through, blocked it somehow. Almost like she reset everyone. How is she doing this?" Melissa said in shock.

The dires locked in each room had already gone crazy, overwhelmed by their new emotions. Further down the levels of absolute horror was what we were looking for.

Dire Mistakes

The noise carrying down to the lab was growing to a roar as the dires beat against their glass cages.

"We have to get out of here." Melissa was right, but there was something that I needed first. The serum that blocked out the shift. I knew Siana had found it. I had seen Henry down it just before she took her own. Although, with her father's serum in her system, I don't think it even mattered. According to Melissa, she had still controlled Ethan. It shouldn't have been possible and yet…

A locked glass cabinet held what I was looking for. The only set back not being the lock, but the crumbled and bloody mass of what remained of Doctor Hawthorne. I reached my hand through the shards of broken glass and took every unbroken vial. A wave of sorrow and fear ran through me as I pictured Siana standing in front of the doctor and ripping him apart. A chill ran down my spine as I uncorked a vial. It wouldn't do anything to stop her if she wanted me dead, but I drank it all the same.

Leaving the doctor behind, we raced up the levels before exiting the RightCorp's house of horrors.

"We should have told her everything!" Anger bursting out as I punched the marble column. "If we had just trusted her, she wouldn't have felt like this was the only choice."

Nira walked slowly toward us, streaks of tears and dried blood on her face. Melissa reached out and stroked her arm.

"I think it would be best for you to stay out here." The sounds of breaking glass punctuating her request.

"What do we do now? Evacuate the city?" Niras' voice was worn but the determination on her face was strong.

Melissa held her close. "I think that's our only option. We don't have time or resources to keep everyone safe while they transition."

"When the dires start feeling everything, they're going to go insane." The blood trickled down my wrist. I turned my hand over to see I had torn open the wide cut that had been healing. I squeezed it closed and bit down on my lip before letting out a slow exhale. I stared out at the city I had wanted to save, destroyed by the woman who had given up everything to protect it. "When she wakes up and realizes what she's done, she will break."

My head felt dizzy as my pulse quickened. The answer was right in front of me. I swallowed and shoved my hands in my pockets, fully aware of the sacrifice I was about to ask of them.

"We already have the answer. Henry." They both looked up at me with cautious hope.

Nira wiped her eyes. "Henry is with Siana. How is he going to help us here?"

"Henry transitioned without hurting anyone because Siana sense shifted him in her dreaming state. He slept through the withdrawals and then Josie helped him cope after."

A shadow fell over Melissa.

"That's great!" Nira shouted.

"I can help them all transition. We can hold them under for a little while until they are through the worst of it and then you can bring them out in smaller groups." She bounced on her feet, turning to Melissa.

"You won't be able to do it on your own." I stared at

the ground. "You're strong, but you'll need an amplifier."

"It seems fitting." Melissa gave a sad chuckle before taking Nira's hands. "The Rightleys started all this pain and suffering. It's only right that I be the one to help end it."

The sound of breaking glass continued to crescendo as the dires inside the labs tried to fight their way out. The comforting sounds of the city were exchanged for ones of pain and anguish, punctuated by the occasional crash or wail. Time froze. Everything that I had tried to avoid had happened anyway, and I was completely powerless to help anyone.

Knowing what they had to do, Melissa and Nira sat on the hard ground outside of the RightCorp building, silent tears streaming down their faces. For Nira, this would be like a vivid dream, living out a memory, but for Melissa—

"If this is going to be my last dream, you had better make it a good one." They both mirrored a sad smile as my heart caved in inside my chest. Hands clasped tightly, they both laid down as the smell of flowers and bread tickled the front of my brain.

As the sense shift took hold, the sounds of breaking glass halted. The wailing and pain stopped as Coranta went silent. My eyes burned as they trailed up toward the sky resting on the white marble arches that now marked the place where the city's new saviors lay: The emblazoned motto now an epitaph.

Everyone Works. Everyone Strives. Everyone Gives, So the Many Survive.

$15.99
ISBN 979-8-218-14234-6
51599>

9 798218 142346